I0586003

THE DRAGON QUEEN

TIANI DAVIDS

Cover art and design by Tairelei

www.tairelei.com

Editing by Carrie Jones

Interior design completed using Canva

ISBN: 978-0-6454774-7-4

To those who hurt but keep going. To those who care, even when it's hard.

Books by Tiani Davids
The Eldrasian Chronicles
The Dragon Healer
The Dragon Kin
The Dragon Queen

Kingdoms of the Fae
Of Glass and Cinders (coming 2024)

CHAPTER
ONE

E LINTA MARCHED DOWN THE entry hall of the White
Palace, shoulders back and chin high, and wished she could
be with the dragon who had just dropped her off outside rather
than on her way to another meeting with the royals. Zhayra had
tuned into her ears and eyes the moment she'd entered the ruined
palace, but this time Elinta didn't look around for the dragon to
absorb the sights. All around her were people: people who looked
at her with hardened eyes or, very rarely, curiosity.

So, Elinta kept her newly whitened, slitted eyes—a mark of
her bond to Zhayra—facing forward. And she tried not to think
about ... anything. Not the sting in her many wounds. Not the
damage to the palace, not the fake deal Prince Mazen of Liyarna

had offered to spare her people in exchange for her and Zhayra, not Blaine.

Blaine.

She'd buried him earlier that day outside of the city. Lorrin, Tamir, Niles, and Zhayra had all been with her, but that was all she allowed herself to remember. That and Lorrin's hand in hers. A lifeline.

Her brother's body belonged in Kethmere, but there was no time to return there. Now he rested near the city he'd died in. A stab of pain went through her heart.

Elinta shook her head to clear it, stuffing the pain down deep inside her to look at another time or maybe never, focusing on the walk to the queen's tea rooms instead. The palace had been damaged by dragon fire during Mazen's attack on the city, and it had been decided that the ground floor was safest. She hadn't been back to her room on the third floor yet, but she'd been told it had survived. Her feet sped up as she turned onto the last hall, wishing that the grey marbled floor would pass by more quickly, and she even offered the man coming from the other direction a small nod in greeting.

Civilians who'd lost their homes in the battle had been allowed to sleep in the palace overnight, and this man's ruffled, dirty appearance marked him as one. A smear of blood had turned the left sleeve of his shirt crimson. His eyes reminded her of her own. Empty.

He stepped out to block Elinta's way, and she startled at the coldness that settled in those eyes as they raked over her. They lingered on her own eyes and the sword at her hip. His lip curled. But he said nothing. Instead, he drew back his head and spat on her. The glob landed on her shirt, and the man walked on as though nothing had happened. Elinta didn't say anything. She didn't move. Perhaps she'd deserved that. Not because she was

Zearla lurai, kin of the dragons, but because she'd let her brother die.

"Elinta."

She turned numbly, following the voice to find Ford Mayes, the palace historian, his dark green cloak billowing behind him as he strode up the hall. He was young for someone in his role, looking to be in his early-to-mid-thirties, a fact that had always intrigued her. Elinta had never seen Ford angry, but a flicker of rage lit his dark eyes as he passed the man who'd spat on her. Zhayra's own anger, a fire in her large belly, calmed as she saw Ford through Elinta's eyes.

"You didn't deserve that," he said as though he'd read the thoughts going through her mind. He stopped in front of her, pulling a tissue from his pocket and handing it to her. She dabbed at the patch.

"Are you coming to the meeting?" she asked, shoving the dirty tissue into her healer's satchel.

She hadn't seen Ford since the meeting the royals and their advisors had held in his house the day before. After the battle. She'd been there and she'd spoken to them all about Zhayra and their bond, but she couldn't remember much of it. Perhaps that was a good thing.

"No, I was only at the last one because it was my house," he said, a self-deprecating chuckle hiding in his words. She'd actually attended another meeting since then, one earlier that morning, but she knew what he meant. Elinta had wondered where he'd been.

Ford pushed a bit of hair back from his forehead, revealing a small cut, and Elinta scanned him quickly. She'd tuned into her dragonsight as soon as she'd awoken this morning, allowing her to see everything with the strength of Zhayra's eyes. She felt safer with it on. Relief spread through her as she noted only a couple other minor cuts on his body. He'd fought well yesterday. Very well.

"Will you come with me, anyway?" she asked.

Ford had helped her in many ways since she'd come to Nevira, and she valued his advice and opinion. If the king and queen couldn't see what an asset he was, especially with his knowledge of dragons, well, then that wasn't her problem.

Ford tilted his head, a lock of his dark hair sliding down his forehead again. "Of course."

She led them down the hall in silence. Something about Ford's presence made her feel a little stronger. It was like, perhaps, she was now more prepared for the meeting she was about to face. At least there would be one more person on her side at the table. As they neared the tea rooms, Prince Lorrin ducked out from within, his blue eyes lighting as he saw her and Ford. He didn't say anything about the historian joining them, but he did nod with approval.

"Is everyone here?" Elinta had purposely arrived at the palace right as the meeting was due to start so that she didn't have to spend time in the company of anyone other than her friends. Especially Shae, one of the king's advisors, who had always hated her. Even before knowing what Elinta was.

"Yes," Lorrin said as they drew level with him. His walk revealed the small limp from an injury received in the battle; she knew it would heal well with time. He glanced at the room behind him.

Elinta had been to the tea rooms many times before as a guest of the queen. But that felt like a lifetime ago. A whole other person ago. Looking at the rooms now, she felt a spark of nerves.

"Ford," Lorrin said, clasping hands with the man.

"Your Highness."

Lorrin's eyes landed on the wet patch on Elinta's shirt, but she didn't say anything of what had happened.

"Are you ready?"

Elinta flicked her eyes to his and instantly felt a sliver of calm trying to wash over her. She took a deep breath.

"Yes."

He held her eyes a moment longer before reaching out and opening the door. He led the way into the room.

Everyone was already there, just as Lorrin had said, and Elinta fought the urge to turn and disappear. A long wooden table had been moved in and Mira's small, rounded one taken out. The table was at odds with the brightness of the room. She resisted the urge to look out into the palace gardens, a place she'd been only last night with Lorrin and Niles. The place she'd been after the battle—when she'd told them about Blaine—and instead studied those gathered.

At the table, already seated, were King Aldon and Queen Mira. Niles's father, General Sonnen, his face bruised and his arm in a sling, sat to their left, and General Nash sat a seat down to their right. Niles and Tamir, both with wounds of their own, and Shae (noticeably unharmed) were all there as well.

All eyes had turned to Elinta as she'd entered, and she fought the urge to run her hands over her shirt to smooth out any real or imaginary crinkles.

"Elinta, welcome," King Aldon said, only a hint of strain showing at his shoulders. He was wearing a crown today, a thin *illayas* band that sat low over his brown hair. "And Ford, we did not expect to see you."

"I asked him to come," Elinta said, picking up the question in the king's words. "Ford's knowledge may be useful."

The king's blue eyes locked on hers. She'd never been particularly close to him though she'd found him nice enough. Even yesterday after the battle and finding out about Zhayra, he'd been reasonable with her. Distant, but not unkind. Perhaps she needed to be careful not to push him too far, but she didn't have it in her to monitor her tone. After another moment, the king nodded.

"Please take your seats and we can begin."

The king and queen were at the head of the long table, and Lorrin returned to his seat directly to their right. Elinta took the empty seat next to Niles, thankful that he'd saved it for her, and moved her satchel out of the way as she did. She felt, rather than saw, Ford take the seat by Tamir on the other side of the table.

General Nash, Lorrin's aunt, offered her a small smile before she turned to the others. She had a minor cut above her eyebrow from the battle that looked rather painful. To Elinta's surprise, the general dove right in, not even beginning with any pleasantries.

"Whilst we need to discuss Mazen, there is a more immediate concern. The palace isn't safe for us to stay in anymore, not until it can be repaired. Tentative estimates put re-habitation several months away."

King Aldon nodded, the heaviness in his eyes suggesting he already knew or suspected as much. "There's nowhere in Nevira that would be suitable for us to live in and defend, and I would not want to stay here anyway. The people need time to repair their own homes and I doubt Mazen would give it to them if we remained," he said bitterly.

"Might I suggest Tremass, Your Majesty?" Shae said, her voice deceptively gentle. Elinta knew what hatred simmered under there for her, the dragons, and even the Asali. "Mayor Harlan has been a good friend of yours for many years."

General Sonnen slowly shook his head. "Too far," he grunted. "Mazen would pick us off before we arrived. We'd be making it easy for him."

General Nash tilted her head thoughtfully. "What about Culmar? The mayor's home there is big enough for his advisors and their families. The city is well defended on land and sea due to the trading through there. It's close enough that Mazen wouldn't have time to muster an attack while we're on the road."

General Sonnen and Lorrin both nodded. For the moment Elinta was happy to remain quiet, as were Niles, Tamir, and Ford, it seemed. Though, she found herself wanting to argue against Culmar, a heavy ball settling into her stomach at the very idea of going there. Where *he* was.

"Being right by the sea has its appeal when fighting dragons too," King Aldon said slowly. He turned to General Nash. "Have a message sent to Culmar informing Mayor Cyril of our immediate departure for his city. I would ask Harlan to join us as soon as he is able as well."

The woman made a note on the paper in front of her.

Elinta's heart froze at the decision to go to the port city. Her father had gone there. His last words to her echoed through her mind. *I don't have any children.* It had always been Blaine's dream to go to Culmar and run his own horse business there. Now her father would try his best to start anew there. Without Blaine. Without her. The ache in her heart sharpened. Elinta couldn't remember what it had been like when her mother had died, a fact she was grateful for in that moment. If it had been like this, she wouldn't have survived it as a small child.

Zhayra's chest tightened in response to the growing ache in Elinta's. She didn't have it in her to whisper to the dragon that she was OK. She wasn't.

"What about the people here?" Lorrin asked, drawing her from her ruminations. She forced herself to focus on him and not the thoughts that threatened to drag her down.

"They'll be safer once we're gone," King Aldon said, exchanging a glance with the queen. "However, those with nowhere to stay are welcome to come with us. Only a quarter of the soldiers are to stay behind. The rest will be needed in Culmar."

Shae tsked. "We need to find out why Mazen is doing this, once we satisfy his demands—" she looked pointedly at Elinta, "—he might leave us alone."

Lorrin opened his mouth, anger flashing in his eyes, no doubt about to remind Shae of the decision they'd all made yesterday not to hand Elinta over. The king had recognised that Mazen couldn't be trusted to uphold his own bargain. Elinta cut across Lorrin, her anger rising like a tsunami, unbidden. Shae had been nothing but a thorn in her side since she'd come to Nevira, and the woman wouldn't stop. She was sick of it. She had enough problems without the woman contributing to them.

"We know why Mazen is doing this." The others looked at her curiously, and Elinta found herself wondering why she'd opened her mouth after all, but she dove on. "The dragons are a whole race of beings, and we drove them away with bloodshed. Mazen's bonded to one of those dragons! He wants them to come back and to be safe here."

"And you agree with him, don't you?" Shae asked, her voice turning venomous, a light gleaming in her beady eyes.

King Aldon remained quiet, his gaze sliding between them.

"No," Elinta said. "Not with his methods." She turned away from the woman, dismissing her as she'd done to Elinta so many times before. "I need to go back to Liyarna," she told the king, telling rather than asking. "There's someone there who can offer some insight into Mazen, maybe even help me work out how to stop him."

King Aldon shifted in his seat. "And if they are working for Mazen?"

To Elinta's right, Tamir moved as though to speak, but Ford spoke first. "I don't believe they are, Your Majesty. The Liyarnans have long believed their prince to be dead. Elinta's report that he no longer has a claim to the throne seems accurate with what we saw here yesterday. The Asali fighting in the city were hardly a dent in their overall population."

Tamir nodded, shooting Ford a thankful look. Had Ford known the king would be more likely to listen to him than Tamir? A satisfied grin threatened to break through Elinta's blank expression. Bringing Ford had been a good idea.

"Aldon," General Nash said, her tone drawing Elinta's gaze. She sometimes forgot the general was the king's sister. "Now is the time to send a delegation. We can't afford for them to change their minds and join him."

"I agree, Your Majesty," General Sonnen grunted.

Something small and unknown lit inside Elinta's heart, something she saw mirrored in Lorrin's eyes as his father finally considered what they'd tried to convince him of for months.

The king looked around at the people seated at the table, taking in their faces.

"Very well," he said after a long moment. "I am willing to agree to a temporary alliance if it will stop them from joining Mazen."

"I'll lead the delegation," Lorrin said quickly. It was clear what he was thinking; it would be disastrous if someone like Shae went. "As I've already spoken to the council on the matter, they might be more receptive to me."

King Aldon shot his son a look, one shared by the queen and both generals. "Yes, but this time, guards will be coming with you and Elinta."

But Elinta shook her head. It would take time to gather the men to escort them, and then the trip itself would take at least two weeks with a larger group. She needed to be there *now*.

"I can't wait that long." Elinta looked out the window at the afternoon shadows stretching across the gardens. "Zhayra and I will leave in the morning."

When she turned back, Lorrin held her gaze with his. He didn't want to leave her, but she could see he understood. That, perhaps, he had understood he'd be going after her before she'd even said anything. He nodded. Elinta managed to crack a small smile for him, one she hadn't known she had in her still.

"I will come with you," Tamir said. "I can prepare the council for Lorrin's arrival."

"I'll go with Lorrin," Niles said after a moment. "We'll meet you both there." Zhayra would fly faster with just two, a fact he seemed to realise.

Queen Mira looked uncertainly at Tamir. The royals had refused to speak with him about the Asali or the council when Elinta, Lorrin, and Niles had first brought him back to Nevira with them. Elinta could already hear what the woman would say.

"Perhaps it would be best if you didn't speak with them, Tamir," the queen said, her green eyes studying him. "Your interest does belong with your people, after all."

Tamir tilted his head, his dark grey eyes revealing nothing.

"I need him," Elinta said. She didn't, really. She could get by in the city without him, though his presence would smooth over her interactions with the council. But she wanted him with her. Not only that, but the Asali would be able to heal Tamir's wounds, and his wife was in Liyarna, waiting to see him. He should be allowed to go home whenever he wanted. He should be allowed to see his family.

"Elinta and Tamir are the best people to go ahead of us," Lorrin said. "If it's important that Elinta gets there as soon as she can, then that's the way it'll have to be."

Elinta fought to keep her eyebrows from raising. Lorrin had never spoken like that to his parents. It didn't go unnoticed by King Aldon, but there was almost a spark of pride in his eyes as he looked at Lorrin, even if he'd made his opinion on the Asali clear.

"You'll follow on behind them in a couple of days. Jaida," the king said, turning to General Nash, "I would like you to join them."

"Of course."

"There is one more thing that needs to be addressed," Shae said, her tone as though what she had to say was deeply important. She hadn't acknowledged anything that had been discussed about the Asali. "Your cousins will be on their way here, Your Majesty."

"Yes." The king waved his hand. "A messenger will have to be sent out to them to return home. It won't be safe for them to join us in Culmar."

There wasn't much more to discuss after that. Everyone there had things they needed to do, and the meeting had been called to make some quick decisions so they could all get back to work. Elinta was the first to rise from her seat when the king dismissed them, and Lorrin caught her eye. They and Niles and Tamir would need to talk now. Elinta nodded but hurried from the room. She'd wait for them in the hall.

CHAPTER
TWO

E LINTA WAITED A FEW metres away from the double doors
in the hall, leaning against the stone wall. To anyone else,
she would seem to be staring unseeingly at the floor, but she was
actually looking through Zhayra's eyes. She knew the dragon had
been listening to the entire meeting in the tea rooms, and she'd
even whispered to the dragon that she had to meet with Lorrin
and the boys. But she'd taken the moment to check on Zhayra, to
see where she was and that she was OK.

Zhayra had returned to the woods outside the city by the
Afonlin river while she waited. It was the place she'd been hiding
in for months. And while everyone knew about her now, it wasn't
safe for her to be in the city. Not that it was likely anyone could

hurt her, since there were only a couple of *illayas* weapons left. But her presence would lead to problems from the people who had just been attacked by other dragons.

"You alright, kid?" a gruff voice sounded nearby, startling Elinta as she was still gazing into the river with Zhayra.

She pulled back, letting the image of Zhayra's reflection disappear, and focused on the man who'd spoken. "Yes," she said, meeting General Sonnen's gaze. "Just checking on Zhayra." She didn't elaborate.

General Sonnen's lips twitched. "You've had a dragon all this time?"

"Yes."

"My son and Lorrin always knew," he said, a spark lighting in his eye. Elinta considered his words. It was a statement, confirming what he and the others had learnt yesterday after the battle. But Elinta still felt the need to confirm it.

"Lorrin always knew, but Niles has known for a long time."

"Hmm." He tilted his head, his greying hair falling around his face. He nodded and moved to walk past her. But he turned back after only a few steps. "Your brother was a brave man, Elinta."

She swallowed the thickness in her throat, unable to respond as the general walked away. Not for the first time, she wondered about that deep, twisted scar trailing from behind his ear and down his neck.

Elinta turned her attention back to the tea rooms as Lorrin, Niles, Tamir, and Ford all emerged together. Ford and Tamir were talking quietly behind the boys.

"We'll need to find somewhere to talk about your trip," Lorrin said, stopping beside her. She could already see his mind working behind those blue eyes.

The king and queen walked by them, offering only the barest of acknowledgement as they hurried to their next meeting.

"The gardens?" Elinta offered. It was still the most peaceful place in the city, even with the memories that it now held, and it would offer them some privacy.

The boys turned in that direction, but Ford stepped forward. "I'm afraid I have work to do, but I would like to speak to Elinta first?"

"Of course," Elinta said.

Lorrin, Niles, and Tamir moved further away to give them some space and instantly began talking, their voices a soft buzz in the hall.

"Ma arin iri," Ford said in a low voice. His use of Asalin startled her for a moment that it was a full beat before she tried to translate his words. *Be careful,* with the future tense. Be careful—in Liyarna.

Elinta looked at him, stunned, but caught a glimpse of Lorrin over his shoulder. She'd wondered who had taught the prince Asalin. Perhaps it had been the mysterious history teacher. His dark eyes were fixed on her.

"I will be." Elinta looked over him again, seeing him differently. She'd guessed Ford had known about Zhayra for some time, though they'd danced around it. He hadn't treated her any differently when the dragon became public knowledge, or when her pupils became slits and her irises turned as white as the dragon's scales. This man ... how he'd treated her despite hardly knowing her meant the world.

"Thank you, Ford," she said.

"Of course." Something light and musical clung to the words, but Elinta couldn't place what it reminded her of. Ford walked away, his cloak billowing behind him, and she joined her friends.

The door to the palace gardens had been repaired and no longer stood ajar. Perhaps it had been fixed simply because of how close it was to the tea rooms and the security risk it posed. Regardless,

Elinta was glad for the sign that the city was already rebuilding. Despite all that had happened, the garden was still intact and as beautiful as ever. The track Elinta and Lorrin had worn around the garden during their morning runs was still there. The small scarlet crown plants, and the hedges, and rows and rows of flowers were still there. This little spot was untouched by dragon fire.

They hadn't even sat on the soft grass before Niles was asking questions.

"So, what's really going on in Liyarna?"

But Lorrin intervened. "Is Zhayra still listening?"

"Yes."

All the boys looked at her expectantly, though Tamir carefully sat down to ease the wound in his side. Though the Asali could heal others, like the rest of his kind, Tamir couldn't heal himself. And though he'd offered to help the three of them, all having sustained minor injuries in the battle, they'd all refused. He needed time to heal naturally.

"I need to speak with the *Zearla lurai* there," Elinta said, unable to lock eyes with any of them.

Lorrin frowned. "What about?"

"I—I'll tell you when I get back," she said, a hint of her fear slipping into her words. She didn't want to share her theory with the boys about Mazen having a bond with the other dragons until she'd heard what Aesira thought. They'd known Mazen was bonded to Vaherin, a large maroon dragon. But more than one? Elinta didn't know if that was even heard of. But Mazen had seen and heard things in the battle that he couldn't have on his own or through Vaherin. What would she be able to do against someone with that much power?

"Do you think they can be trusted?" Niles asked, breaking through her spiralling thoughts. He pulled an apple out from an inner pocket of his jacket, biting into it.

Elinta exchanged a look with Tamir. He was the only other person among them who knew that Aesira was Mazen's grandmother. She hadn't told the boys, both wanting to maintain Aesira's privacy and because she wasn't sure what they would say about her connection to Mazen. But ... she wanted them to know. Because Aesira was a resource, and a trustworthy one, who deserved to be recognised.

Tamir saw the resolution in her eyes and reluctantly nodded.

"There's something you should know about her." Elinta cleared her throat. "But please believe me when I say she can be trusted."

Niles and Lorrin both gave her concerned looks.

"The *Zearla lurai* is Mazen's grandmother."

"What?" both exclaimed at the same time, their eyes going comically wide. Niles winced as the movement pulled at his black-eye and quickly adjusted his expression to ease it.

"You met with MG?" Niles asked, his voice loud and reverberating off the garden walls.

Elinta rose her eyebrows at that.

"Mazen's grandmother," he elaborated around another bite of fruit.

"Yes," she said, shaking her head at him. "And I really think she can help me."

Lorrin's brow was furrowed, but he eventually nodded. "If you're sure."

"I am," she said.

Tamir didn't say anything, but relief seemed to etch across his features. It had been clear to her from the beginning that he loved and respected Aesira. No doubt he would have jumped to her defence, as Elinta would have, too, if the boys had said anything against her. He shifted to ease his side again. His glow was already becoming more obvious in the afternoon light.

The shadows had begun to deepen in the garden as they'd talked, and the three boys grew strangely fidgety in the quiet that settled over them, exchanging looks and glancing at the sky.

Elinta immediately knew why. It was an hour until sunset. Mazen's cut off time for his deal. "I'm not going to him," she said to the awkward silence that had descended. Mazen had wanted both her and Zhayra, and she could never give up the dragon. Never.

Lorrin's eyes softened. "We know," he said, his hand twitching as though he wanted to reach for her. "But we're worried for you anyway."

Niles nodded. "We don't want to lose you."

"You won't." She shifted. "I should go pack."

It was funny, when she was alone, all she wanted was to be with the boys, but when she was with them, she just wanted to be alone.

"We'll see you at dinner," Lorrin said.

She merely nodded before turning and making her way back through the palace to her room on the third floor.

Cracks had appeared around the bay window in her bedroom and the scent of smoke lingered in the air. Elinta looked around her. Nothing had changed in the time she'd been away searching for her kidnapped family. Neva had kept the place tidy for her while she'd been living there, so she doubted the maid had even been there since the night Elinta had left. Where was the maid now? A flash of worry and guilt lit in her stomach, and Zhayra's own stomach tightened in response. Was Neva even alive?

Elinta pulled her satchel in front of her and flipped it open. There was enough room for a small bundle or two of clothes next to the few herbs and cloths left behind after she'd treated her own wounds. And the other thing. The one she didn't want to look at or acknowledge. The thing that had taken Blaine's life.

She quickly stuffed in a couple of changes of clothes, and on top of it, she placed the special Asali jumper Ciar had given her in the White Mountains. There was nothing else to grab. Her sword was on her hip, her mother's necklace at her neck. Her bag and Zhayra's harness were with the dragon in the woods. She'd decided not to fly to the palace with the harness today so as to spare Zhayra an uncomfortable day with it on. The flight had been smooth, but Elinta's fingers and legs had been aching when they'd landed. A small price to pay for the dragon's comfort.

Someone had brought Blaine's sword to her room sometime during the day. It was the only thing of his that she had now. Her father had taken what few belongings Blaine had brought with them from Kethmere with him to Culmar. She fingered the hilt. No, she couldn't take it with her. Elinta carefully picked it up, carrying it over to her wardrobe and tucking it inside. Her chest ached as she closed the door and rested her head against it. Memories of the burial threatened to surface, and she shoved them down, taking a deep breath. She'd come back for the sword once things were finished with Mazen.

After a long moment, Elinta twisted her head to look out of her window, her head still against the wardrobe. It faced north, out over the palace courtyard and the damaged city. Faint streaks of orange and pink had begun to filter across the sky. Sunset. Elinta tugged at her satchel and left the room, following her feet.

No, she wouldn't go to Mazen. Not when it wouldn't make a difference. But ... she needed to watch this moment pass. Needed to feel it. So, she went down to the ground floor, to a room that was intact, empty, and had beautiful large windows looking out at the world and the sunset. The ballroom.

She hesitated in the doorway, the echo of the music from the king's birthday in her ears. The room was huge, bigger than she'd thought during the ball and the Eggslaying festivities, when it had been full of laughing and dancing people. Elinta trailed inside, her steps echoing across the polished wooden floors as she made her way to the large windows. They stretched from the floor nearly all the way to the painted ceiling. She stopped by one, and stared out at the palace grounds, the walls, and the ruined city thrown into orange hues by the tainted sunset and knew that Mazen watched it as well. He watched over the same descending sun at their meeting place in Bradfin with Vaherin and waited. The oranges began to deepen, and a streak of pink slit a large patch through the middle. The colours were even more beautiful since she looked through dragonsight.

Mazen would be surprised when she didn't turn up. He'd revealed yesterday how little he thought of the royal family, and how little he thought they'd now think of her. He probably thought she was late because they'd hog-tied her and left her out as an offering. The image of his surprise almost had her lips twitch upward in grim satisfaction.

She didn't know how long she stood there while the sky darkened, and the striking colours slowly faded. Zhayra had continued to look and listen through her, a welcome comfort that reminded her she wasn't truly alone.

"Elinta?"

It was the slight note of panic in his voice that made her turn, her hand falling from her mother's necklace around her neck.

Lorrin stood under the frame of the left door, the one she'd left slightly ajar. His hair was slightly ruffled, and relief etched its way across his face as he caught sight of her.

His steps echoed in the dimly lit room, just a little uneven still. The chandeliers were dark, and only two torches by the door cast any light into the large room. The shadows settled into the circles under his eyes, making him look exhausted. But his manner showed none of it.

"Were you watching the sunset?" he asked, stopping in front of her and not saying what he was really thinking and what had made him look so scared before he saw she hadn't left the palace at all. "It was beautiful."

"It was," she said, glancing over her shoulder at the window. When she turned back, Lorrin had moved a step closer, closing the distance between them until the memory of the way he'd once held her as they'd swept around the room forced its way into her mind. The warmth of it pressed against the coldness that had been latching to her all day.

"Dance with me," he whispered, slipping his arm around her waist.

"OK," she whispered back.

It wasn't like the dances they'd had at the king's ball. Lorrin merely held her close, and they swayed to some invisible music only he could hear. She rested her head against his shoulder, her face turned toward him. Only a single tear came, which he gently wiped away as they continued to move in time together.

🔥🔥🔥

Elinta returned to the palace in the morning with Zhayra after another night in the forest, bracing herself to say goodbye to Lorrin and Niles. She'd already put the harness on the dragon and clipped the empty bag to a strap by one of her front legs. Elinta's satchel was slung across her shoulder. She'd turned dragonsight on again as soon as she'd woken, determined never to go without it again.

Lorrin, Niles, and Tamir came out to the courtyard to meet her so the boys could say goodbye to not only her but also to Zhayra. The dragon's spirits seemed to lift as she realised this.

Lorrin pulled Elinta in for a hug first, and she breathed his scent in deeply, remembering their dance last night and the embers it had fanned back to life in her. Embers that were still burning.

"Be careful," he murmured.

"Of course," she said, pulling back only to be yanked by Niles into a bearhug.

"You better come back," he said, his cheek pressed against her head as he squeezed her.

Lorrin grasped Tamir's hand while Niles finally released Elinta so he could do the same.

"I will look out for her; you have my word." Tamir glanced her way, a flicker of pride in his shining eyes as they settled on her sword. "But I don't think she will need my protection."

"No, but it's appreciated anyway." Lorrin's gentle eyes flickered to hers, holding them, holding her.

"Zezayn malli—mally—uh, you know: may the sun continue to shine on you. Both," Niles said, waving his hand at his awkward attempt at the Asali parting phrase.

A chuckle escaped Elinta's lips, the first in what felt like a lifetime. "You too," she said. "We'll see you in a couple of weeks."

"Right," Niles said, rubbing his hands together. "And then we'll finally kick Mazen's butt with the Asali on our side."

CHAPTER
THREE

T HEY FLEW HARD AND fast, going at the quickest pace
Zhayra could maintain for the long journey. Elinta slowly
counted down the landmarks as the ground whizzed by. The
river. The grasslands. A giant grey and white boulder. She hadn't
wanted to waste any time in getting to Liyarna. But even so, they
had to stop a few times throughout the day to rest and when dusk
came, they landed to set up camp for the night.

Elinta rested her back against Zhayra's side as the dragon slept
after the long day, curled into a ball. Despite his injury, Tamir
sat with his back inches from the white dragon as they ate their
meal of roasted potato and fresh coffee heated on the fire. She'd
already checked on his wound, a deep cut he'd received in the

battle, and redressed it. Her own—cuts that littered her arms and legs—were relatively minor. In fact, her aching and strained muscles bothered her more.

"Do you think the council will listen to us now?" Elinta asked, cupping her mug of coffee in her hands. The question had been on her mind all day, but she hadn't asked, hadn't dared to hope. But now it spilled out of her as though pulled out by the comfort of the fire.

Tamir paused, tucking a strand of his shoulder-length hair behind his ear. "I don't know," he finally said. "The council would prefer not to become involved, but they cannot deny the danger Mazen is to all of us now."

Elinta mulled over his words. If the council tried to ignore them, tried not to become involved ... Elinta sat up straight. She thought back to her last trip to the city, furiously examining all her interactions with the council and the other Asali. They wouldn't have!

"Did they tell anyone else about Mazen? Does the rest of the city know?" Elinta finally asked, but deep down, she already knew the answer.

"No." Tamir lowered his mug and looked at her with wide eyes. "I do not think they told anyone while we were there."

"They lied!" Elinta growled, slamming her coffee down on the hard earth. The black liquid spilled over the sides of the mug, but she didn't notice. "They said no one would support Mazen, but they didn't even tell them he was back?"

Well, she'd make sure they all knew. She wasn't going to play whatever game it was the council members were trying to play with her. Not after—after everything they'd lost. *Who* she'd lost. She swallowed thickly.

"They cannot hope to keep it from the people forever. News of Nevira would have reached them soon even if we were not travelling there ourselves."

Elinta nodded, her thoughts still on what would need to be done when they arrived. Fire burned ugly and bright in her stomach.

"Elinta," Tamir said, his voice turning quiet and drawing her attention. His dark grey eyes were studying her carefully. The reflection of the fire was strangely dimmed, suppressed by his own shine. "I told Lorrin and Niles I would look after you, but I do not think they realised that may include protecting you from yourself. Please do not make any reckless decisions when it comes to Mazen."

"Don't worry," she said, "I—I'm not planning anything reckless with him."

He tilted his head and she waited for another word of warning, but instead a small smile lit his lips. "Very well. I believe the council may respond to whatever you are planning." There was a pause, then the warning came. "As long as you are careful how you do it."

Elinta returned his smile, swallowed the last mouthful of her coffee, and settled down to sleep.

The green and silver trees of the Calaza Forest came into view at noon, and despite herself, Elinta found her strengthened eyes lingering on the strange trees once again. They were stunning with her normal eyes, but with Zhayra's strength they were beyond beautiful. Silver bark hung from the tallest trees like ribbons, their clumps of leaves reminding her of cushions or pillows. Her mind flew back to that first time she'd looked through Zhayra's eyes and saw the very same forest. Nothing could compare to that experience. It hadn't been so long ago, but already she longed for those easier days.

Zhayra tilted her course to aim for Liyarna, her wings beating faster. The city was almost invisible from the air, but with her dragonsight on, Elinta could see the training field where Zhayra had slept on their last visit. But she could also see the small clearing where the council met. It was there that Elinta called for Zhayra to land. The dragon didn't need to be told twice. Her stomach clenched in anticipation of what was to come.

Tamir's grip around her waist tightened as Zhayra descended, aiming for a spot directly in front of the council table. Elinta steeled herself for the meeting she was about to thrust on the three rulers. It had to be done. They'd brought it upon themselves.

As Elinta had hoped, their surprise arrival drew many Asali toward them so that when they landed, there were at least a dozen already waiting on the outskirts of the clearing with more arriving. Their faces ranged from curious to wary, their bodies shined equally bright. The three council members, Nakiah, Aisla, and Piran, were already there as were a couple Asali standing before them at the long stone table.

They'd arrived during a meeting. Elinta grinned in satisfaction. They couldn't have arrived at a better time. She unclipped herself from the harness and slid to the ground. Her feet landed silently on the grass.

"*Zearla lurai*, we were not expecting you," Aisla said, her long grey-blonde hair hanging freely down her back. Her face was welcoming, unaware of what was about to happen.

Piran's face was perfectly calm, but Nakiah's had darkened at their unannounced arrival. If they were surprised by the change in the appearance of her eyes, none of them showed it. She knew her hair would also be a tangled mess after the flight, but she didn't bother trying to smooth it down. She charged on.

"No, I didn't think you would be. Though the news I have for you shouldn't come as a surprise given my last visit," Elinta said, striding forward and coming to a stop beside the Asali the council had been meeting with. They gawped. At her tone or her arrival? She didn't care. As long as they were there. Witnesses were what she'd been missing last time. Tamir dropped softly to the ground behind her a moment later.

Piran's dark eyes turned cautious, flickering to take in the people beside her as well as behind. "Perhaps you would like to rest and regain your strength first after such a long journey?"

Oh, I don't think so. "No, actually, I'm feeling quite well. Are you feeling well, Tamir?"

"I am well rested," he said.

Elinta fought the urge to grin at his windswept hair as she glanced at him. "Well, there you go. Which honestly is quite a miracle given your injury. Anyway, I really don't think what I have to say can wait."

Nakiah opened his mouth, but Elinta didn't allow the man to speak. He was the one she was most worried about, as he was openly the least receptive of the three, and he was always the coldest with her. She couldn't afford to let him get a word in before she had said what she'd come to say.

"Prince Mazen—you know the one I told you weeks ago was still alive?—attacked Nevira. He was accompanied by Vaherin, six other dragons, and members of *your* people." Elinta's words reverberated around the clearing. Her harsh tone was strange even to her own ears, but this was the only way to tell the council, and to make sure the people heard. And they did. Murmurs filled the clearing as her words spread. Elinta kept her eyes locked on the council members. "The damage was significant and—and many lives were lost."

Aisla and Piran looked at her in shock, but she wasn't sure if it was at her words or who she'd said them in front of. Nakiah's eyes were glued to the whispering people around them. They couldn't stop it now even if they tried. There was no taking it back. Elinta fought to keep the triumph she felt from showing on her face even as her sorrow threatened to rise again.

"Prince Lorrin will be here in a couple of weeks with a delegation to meet with you. I'll return tomorrow to speak with you further, but right now, Tamir still needs to be healed from his wounds sustained in the battle." She turned her back on them, taking in the stunned faces of the growing crowd behind them. "Against Mazen Elliar."

Tamir's face was carefully controlled as she crossed to him.

"I can—" she began.

"Tamir!" a barely restrained voice called from the crowd, cutting her off. Elinta's eyes flickered over his shoulder, landing on the willowy form of Serren, Tamir's *ngaparta*. Tamir's already shining face lit up at the sound of his wife's voice and he twisted so fast Elinta was sure she heard him wince.

"Serren," he said, hurrying to where she pushed her way through the crowd that had more than doubled since their arrival. Her long, brown hair was swaying loosely as she practically shoved people out of the way. Elinta had never seen the woman so forceful.

Smiling, Elinta watched them embrace—a somewhat awkward action given the injury to Tamir's side—then called out, "I'll see you later."

Without looking back at the council, Elinta jumped onto Zhayra's back and the dragon shot into the air. Serren could heal Tamir properly now and then the two could finally catch up. She fought against the hollow feeling settling in her chest at the sight of their embrace.

Zhayra landed in the large training field at the invisible border of the city, startling a couple of Asali locked in a sparring match. The pair looked at Zhayra in wonder, sweat trailing down their shining faces, before restarting their training. The sight reminded Elinta of the times she'd trained here with Lorrin and Niles. It would be around a week and a half before she would be with them again. And in that time, she'd have to put up with the council members and any other Asali who might not be hospitable to her. Aisla had always looked at her with respect in her eyes, and Piran had been nice to her, but she wondered whether that would continue now that she had made sure the Liyarnans knew about Mazen, and that the council members had been keeping it from them. But she shrugged. It wouldn't have happened this way if they had been honest. Maybe a lot of things wouldn't have happened.

Elinta sat against one of Zhayra's large, white, scaled feet, and tuned into the dragon's hearing, trusting that Zhayra had better control than she did. She'd accessed the strength of Zhayra's ears twice before—both times during the battle at Nevira—but this was the first time she'd listened through Zhayra's ears. Elinta did it in much the same way as when she used the dragon's eyes. Focusing on her ears and nothing else, and straining to hear what she heard. It came easily.

Zhayra cocked her head, and slowly low voices began to reach them. At first, they couldn't make out any words as the speakers were too far away, but their tones told them plenty. Worry and anger seemed to be the most popular reactions to Elinta's news, and soon the voices cleared as the news spread further through the city, coming right up to the edge of the training field.

Shouts of Mazen's name reached them, dismayed whispers of the damage to Nevira, and angry comments at the council's secrets. Some even spoke of going to see Nevira with their own eyes. The two Asali on the field stopped their sparring again, exchanging confused glances before they hurried into the city to hear the news for themselves. Elinta pulled back from Zhayra's ears and smiled.

"We did it," she murmured both to Zhayra and to the image of Blaine sitting in her mind. Now the Green City knew what

Mazen was doing. And she doubted they would let it continue. She wouldn't let her brother's death be in vain.

Zhayra grunted, blowing a puff of hot air over Elinta. Elinta glanced up at the dragon, who had tilted her head to look at her.

"What?" Elinta said, trying to lock onto what the dragon was feeling.

Zhayra grunted again, a warmth spreading in her chest. Pride.

Elinta smiled and reached out to touch the dragon's cheek. "I love you," she said, leaning her head against the dragon's chest.

As night descended, Elinta decided not to venture into the city to find food, and she sent away the person who came to offer her a dinner with the council. She told them the council had much to discuss and she didn't want to interrupt them, but really, she just didn't want to be anywhere near them tonight. Her anger still simmered beneath the surface, a force she wasn't sure she would be able to keep contained if she had to play nice with Nakiah and the others.

Instead, she scooted down to rest against Zhayra's side, and the dragon spread her membrane wing to cover her as she had so many months ago in the cold of the White Mountains. She still had so much to do and so much to figure out. Perhaps things with the Liyarnans had taken a good turn—though only time would tell—but after all of this was solved, after Mazen was dealt with, she still had to work out how to fix things with the dragons. She still had to find a way for their races to communicate and one day bring the dragons home. An idea had been lingering in the corners of her mind for some time, but whenever she tried to look at it, it slipped away. Sighing, Elinta shoved her mess of thoughts aside, pressed closer to Zhayra's warmth and closed her eyes.

But when sleep came, so did the dreams.

Dreams of Blaine's blood on her hands, his unseeing eyes, and Mazen's cruel laugh echoing over her. She looked up from

Blaine's body, only to see Niles lying beside him, the same *illayas* dagger protruding from his chest as the one in Blaine. A sob pushed its way out of her. She looked away, but there was no relief. Lorrin was beside her. His throat slit, dark blood bubbling out of his mouth as he took one last, gurgling breath.

"NO!"

Elinta woke with a start, sitting up so fast she bumped her head against Zhayra's chin. The concerned dragon had been staring down at her.

Gasping, Elinta turned to face Zhayra. A low keen came from the dragon. Zhayra tilted her head further so that her amber eye locked on her. The night was dark, darker still because Elinta had turned off her dragonsight before bed, but Zhayra's white scales still shone in the moonlight.

"I'm OK," she whispered, wiping the sweat from her face. Her hands were shaking. "I'm OK. It was just a dream." She reached out for Zhayra's face as the dragon lowered her head. She pressed her cheek against the dragon's. "He would have been twenty-one next week."

Zhayra slipped her head over Elinta's shoulder and nudged her closer. Elinta let herself fall against the dragon's shoulder as Zhayra wrapped herself around her. Enclosed in one massive hug, Elinta drifted off again.

CHAPTER
FOUR

S TILL ENVELOPED IN ZHAYRA'S hug, Elinta awoke with the knowledge that Lorrin would finally be on his way to them, and she smiled despite the lingering images of her dream. She gently nudged Zhayra's face so she could have room to stretch, and she tuned back into the dragonsight.

Zhayra grumbled, not opening her eyes as she moved so Elinta could get up.

"You're such a grouch in the mornings," Elinta teased, rubbing a hand along the dragon's cheekbone.

Zhayra shifted her head and grumbled again.

"I'm going to check on Tamir."

Elinta left Zhayra to her sleep. Despite her teasing, the dragon did need to rest after the long flight from Nevira. She may as well enjoy the lazy mornings ahead of them while they waited for Lorrin.

Elinta set off into the city and once again looked around her in amazement. Every building had been built in and around the trees, the trunks and branches woven into the design. The air in Liyarna was the freshest she had ever breathed, the scent full of the natural perfumes of the flowers scattered around the buildings. Liyarna was truly a beautiful city, filled with beautiful people, people who watched her with openly curious expressions as she passed. There was none of the hostility she'd seen among her own people. She knew how she must look to them, too. Even if she'd only been in the city recently, she'd changed. Her eyes, once brown with rounded black pupils, were now white with black-slitted pupils. She could have almost passed as Asali if her pupils had been white and more ovular. She knew that her manner had changed too, especially in the way she'd dealt with the council. But she ignored the stares—she was growing used to them—and kept walking among the silver trunks the city had been built around.

It was only when she drew near to the pod-like building she, Lorrin, and Niles had stayed in on her last visit that Elinta realised she didn't know where Tamir lived in order to make sure he was OK. She sighed and stood awkwardly by the building. It was a surprisingly overcast day for the end of summer, but the city was aglow with the shine of its people. Since the people could never truly be in the dark, she'd never seen a lantern outside of the ones in the building behind her. A flock of blue and white birds swooped down and landed on the path only metres from her, chattering softly.

Elinta turned to head back to Zhayra to rifle through her bag for some food when she heard her name called by a familiar voice.

Twisting, she found Tamir walking her way, a tray of food in his arms. She ran her eyes over him, glad to see that not only did he move as though his side had been healed, but there was also no trace of the cut on his head that he'd sustained too.

"I was just coming to wake you," Tamir said. "I should have known you would be up already."

She nodded. She'd long been in the habit of rising early because of her training to be a healer in Kethmere, her home village. Despite having left months ago, Elinta hadn't been able to break the habit.

"We can go back to Zhayra to eat," he said, gesturing with his head at the food he carried.

"She's still sleeping," Elinta said.

"Ahh." He glanced around. "Come, this building has been set aside for you again. We'll eat in here."

He walked toward the building she'd been standing in front of, and they slipped inside. The interior was exactly the same as when she'd last been in the building. They entered the main room. It had three comfortable chairs in the centre and a table with wooden chairs to the side. Three doors led from the room to the bedrooms she and the boys had slept in during their last visit. The walls were rounded with real tree trunks built in around the wood, stretching up through the ceiling to join the unseen canopy above them.

Tamir set the food on the table and drew her a seat before sitting beside her.

"I can heal you now," he said, reaching for her. He'd given her and the boys many guilty glances since the battle, but they'd refused his offers to heal them, insisting that he'd needed to rest. Now that he was better ...

"No," she said, half surprising herself. "No, that's OK."

Elinta hadn't gained any serious wounds during the battle, though there were many of them. Tamir frowned, his eyes searching hers as though she'd spoken some strange riddle.

"I ... I want them." The numbness she'd felt directly after Blaine's death, while it had helped her tell the king and queen about Zhayra, had scared her. The pain ... it had been one of the few things she had felt once the adrenaline of battle had faded. It reminded her she was alive. And she'd fought to be. Had fought so very hard. She wanted her wounds to fade naturally. Well, naturally for her.

Tamir's face had cleared, understanding lighting in his eyes.

"How's Serren?" Elinta asked, quickly changing the subject and grabbing a piece of fruit.

"She is well." A huge smile lit his face. "She must work this morning, but she proposed we all have dinner tonight with Zhayra?"

"That would be great. Zhayra would love that." She paused. "I'm going to see Aesira this morning. As soon as Zhayra is awake."

"I'm sure she will be glad to see you," he said, around a mouthful of a grain-filled bread. He didn't ask about her reasons, likely remembering what she'd said at the meeting with the royal family. She'd share when she had answers. And she desperately hoped she was wrong.

"It's good that you visit Aesira," Elinta said. "It would be lonely out there, especially for her." Elinta couldn't imagine spending so many years bonded to a dragon only to lose it, in addition to her family. There would be an emptiness inside of the woman that could never be replaced. Never be filled. Her stomach churned at the very thought.

"I would always see her with Mazen, and then would visit when her foster son lived with her. When he left, I promised her foster son I would continue to see her. It was not a difficult promise. I had no intention of leaving her alone."

Foster son. Aesira had mentioned him before, but Elinta had had too much to think over at the time to dwell on him. The dead king had a foster brother, though they'd never met. The man might not be considered an heir to the throne, but why hadn't he stayed in Liyarna? Aesira said he'd left fifteen—or sixteen?—years ago. Where had he gone? And why?

She mulled over her questions in silence as she took a hunk of bread. She paused. Mazen had mentioned the man. Wait. Elinta's eyes widened. Mazen had mentioned a *human*.

"The—the foster son," Elinta stuttered, "was he human?"

Tamir tilted his head. "Yes."

"But how?" Elinta swallowed the last of her bread. And how much had Mazen learnt about Aesira and Liyarna through the Asali who'd joined him? Did he know who the foster son was? Did he know where the Liyarnan *illayas* sword was kept?

"Aesira found him wandering the forest as a small child after his parents died of a sickness. He had no family left, and neither did she. She could not bear to leave him there to die."

Elinta mulled that over before she finally smiled. That time, however small in the grand scale of Aesira's life, would have been special to the older woman.

"I should go," Elinta said eventually. "My questions can't wait."

Elinta and Zhayra flew up to Aesira's small hut on the side of one of the mountains in the Benhurst Ranges, the Calaza Forest sprawled out far below it. Despite the reason for her visit, Elinta couldn't help a twinge of excitement lighting in her. The feeling was something that Zhayra mimicked. Aesira was the one person who could truly understand what it was like to be bonded to a dragon. They landed in a rush of wind, pushing leaves and dirt running along the ground.

The little silver and brown hut looked the same as the last time she'd seen it, nestled on the mountainside in the middle of nowhere, with only rocks and scarce trees for company. But it was beautiful. It had an air of home about it, though it was nothing like the one Elinta had left behind in Kethmere.

"*Inna ayn nai rayni?*"

Elinta twisted on Zhayra's back to see Aesira standing behind them, a bony finger pointing at the leather harness on the dragon. The skin around her peculiar green eyes was crinkled. Her back was stooped, but Elinta knew that the appearance was deceptive. She'd seen the way the woman could move, even on the rougher parts of the mountain.

Elinta couldn't help a small smile from tilting her lips. "Prince Lorrin and Niles gave it to me," she said, unclipping herself and dropping to the ground. Leaves crunched beneath her feet. "It's fantastic!"

Zhayra hummed in greeting.

Aesira's eyes—the same as the dragon she'd lost—sparkled as they flitted between Elinta and Zhayra. "I suppose progress is progress even if Zhayra must bear to be a pack horse."

The old woman's expression turned heavy as she looked at Elinta's face again. Elinta wondered what Aesira saw there as the woman said, "You have much to tell me."

"Yes."

Aesira said nothing of the cuts still littering Elinta's arms as she stepped forward. Instead of leading Elinta and Zhayra back up the mountain to where they had talked once before, Aesira crossed the distance between them and sat on the ground. Once again, Elinta was astonished at how well the old woman moved despite her age and bent back.

Elinta joined her, knowing they didn't go into the hut for any lack of hospitality. It was so that Zhayra could be involved. The dragon settled into a crouch, content, and Elinta began her tale of Mazen's attack on Nevira. It was hard to begin, but once she had, she found the words pouring out of her. While necessary, she hadn't expected it to be so easy to speak to Aesira about it all.

When Elinta had finished, they all sat in silence for a long moment. Aesira's face had fallen, sorrow etching across her features in a rare display of emotion.

"I am sorry for your loss. *Zetayn elai pepyan eka ayn air kli nalliyan.*" It was an altered version of the death blessing—changing the pronoun to suit—and it touched Elinta to her soul, but she stopped her tears from falling.

"Thank you," Elinta said, rubbing at her eyes. Now was not the time. She took a deep breath. "But there's something else. I—I think Mazen has the *ngaran* with at least one other dragon."

Aesira stared at her for a long moment in stunned silence, her mouth dropping open. "I—I have never heard of this ... though I cannot see why it couldn't happen. The dragons do, after all, have hundreds of bonds with each other. But one *ngaran* is rare enough, two or more...." It wasn't wonder in her voice. It was dread.

Elinta watched Aesira curiously. This was her grandson they were talking about, but it was more than clear Aesira had no loyalty to him. Mazen had severed this last familial tie bit by bit over the many years since he'd left.

Aesira sighed deeply. "Perhaps now is the time to share more about the legend of the Dragon Asali."

Elinta frowned, thinking back to the story Aesira had shared with her on her last visit. What did that have to do with anything? The man, real or fictional, had forgotten how to speak to his son. What more could there be?

"You are an open book with your thoughts," Aesira said, a smile tilting her thin lips. "The legend is true, and there is much more to be learnt."

"OK," Elinta said, shifting to become more comfortable. She wasn't about to argue with the woman. Zhayra lowered her head to the ground.

Aesira launched into the story, not even needing a moment to gather her thoughts. "As you know, many years ago a *Zearla lurai* lost his wife. He was distraught to the point that nothing and no one could comfort him, only his dragon. The man left the city, left his young son, to join the dragons in the Ash Mountains. He stayed there for many years. But in that time, he came back to himself enough that he began to wonder about the son he'd left behind, and he wished that he could know that he was alright. He thought of the way he could see through his dragon's eyes and tried to do the same with his son. He was astounded to find that he could."

Elinta gaped at the woman, listening half in wonder, half doubt. How could this be possible? And how did Aesira know about it?

"But the man didn't realise that as the dragon could tell when he looked through his eyes, so could the man's son. The son recognised the feeling instantly from the stories his father had shared with him as a child about the *ngaran*, but it was many years before he set out to find his father. Bitterness and love had long waged inside him at the thought of the man who had abandoned him. When he arrived in the Ash Mountains, he didn't know whether to hug his father or berate him for all that he'd done. He spent only a week there but couldn't bring himself to ask his father to stop checking in on him, though he felt it was a deep invasion on his life. He was not yet ready to sever that tie."

"How—"

Aesira spoke over her. "My husband returned home and never saw his father again."

"Your—your husband?" Elinta choked. "The Dragon Asali was your father-in-law?"

"Yes," Aesira said. "Though I have no memories of him as king. He left when I was a very young child."

"And—and he really could look through his son's eyes? How is that possible?"

Zhayra grunted, her eye swivelling between them, but Elinta wasn't sure what the sound meant.

Aesira nodded. "I couldn't believe it at first, but when my husband made me promise never to do it once I became *Zearla lurai*, I knew it had to be true. His aversion to it was real."

"Did you ever try it?" Elinta asked after a long moment. Her heart pounded in her chest. Mazen. She could see what Mazen was doing.

"I did not mean to," Aesira said, her green eyes becoming distant. "One day my husband asked me to go to our people in another part of Eldras, and I missed him terribly. That night, as I was thinking about him, wishing to be with him and know what he was doing, I slipped into his eyes. I pulled back immediately and explained what had happened when I returned. I never tried to do it again, but I can tell you with certainty that it won't work with just anyone." Aesira looked at her meaningfully. "This kind of bond is for kin, for people that you love and who love you dearly. It is not ours but the dragons', so it is harder for us. I believe it would only be for the strongest of ties, in the way that it was for my husband's father and for me."

"So, I couldn't watch Mazen." Elinta's shoulders slumped, but another name whispered through her thoughts. She decided not to focus on that name. Not right then.

"No, you cannot."

"Do you think he knows about this? That he could do it?"

Aesira slowly shook her head. "The only one he cares about now is Vaherin. He has no reason to try."

Elinta turned to Zhayra. "Did you know that was possible?"

Zhayra's amber eye locked on her. After a long moment, she blinked once, yes. It was a system they'd developed the last time they'd been in Liyarna, where two blinks would have indicated a negative.

"Huh." Elinta turned back to Aesira. "Is it two-way? Like the bond?"

"I do not know," Aesira said, twisting a loose strand of her grey hair back into her bun. "My husband never tried. But you wouldn't be able to initiate such a bond unless you were *Zearla lurai*. He had no echo of the bonding, so it would not have worked. Once the bond has been opened ... I do not know."

Silence fell over them as Elinta processed everything. This new aspect of the bond was certainly interesting, but it did little to help her against Mazen, especially if he had more than one *ngaran*.

"What—" she cleared her throat, "—what do you think it'll mean for him? These extra bonds?"

Aesira shook her head as if sensing what Elinta was truly asking. "I do not think it would affect the strength of his senses in any way. Because of the dragons, he will be able to hear and see things in more locations through them, and their numbers will bulk his army, but that is all." She looked down the mountain. "It is their willingness to bond to him that concerns me."

That was a relief though, but it didn't change the fact that Mazen was still too strong for her to face alone, if it ever came to that. She wrung her hand in her shirt.

"How am I supposed to stop him?" Elinta whispered. "How am I supposed to master all these senses in time?"

"All?" Aesira grunted, refocusing on her, her skin crinkling around her eyes. "Who said anything about all? You only need to master a few, or you will only be, at best, mediocre with all."

"But—"

"Elinta. You are right in worrying about Mazen's experience, but he will also underestimate you because you are human, and because you are such a young one. You must be smart. Choose the senses that will help you the most and learn those."

Elinta opened and closed her mouth, a sudden fear knifing her in the stomach. "Well—well, maybe it won't come to that. If the council helps us, Mazen might just give it up."

Aesira looked at her sternly. Elinta half expected her to raise one of her bony fingers and point it at her. "You are the only one to stop my grandson. And he *must* be stopped. The council joining your cause will help you against the people Mazen leads, but not against Mazen himself. You are the only other *Zearla lurai*, Elinta. No one else would stand a chance against him."

Elinta's shoulders slumped again. "I know," she whispered. She'd known for a while and there was no hiding from it. She couldn't. For Blaine. He deserved better. Even if doubt and fear continued to eat at her. It felt like those feelings would never go away. But there was only forward, never backward.

Zhayra shifted beside her, twisting her head to study her. Elinta absently rubbed the dragon's smooth muzzle. "What senses should I learn?"

"Ahh no, that is one for you to discover."

Elinta let out a frustrated moan and rested her head against Zhayra's. The dragon's stomach tickled in amusement.

Aesira chuckled. "I do not know what your faults are. Your deficiencies. I could tell you to practice one thing when you need to focus on another. I would suggest learning about the senses and weighing up the benefits of each. You are doing well, Elinta. Do not doubt yourself."

"I looked them up in Nevira," Elinta murmured, her thoughts trailing. There was one moment, one instance, that she'd blocked thinking about where she knew she had used more senses. Ones she had never even tried to access before. Elinta raised her head. She had to have been in that moment. There was no other explanation.

"What is it, child?"

"When Blaine—" she choked "—died. Before I knew he was gone, I remember fighting like I'd never fought before so I could get to him. I moved so quickly, and I just knew what I was doing, where each part of me was. Beyond what's normal ..."

Aesira's face softened. "Often great emotional stress can help in accessing the senses. It sounds like you did then. But you mustn't rely on your feelings doing this for you again. You must learn."

Elinta nodded. She remembered learning about a sense like that, of knowing where one's body parts were at all times. It was a normal human sense, but what she'd accessed through Zhayra had been even stronger. Clearer. What she'd done that day had been amazing, she knew that, but she didn't like to remember it. She needed to try it again soon, so she could have a new memory associated with the sense. So that she could use it against Mazen.

Elinta sighed. A move echoed by Zhayra.

A twinge of longing crossed Aesira's old face but quickly vanished. "How long will you be in Liyarna? Perhaps you can practice while you're here."

"A while," she said. "Lorrin is on his way with a delegation, but they're still at least nine days away. And then, however long talking with the council will take."

"Plenty of time." Aesira clapped her hands, then pushed herself to her feet. "Come, it is time for you to stop moping and go back into the city."

Elinta shook her head at the woman but rose to her feet, anyway. Elinta was only average in height, but standing next to Aesira always made her feel tall. She was nearly a foot taller than the woman.

"I have nothing more to teach you for now, so I doubt I will see you again before you go," the woman said matter-of-factly. "Will you send my greetings to my son?"

"Son?" Elinta said, absolutely stumped with her thoughts still half on the senses. What was she talking about? King Riah was dead.

Aesira gave Elinta a curious grin and tilted her head. "Never mind then," she said with a laugh. It was, perhaps, the first Elinta had ever heard from the woman, and it was a surprisingly soft sound.

Elinta exchanged a glance with Zhayra, before looking back at the older *Zearla lurai*. "We'll come back to see you soon," she said. Maybe it was good in more ways than one that Tamir visited the woman often, if her mind was beginning to go. Unless ... no, she couldn't mean her foster son? How was she meant to know who that was? Surely, he was an old man by now and he wasn't even in Liyarna.

"I am not that old," Aesira grumbled, somehow reading Elinta's earlier thoughts. The woman shooed Elinta down the length of Zhayra, to where she usually climbed up the dragon, before she could pursue any questions about this mysterious son. "And stop using that harness! The senses will help you hold on."

"So would the fear of dying, but I'd rather not put it to the test again," Elinta mumbled, settling into place on Zhayra's back.

"Get going, *tarsi*," the old woman said, but Elinta wasn't sure if she was talking to her or Zhayra. Maybe it was both. Elinta waved as Zhayra grunted and leapt into the air.

CHAPTER
FIVE

E LINTA HAD ORIGINALLY PLANNED on returning to the
council's table to check on the three members, but she
wanted to talk through what she'd learned with Zhayra. Besides,
Tamir would tell her if anything important happened in the city.
So instead, Elinta asked Zhayra to go further up the rocky mountain to locate somewhere for them to sit in private.

The dragon found a huge outcropping of grey rock jutting
out of the mountain. Scraggy tufts of grasses pushed up through
the cracks. Zhayra landed softly and Elinta slid to the ground
beside her, her mind whirling with everything they'd discussed
with Aesira.

"What do you think?" Elinta asked, turning to the dragon. She had to shield her eyes against the sunshine reflecting off her white scales, but the brightness still sent her squinting. "Do you think Aesira's right about just learning a few of the senses?"

Zhayra tilted her head as though thinking, then blinked once: yes.

"But which ones?" Elinta walked a few paces away and then turned back, too distracted to appreciate the beautiful view of the forest sprawled out below them. "I need dragonsight and the hearing ... and your heat sense has been helpful. But then so would kina—kina—that one where I know how I'm moving, or is that proprioception?" She threw her hands up. "And what about balance?"

Zhayra lowered her head, looking Elinta in the eyes, and grunted. That, coupled with the tinge of humour fluttering in the dragon, told her Zhayra thought she was overreacting.

Elinta took a deep breath, forcing her thoughts to calm. "I suppose that's not too bad. I already know dragonsight, and the hearing isn't too hard. I just need to get used to seeing heat and using sight at the same time so that I don't lose the contents of my stomach anymore. Then that just leaves learning the movement and balance ones from scratch."

Zhayra blinked once. Elinta sighed and walked to the cliff edge, sitting a metre away from the drop with her legs sprawled out in front of her. She sent a small rock flying over the edge.

Zhayra shuffled around to look out across the Calaza with her. The forest truly was beautiful, with its mix of silver and brown trunks, and stunningly green leaves. Flocks of birds moved among them, rising together like a wave before sweeping down on another set of trees. It was deceptively peaceful when she knew the trouble she'd stirred up in the city over Mazen. Trouble she had, admittedly, been ignoring.

But there was one more thing Aesira had mentioned that clung to Elinta's mind. Her stomach tightened. Not at the skill itself, reserved only for strong familial or romantic love, but at the name it had conjured. Lorrin.

Zhayra looked down at her and grunted, moving her head forward as she did. It was as though she was telling Elinta to spit it out. She nearly laughed at the ways the dragon managed to communicate with her. The sunlight flickered across her scales.

"I—" She cleared her throat, then tried again. "It's just—"

Elinta swore that if the dragon had an eyebrow to cock, she would have been doing it right then.

"I don't think I could ever be with him because it would make him even more of a target with everything going on, and he wouldn't be safe, and with everything else going on it might not be a good idea anyway," she gushed, fixing her eyes straight ahead as she spoke.

Zhayra snorted, her chest tingled, and her stomach tightened. Humour and a tinge of frustration.

Elinta turned to the dragon, startled.

"You don't think so?" Elinta frowned, pushing a wayward strand of hair back behind her ear.

Zhayra lowered her head, fixed Elinta with an amber eye, and blinked twice.

"But—"

Zhayra grunted and blinked twice again.

Elinta mulled it over, trying to find the information that had led Zhayra to tell her she was being silly. Lorrin was a prince ... and Mazen had originally been after Lorrin the night he'd snuck into the White Palace and ended up fighting her. Elinta closed her eyes against the reflection from Zhayra and kept thinking it over. Lorrin would probably always be a target in one way or another. Mazen would want to kill him whether Elinta was around or not.

Elinta's spirits wanted to soar ... except. "I don't want to ever leave you," she whispered, opening her eyes. "I couldn't."

It was almost too hard to even think of. There was a time, in the very early days of their bond, when Elinta had planned for her and Zhayra to part ways. But now the thought was unbearable. Zhayra was a part of her and her closest friend. But being with Lorrin might mean she and Zhayra would have to separate ...

Zhayra nudged her gently with her muzzle. The movement sent rainbows of light dancing across the dragon's scales.

"Zhayra," Elinta said. "Wherever you go, I'm going too."

Zhayra held her eye a moment longer, and Elinta got the feeling the dragon thought it didn't change anything.

"But it might," she said, thinking of Zhayra's claim to the dragon throne. "If you want to go home, I'll go with you, but Lorrin couldn't come. He'll be king one day."

Zhayra lowered her head gently to Elinta's lap, her head wider than the length of Elinta's legs. She absentmindedly stroked the dragon's face. She'd forgotten to ask Aesira about the dragons and their royalty with all that they'd discussed. She'd have to ask her during her next visit. Despite what Aesira had said, she was determined to see the woman again.

For now, though, they looked out over the mountain and watched the day as it passed them by as Elinta tried to work out what she would do with her runaway heart.

The next day found Elinta working in the training field as soon as the sun was up, the warm morning light casting a golden hue over the grass. Zhayra snored quietly in the centre, but Elinta was up and determined to learn. They were the only ones on the field, so she was going to take full advantage of it and the cooler morning while she could.

"Right," she said, coming to a stop by Zhayra after running a couple laps around the field to warm up, a habit she'd developed with Lorrin many months ago. She ran through the list of senses she needed to work on and landed on heat vision. There were vast improvements to be made with that one still. For one thing, she could hardly move without getting dizzy.

"OK." Bracing herself as she closed her enhanced eyes, Elinta strained to see the huge dragon mound in front of her.

A colourful lump where the dragon lay slowly appeared in her mind. Red had clumped around the dragon's mouth. A thick line of reds and oranges ran down her neck. The rest of her was also surprisingly warm, only her claws were blue.

"Wow," Elinta murmured, staring at the different colours along the sleeping dragon. An orange cloud left her mouth in time with her breathing.

But that was the easy part. Elinta opened her eyes, letting the image from the heat sense sit next to the image from her eyes. Taking a deep, steadying breath, she made herself gently jog around the grassy field again. She made it barely three metres before the dizziness struck, but she forced her feet to keep moving.

"Urgh." Elinta groaned, placing a hand on her roiling belly as she staggered along. But she didn't allow her feet to slow, even if she was sure she looked like she'd drunk too much wine. Stopping wasn't going to make her any better with the sense. And she had to get better.

Halfway around the field, something changed Elinta's mind. Bile rose in her mouth, and she came to a dead stop. "No," she gasped, bent at the waist, and retched.

Moaning, Elinta made herself keep the sense on and her eyes open as she stumbled across the field to slump against Zhayra.

The dragon was still asleep and totally unaware of Elinta's troubles.

"How do you see like this all the time?" she grumbled, wiping sweat from her brow. Elinta poked the dragon. "Are you going to sleep all morning?"

Zhayra grunted, shifted slightly, and continued sleeping.

"Elinta!"

Frowning, Elinta leant forward to see around Zhayra's bulk toward where the voice was coming from. Tamir strode across the field, his figure lit in a uniform red.

"Morning!" she called, closing her eyes as the dizziness hit again. Any form of movement seemed to be causing it in her. It was even happening when she was the one completely still.

A shove came from behind her, and Elinta grunted in surprise as her body lurched. Turning, still with her eyes closed, she found Zhayra's wing pushing against her, but the dragon's eyes were still firmly shut. Too firmly shut.

"Don't make me come up there, lazybones! Everyone else has been up for a while." She laughed, gently shoving against the wing.

Zhayra had cracked open an eye to watch Tamir as he came to a stop in front of them, but other than the humour tingling in her stomach, she ignored Elinta's remark.

"Are you OK?" he asked, his hands folded behind his back. It was hard to tell in the coloured image, but it looked as though his eyes were scanning her.

"I've been practicing the heat sense," she said, gesturing at her still shuttered eyes.

"Ah," Tamir said. "The council would like to speak with you as soon as you are able." He'd pulled back his hair today, with half up in a bun and the other half loose and barely touching his shoulders.

"We can head there now," Elinta said despite the grumbling in her stomach. She wouldn't be able to eat now, not with knowing the council wanted to see her. And not with her stomach still roiling from dizziness. Yes, she'd get the meeting over with right away.

Elinta opened her eyes, shutting off the extra sense, and she jumped to her feet.

"I thought you might want to." Tamir smiled. "Will we meet you there, Zhayra?"

Zhayra blinked, stretching out her legs with a long groan. Elinta had to jump away as the dragon began to stretch her large membrane wings.

"Let's go then," Elinta said, shooting a teasing glare back at the dragon.

Elinta and Tamir left the field together, heading back through the awakening city. It was cooler under the canopy of the large trees, but she could already tell by the heaviness in the air that it was going to be another hot day.

"Can we just quickly stop so I can wash my face?" Elinta asked, wondering if she looked as ill as she felt. "I, uh, had troubles with the heat sense again."

"Of course. I'm sure it will become easier in time, *tarsi.*"

She nodded, thinking of the last time she'd had to rely on it. It had been when she and Tamir had snuck through the desert in search of her brother and father. She'd had to move with her eyes closed while using the extra sense because of how sick it had made her feel then. She tried not to linger on the reason she'd been there in the first place.

Fifteen minutes later, Elinta and Tamir arrived at the council table. Zhayra landed instantly. Aisla, Piran, and Nakiah were waiting for them and were already seated at the table, their faces carefully neutral. They seemed as neat and collected as usual. No one else was there.

"*Layzun, Zearla lurai* and Zhayra," Aisla said, using the formal greeting. "Tamir, welcome home."

"Thank you," Elinta replied, willing for the moment to let the council play out whatever scenario they'd planned since she'd last seen them. Tamir merely nodded.

"We have long discussed your news and are willing to meet with Prince Lorrin and the delegation," Piran said, his deep voice reverberating around the clearing. His long hair swayed in a light breeze. "Though we must stress that we cannot promise anything."

"Thank you," she said again, keeping it short in case her impatience shone through her tone. Now was not the time to offend them again, but his words were somewhat redundant when Lorrin was already on his way.

Tamir remained silent by her side, and she wondered whether it was for the same reason. He'd joined her in Nevira because he'd disagreed with the council's original decision not to pursue Mazen. He'd even gone so far as to help her rescue her family from him.

"But," Nakiah said, his high voice grating on her. She braced herself for what he was going to say. "You must know that we did not sanction or support Tamir's involvement in the attack at Nevira, terrible though it was."

"Of course," Elinta said, smiling sweetly even as her blood boiled. "You needn't worry. This council has made its position quite clear."

Nakiah's eyes darkened, but he didn't say anything, perhaps because Zhayra shifted her large body at that moment, letting out a quiet huff. Or maybe he was playing the same game Elinta was. He brushed a strand of brown hair from his eyes.

"I look forward to your meeting with Lorrin and whatever results it may bring. I know I speak for all of us when I say Mazen is a threat that can no longer be ignored." Elinta hid a smile at her own words, knowing that her arrival yesterday and subsequent announcement in front of so many civilians had *made* Mazen impossible for the council to ignore. No matter how much the council might wish it, the Liyarnans wouldn't simply forget their long-dead prince was actually alive and trying to enslave the humans and kill a dragon.

Nakiah scowled. Elinta could have scowled right back, but she stopped herself. *Careful*, she reminded herself. *Careful.*

"We ask that you join us for dinner tomorrow night, Elinta," Aisla said, her own emotions carefully hidden. "We are pleased to have a *Zearla lurai* among us again."

Zhayra's stomach flickered with irritation at the words, and Elinta tried to give her a calming glance, understanding her feelings immediately. Despite their happiness at having a dragon among them again as well, it seemed the council didn't want to eat with her, too. Though the dragon usually hunted for food in the forest, she would have liked to have been involved. Elinta would have refused the invitation, especially for Zhayra, but she was still playing the game and had to choose her moves wisely. Zhayra, she knew, would understand.

"I'd be happy to," she said, facing the council again, "though I'd like to request Tamir and Serren be invited as well." There was no way that she wanted to be alone with the Asali Council for that long, especially if they invited Maaka again. The warrior had refused to speak the common tongue the whole night at the last dinner unless he was speaking directly to Elinta. It had made for an awkward meal where Lorrin had attempted to translate for Niles and Elinta as best as he could.

"Of course," Piran said.

There was a beat of silence where it seemed the council had nothing more to say, but neither did she.

Elinta shuffled her feet. "Uh, well, I have some things to ... do."

"Yes, very well. We'll send someone for you tomorrow night," Nakiah said. Elinta half expected him to wave his hand dismissively in the air, but he didn't.

Aisla's brow crinkled slightly, but she nodded. "*Layzulla.*"

Tamir whispered from beside Elinta. "I have some things to attend to while we're here, but Serren and I will see you at lunch."

"Thanks," Elinta said.

Tamir hurried from the clearing while Elinta mounted Zhayra. The dragon took off, leaving the vined netting behind the council swaying again.

For the next hour, they flew together over the Calaza. Though Elinta had become more comfortable flying since Niles and Lorrin had given her the harness, she wanted to keep at it, to keep practising. Besides, as pretty as the city was, Elinta was an outsider there and time seemed to drag. If there was one thing she knew about herself, it was that she needed to be kept busy. And preferably away from the Asali. So Elinta let Zhayra have free rein, trusting that the dragon wouldn't do anything too crazy while Elinta clung on to her neck. Zhayra's happiness radiated through her.

The wind rushed into Elinta's face, surprisingly cold despite the heat of the day, and sent her blonde hair flying out behind her. She'd lost many hair ties while flying though she permanently kept one on her wrist to help her with accessing and turning off the senses. No matter how tightly she did her hair up, it always seemed to come out. Perhaps she'd have to get Neva to teach her how to do tighter braids the next time she saw the maid.

Zhayra sped up, tilting her body to the side, dropping several metres, and abruptly catching updrafts that shoved them upward. Elinta's stomach dipped at a particularly sudden drop, but a burst of laughter quickly followed. It was quickly met with a stab of guilt. She shouldn't be laughing. Not now, not after—

Zhayra grunted, turning her head as she flew to look at Elinta.

"What?" Elinta said, shifting to catch the dragon's eye easier.

Zhayra grunted again, then made a series of noises that sounded distinctly like a laugh, moving her head joltingly up and down. Zhayra then blinked once.

"I—what?" Elinta frowned. That was a grumpy grunt, a laugh, and then a blink for yes. "Are you trying to tell me not to feel guilty for laughing?"

Zhayra blinked again.

Elinta shook her head, but a smile tilted her lips. "OK, but could you please concentrate on where you're flyi—" She broke off into a scream as Zhayra's wings billowed in a sudden updraft of wind and they shot into the clouds.

"There you are!" Tamir called as Zhayra landed in the centre of the training field a couple of hours later. "Serren and I were beginning to wonder where you two were."

"Sorry," Elinta said, untying her legs and unclipping her belt from the harness. "We were getting some flying in and lost track of time." She slipped to the ground. At least the wind had helped her dry off after their unexpected trip through the clouds. But she didn't dare run her fingers through her hair. It felt like a rat's nest.

Zhayra grunted and trotted over to where Tamir and Serren were seated with several plates set out before them.

"I brought some meat for you," Serren said to Zhayra. Elinta trailed after the dragon, trying in vain to flatten her wind-swept hair with a flat hand. "We weren't sure when you last ate."

Zhayra pulled back and roared.

"Thank you," Elinta said with a laugh as she sat between the couple. Zhayra had certainly been communicating more vocally lately. It warmed Elinta's heart to be able to have deeper conversations with her.

In one go, Zhayra ate the small piece of fresh meat Serren had sourced, then she stretched out on the ground in the sun beside them. Her belly was warm and her chest light. The tip of her tail disappeared into the trees.

"How did it go with the council?" Serren asked, handing Elinta a cup of sweet tea.

"Um, well, they'll meet with Lorrin, but I don't think he would have let them say no," she said, sipping at the tea while Serren unpacked the bag she'd brought containing their food. The woman set the various dishes down in front of her as she sorted through them.

"That is good news, though not what you were hoping?" she said as Tamir reached over to help her organise the food. They worked seamlessly together, seeming as aware of each other as they were of themselves.

"No, I thought maybe they'd want to help as soon as they knew what Mazen was doing," Elinta said, her heart sinking again at the very thought.

"Lorrin and his aunt will explain everything to them. It is in both of our interests, after all. I'm sure they will see that, *tarsi*," Tamir said.

A weighty silence fell over them. Serren pushed her long brown hair back from her shoulders and gently reached out to take Elinta's hand. "I am sorry for your brother. Tamir tells me he was a great man."

Elinta's throat bobbed. "Thank you."

Elinta took the bowl of salad Tamir offered her. It looked like a mix of grains and strange berries. But as she took it, her eyes landed on the blue *illayas* bracelet on Tamir's right wrist. Serren, she knew, also wore one but on her left.

"What do your bracelets mean?" Elinta asked, glancing between them, glad to be able to change the subject from her brother.

"Oh." Serren laughed, tugging at the hem of her dress as she shifted to put the bag behind her. "They're how we show marriage. We are joined together." She held her hand with the bracelet next to Tamir's. The metal glinted in the sunlight.

"I wondered why you didn't have rings. I guess that's a human tradition then?"

Serren nodded. "We are lucky to have our bracelets made from *illayas,* as is tradition. Since the Eggslaying, we've not had any new ones made."

Because they needed dragon fire to melt and shape the rare metal, Elinta knew. She frowned.

"How did you get yours? You were married after then, weren't you?"

"Yes," Tamir said, swallowing a mouthful of food. "Aesira gifted hers and her husband's to us. It is a great honour. The bracelets are usually never removed."

Aesira and Tamir must be really close then, Elinta thought with a smile.

Serren turned to Zhayra. "The harness looks very good on you," she said. "I hope that you find it comfortable. It has been a long time since this city has seen one."

Zhayra blinked once, happiness bursting in her stomach at being addressed.

"It's been really good," Elinta said after translating the dragon's response and spooning more food into her mouth.

Their conversation drifted off, jumping from topic to topic as they enjoyed each other's company. Liyarna, despite being so big, was strangely lonely, but with Zhayra, Tamir, and Serren, it didn't feel too bad. For just a moment, Elinta's shoulders didn't seem so heavy, and she let Zhayra's contentment wash over her.

That afternoon, Elinta resumed her training. Just as she had that morning, Elinta tried to run around the field with heat vision on and her eyes open.

"You are going well," Tamir called as he arrived at the edge of the field.

"Thanks!" She'd made it halfway around the field and so far had only had one major dizzy spell. She'd also managed to keep the contents of her stomach down this time. The trick seemed to be focusing more on one image while letting the other become almost like peripheral vision. There, but not the focus.

The ground shook slightly, in time with Zhayra's large bounds as she followed along behind Elinta, waiting for her to draw ahead some way before covering the distance in one large leap. The shaking wasn't helping Elinta's balance, but she couldn't bring herself to tell the dragon to stop when she was clearly having fun.

After one successful lap, Elinta stopped beside Tamir with a huge grin, but it faded when Tamir smiled back and drew a sword from his belt.

Elinta groaned. "You'll cut my arm off the second I stop to catch my balance!"

"I will not," Tamir said, now pulling a knife from his belt. "These are training blades."

Elinta's shoulders slumped. "OK."

She took the sword and stood at the ready, making sure the heat sense was the vision to the side. Zhayra backed away to give them space, her stomach lighting in interest and her tail swinging slowly behind her.

Tamir struck, his blade darting toward her knee. Elinta blocked, stepping forward as she did to get inside his reach. He spun to the side, keeping his blade in close but with the edge sticking out. It harmlessly slid across her arm as he moved. Not even three seconds in and he'd already landed a blow.

Tamir had slowed his movements down, too, matching the loss in her own speed because of the extra sense. Her concentration was now split, with a large focus on trying to maintain control of her vision as well as her swordplay.

She dove back in, feinting a strike at Tamir's side before letting her sword drop and run along his leg. But the movement sent Elinta's stomach jolting and bile rose in her throat.

"Are you well?" Tamir said, his training dagger dropping as she stepped back. "You are looking pale, *tarsi*."

"I'm f—" She folded in on herself, emptying the contents of her stomach. "Urgh." She groaned, arms folded across her middle.

Zhayra shifted beside them but didn't make a sound, though her throat seemed to tighten.

Tamir gave her a moment to collect herself before insisting they continue a few metres away. Elinta trudged after him. The fight lasted another two minutes before Elinta lost her balance and fell straight toward the tip of Tamir's fake blade. He turned it down at the last moment and caught her as she crashed into him.

"I think we can leave it there for today," he said, helping to righten her on her feet.

She moaned her agreement, pressing a hand to her head. It took her only a second to turn the heat sense off. At least she was improving there.

"That was not fun," Elinta said, handing the sword over and shaking her head.

"You did well."

"I didn't," she said, thinking over the fight now that she no longer had to argue with the strangely coloured vision. "That was the quickest session we've ever had."

"And they will get longer. You're right to want to train it, *tarsi*. It was a great help in Bradfin."

"It was." The reminder of her brother sent her throat clogging, but she swallowed heavily. "So were you."

Tamir smiled.

"Why did you stop being a warrior?" Elinta asked, running a hand through her hair. It had taken Serren's help to finally get the bulk of the tangles out. "When I first came here, the council said they'd asked you to come back before. So, you must have left at some point."

Zhayra grunted, fixing one of her amber eyes on him.

Tamir glanced down, and she got the feeling it was something personal that had stopped him from explaining. Perhaps she shouldn't have asked him so bluntly, but her curiosity had been bubbling away for some time.

"It was just after the Eggslaying," he said, looking back up. "We had lost King Riah, Mazen, and the dragons. I had just ... had enough."

She could understand that.

"Thank you," she whispered, "for coming back."

"Mazen has gone too far. He needs to be stopped."

The overpowering urge to tell him he didn't know all of what Mazen had done hit her, but she shoved it down. She'd tell him about the other dragon, or dragons, Mazen had bonded with once Lorrin and Niles arrived. Until then, she'd work hard practicing the senses so that when she told them, there'd be some good news along with it. For now, she'd bear the knowledge alone. Her sole comfort was that the *ngaran* didn't allow anyone to control a dragon, only communicate and use the senses. But now, Mazen could have eyes all over the country, ready for him to look through whenever he wanted.

Elinta lay beside Zhayra that night, her mind whirling despite hours of trying to calm her thoughts. She stared up at the night sky, studying the stars with her enhanced eyes. She'd never tire of the details the sense revealed. The colours she wouldn't usually notice. Zhayra watched with her. No words passed between them, but Elinta knew the dragon was thinking along the same lines as her. Mazen had consumed their thoughts for a long time now. Sighing, she snuggled closer to Zhayra, wondering whether the day would ever come when they'd be free of the worry and the fear. But what prison would ever hold him, when *illayas* could break through any metal? Was there even enough *illayas* left to make one? Her eyes slowly, finally, closed, and she drifted into a sleep plagued by an Asali with maroon eyes.

Elinta jolted awake, finding herself pressed against the smooth scales of Zhayra's belly in the darkness. Liyarna was silent, a weighty silence only found in the dead of night, but a deep foreboding sat on her chest. Elinta strained her ears for any sign of something being amiss and knew Zhayra was doing the same. She felt sleep trying to tug her back under, but still she waited, listening, knowing deep in her bones something was wrong. Smoke wafted in the air.

Then a scream ripped through the night.

CHAPTER

SIX

A NOTHER SCREAM ROSE TO meet the first and soon the city was alive with shouts and cries. Elinta and Zhayra were on their feet in seconds. Where only a moment ago the training field had been dark, orange flickering light now illuminated it. The light came from the other side of the city. Fire.

"Mazen's here." There was no question about it in Elinta's mind. No one and nothing else would do this. She spun in place to lock eyes with Zhayra. "You need to get out of here."

It wasn't safe for the dragon in the city. Not when Vaherin could fly over and spot her in an instant on the open training field. Her throat clogged up at the very thought of him finding Zhayra.

Zhayra growled deep in her throat and blinked twice. Her scales reflected the orange light pouring over them.

"No, listen to me. I have to find Tamir and Serren. We can't leave them here. You need to get away from the city and out of sight." She paused, wracking her brain for a place they could meet outside of Liyarna. "Do you remember where we first met Tamir in the forest?"

Zhayra blinked once. Elinta could feel her acceptance seeping in.

A cloud of smoke spread over them, and the screams grew louder. And what about the council? What would happen now? Could she get them out too? But Zhayra wouldn't be able to carry them all. She'd have to send them into the forest to hide and then come back for them.

"We'll meet you there. Promise me, Zhayra. Promise me you'll go there."

Zhayra keened quietly, nudging her gently with her nose.

"I'll see you there," she whispered.

Zhayra blinked once and turned into the trees, her heart a weight in her chest. Elinta's eyes grew heavy as soon as the dragon's tail disappeared.

Elinta grabbed her satchel and the bag containing Zhayra's harness from the ground, slinging them over her shoulder, and turned to face the burning city.

Elinta studied the buildings, seeing them with sharp clarity. Too sharp for her normal eyes ... She'd forgotten to switch off her dragonsight before falling asleep and it was still on! Just like her emotional link to Zhayra, it hadn't shut off overnight.

Smiling grimly, Elinta drew her sword and ran into the city. Mazen's *illayas* dagger was still in her satchel, the only weapon that would pierce his armour, but the thought of touching the weapon that had killed her brother made her skin crawl. Her grip tightened on her own sword.

Elinta had made it barely three metres off the training field when she stumbled in her steps, the Green City stretching away in front of her. She still didn't know where Tamir lived. How would she find him in the chaos surrounding her? Elinta stared around at the huts woven in between the trees and jolted.

An Asali was running toward her, the man's face streaked with ash, sword in his hand. Elinta raised her weapon, bracing herself. She'd try to get the first strike in, she thought as she watched him draw closer. But the man simply ran past her. Elinta stared after his disappearing form, heart thudding in her chest. A sick dread settled over her. She was the only human in a city of Asali and any one of them could be working for Mazen. Any one of them might try to kill her. And she had no way of telling which ones they would be until the moment they attacked.

Zhayra's own heart was tight as she watched through Elinta's eyes.

Elinta shook her head and forced herself to think over the deafening screams and the rush of flames that had risen to meet them. Her skin grew sweaty as the air trapped under the canopy began to heat. Tamir wouldn't just sit around in his home. He'd go looking for her. Either at the training field or at the house where she was meant to be. She came to her decision. She'd go to the house since Tamir would have to pass it on his way to the field. Depending on what she found there, she would make another decision.

Elinta ran, ran as hard as she could, her bags bouncing wildly against her body while her gaze snagged on every single Asali that came her way. She dodged them as best as she could, brushing against bodies in their frenzied rush to flee the city. But none tried to attack her. Maybe Mazen's warriors hadn't made it this far into the city yet. But she didn't let her guard down and kept her weapon ready.

Her little building came into view. The trunks in the walls shooting up into the air. The canopy to her left was on fire. Smouldering leaves drifted down to the grassy floor. The fire around the city had oddly helped her, lighting up the buildings in place of the lighting the Asali didn't have or need. She pushed her legs harder. Too hard. A brown-haired Asali ran out from beside the building, and they were on a collision course.

The man turned at the last moment to see her, and she dimly recognised Nakiah as she slammed straight into him.

"There you are! Where's Zhayra? We need to get out of here," the council member said, scrambling to his feet and staring at her with wide eyes. His earlier haughtiness was gone. Crimson soaked the front of his grey tunic and coated his arms like sleeves.

"Are you alright?" Elinta grabbed his arms, searching him for any sign of injury. The blood shined with his light behind it.

"My—my wife," he murmured, following her gaze.

Elinta swallowed. "Zhayra's waiting in the forest. Go to the training field, and I'll lead you to her once I've found Tamir." She could have told him where the dragon was, but in the darkness, he would never have found her, not even by the light of his body.

"No, we both need to go now," he said, clutching at her arm painfully, fear making his already high voice even higher. He pushed a lock of hair from his eyes, smudging blood across his face. Orange light flickered across his glowing form.

"I need to find Tamir. I'll meet you out there!" She wrenched herself free from his grip, blood smearing along her arm and ran on without another word. If Tamir wasn't waiting for her here, then maybe he was trying to help Aisla and Piran.

The beating of heavy wings sounded, and Elinta instinctively ducked as a large shadow passed over her, pushing the smoke down onto her. The screaming intensified, so loud that Elinta's ears ached with it. Was it Vaherin or one of the other dragons flying over? But she couldn't tell through the canopy. As soon as the shadow was gone, Elinta jumped to her feet and forced her legs on. Her breath came in shallow gasps, her chest constricting against the thick smoke, but she kept going.

Elinta ducked once again as a flock of birds flew over her screeching, flying so low one of their wings grazed along the side of her head. The sound was echoed by a set of larger wings returning above the canopy. It blocked out the fiery glow and left the city lit only by its occupants for a moment. While it may once have been normal for Liyarna, it was now eerily frightening.

The shadow cleared and Elinta realised she'd stopped in her tracks, just like the only other two people still in that part of the city. As the firelight returned, the others unfroze and ran into the burning forest. Flaming leaves drifted down around them. Ribbons of smouldering silver bark following close behind.

Elinta paused. The council table was close. Just up ahead was the nearest building to the clearing, all she had to do was pass it and turn right ... but something told her not to go charging in. A heavy foreboding sat on her chest when she looked toward that clearing. She glanced around her. There was no one else here now, something that sent her internal alarms blaring even louder. Elinta pivoted and crept through the city in a wide loop, coming in behind the council table. A clump of low trees sat to the right of the vine netting spread across the space behind the stone table. The sweet scent of those beautiful flowers decorating the curtain reached her, but she hardly registered it as she ducked to her belly behind the trees. Something else was in the air. The sharp tang of blood.

A cold sweat broke across her face, and she clamped a hand over her mouth to keep the gasp rising in her throat from escaping. Mazen was in the council's clearing. And he'd found the *illayas* sword the council had kept. One of the last two remaining in Eldras. Zhayra's stomach dropped just as quickly as Elinta's at the sight of the weapon clutched in his hand.

The exiled prince was locked in a fight against a stocky Asali with close-cropped black hair and shining white eyes. Elinta recognised him immediately: Maaka, one of Liyarna's best warriors, a man she'd met on her last visit. They whirled around each other, their swords flashing in their own light and the light of the fires raging behind them in the forest. Mazen, in his maroon dragonscale armour, moved like lightning, and Elinta knew for certain that she only kept up with his movements because of her dragonsight. She tore her eyes away from them, glancing around the clearing for any sign of Tamir, and gasped.

Piran lay sprawled under the table, his face turned away from her with his long hair spread out behind him. She'd seen enough injuries to know the blood soaking the grass around him meant that he was dead, but his body was only just beginning to dim. Aisla, her leg strangely limp, dragged herself across the ground toward him. Her hair was a tangled mess, streaked with blood and dirt. Her eyes were glued to the two fighting figures as she clawed through the grass, but the woman didn't allow an ounce of fear to show on her face. Tamir was nowhere to be seen.

A loud clang echoed across the clearing. Elinta's eyes darted back to Mazen in time to see his sword sinking into a weapon-less Maaka. The warrior fell to his knees, deep gurgling gasps coming from his mouth. Blood splattered down his chin. Mazen yanked his sword from the man's chest. Maaka's bright eyes dimmed, and he sunk to the ground. His light instantly began to leave him.

With a cocky grin, Mazen slowly turned in place. Flecks of Maaka's blood had spattered across his face, but he either didn't notice or didn't care. His maroon eyes landed on Aisla.

"Is that really the best you have?"

He strode toward the woman, flicking Maaka's blood from his blue blade. Large drops of it landed on Aisla's pale face. He was mere steps away from her.

The movement snapped Elinta back to herself and she grabbed her sword from where she'd dropped it beside her. Closing her eyes, Elinta braced herself, then began to rise to her feet. She couldn't let Mazen get away again. Couldn't let this continue.

A hand yanked her back down into the dirt. Tamir stared from beside her with wide eyes and slowly shook his head. She turned back, unable to keep from watching Mazen.

"I guess I shouldn't be surprised you were chosen for the council," he said, standing over Aisla. "But did you really think you had any real power over *me?* That you could stop me from returning to take *my* throne?"

Elinta grabbed a fistful of dirt. His throne. *No.*

A stone clogged Zhayra's throat.

Elinta pulled against Tamir's grip, but he didn't release her.

"You will never be a true king," Aisla said raggedly, no longer trying to move away from him. She coughed at the smoke thickening the air. But still she showed no fear looking up into the face of the exiled prince. In that moment, Elinta wished she'd known Aisla better, had gotten to know the brave woman staring up at death so fearlessly.

"I beg to differ." He struck, sending the sword straight into the woman's heart.

Elinta's head whipped round to look at Tamir. His face was deathly pale, and his lips parted as though to speak. Elinta slammed her hand down over his mouth, stopping the death blessing in its tracks. Tamir's eyes widened, a flash of panic in his eyes as if he'd realised what he'd been about to do. Even a whisper might carry to Mazen if he was listening with the strength of Vaherin's ears. And though she wanted to stop the man, fear made her quiet Tamir, rooted her to the spot.

Mazen twisted in place again, surveying the bodies and the burning city. His eyes seemed to shine, but not just from his own natural glow.

"Vaherin," he said as though the dragon were right beside him. "It's done. Hurry." He strode out of the clearing, the *illayas* sword held point down at his side. Crimson blood dripped from the end and soaked into the ground. All was still in the council's clearing.

They waited two full minutes before they dared to move, and in that time, the screaming in the city doubled, the rush of fire grew stronger, and the smoke settled like a thick blanket over them. Vaherin was burning the forest around the city. Blocking everyone inside.

"We need to go now!" Elinta yelled over the roaring of the fire. They'd be trapped if they couldn't get to Zhayra before the way was overtaken by flames.

Tamir was up beside her in an instant and they were running through the trees on the outskirts of the city, scarcely paying attention to their surroundings. If they couldn't get out, if Mazen found them ... They had to get out now.

Smoke hit the back of Elinta's throat, and she coughed violently, but didn't dare slow down to recover her breath. Tamir kept pace beside her.

She jolted to a halt. "Tamir! Where's Serren?"

He turned, having stopped a few steps ahead, his face unreadable. "She is not coming."

"What?"

"We do not have time to stop, *tarsi*." He hurried back and grabbed her arm, dragging her back into a run. "She wishes to stay and help our people."

"But Mazen, he'll ..."

"He does not know who she is. We were not together when Mazen lived here." He coughed, shaking his head at her to stop the argument on her lips. His eyes were heavy, betraying his worry, but Elinta didn't argue.

Serren. Elinta silently wished the woman all the luck she could possibly have and pushed herself on. The training field came into view, and there was Nakiah hiding under the trees at the far end, peering around a silver trunk.

"Nakiah," Tamir breathed. "He survived."

"I found him on the way into the city," she said, her voice already husky from the smoke, then added, "He wanted to leave you here."

Tamir smirked, but the expression cleared when the blood on the man's clothes and arms became clear.

"There you are!" Nakiah gasped, stumbling forward. "The forest is burning!"

"Where is Raelynn?"

Nakiah stared blankly at Tamir, his blood-soaked arms limp at his sides.

"Nakiah—" Tamir grabbed the man's shoulders "—where's your *ngaparta?*"

"She was fighting," he said blankly. But when his gaze landed on his bloodied hands, his eyes welled.

"We have to go," Elinta said, snapping Nakiah out of it. In a distant part of herself, she realised she hardly recognised the grieving man. But there was no time to offer comfort. No time for anything. "Both of you need to hold on to me as tightly as you can. I'll lead you through to Zhayra."

Tamir grabbed the hem of her shirt while Nakiah latched onto the strap of her satchel, leaving her sword arm free. She stared into the forest, the shadows swallowing up the trees within a few metres despite the fires igniting around the city. If any Asali had come with Mazen and were patrolling the forest, their glow would give them away up close, but from a distance.... She'd need more than dragonsight to lead Tamir and Nakiah safely through there.

Gritting her teeth, Elinta switched on her heat vision. The second, coloured image appeared in her mind, but she forced herself to focus most of her attention on her eyes for the moment. She could do this. She didn't have a choice. She shoved her hair back from her face.

"Let's go," Elinta said, and ran into the shadows.

Tamir and Nakiah's light illuminated the ground in front of them, helping Elinta's eyes to pick a way through. The strength of Zhayra's eyes had already made the night a little less dark, letting her see barely twenty feet around her, rather than just a hand directly in front of her face. The glow added another three feet. The heat sense, though, gave her up to forty feet. The trees were a light blue, the space between them a deep blue-black. She navigated the coloured world as best she could, swapping her focus to it.

"I cannot see anything," Nakiah gasped, tripping on a root, but his iron grip on her didn't falter.

"I can," she whispered. Though they were no longer in the city, the screams still echoed around them. The heaviness of the city's dread was as thick as the smoke in the air. She couldn't bring herself to raise her voice beyond the softest whisper.

"Get down!" Tamir tugged hard at her, and she allowed herself to go down. The three of them lay sprawled in the dirt and leaves as wing beats thundered overhead and Vaherin's maroon form flew by. He was too far away for her heat sense to see him, which meant he couldn't see them. Zhayra's gut was clenched so tightly Elinta could almost feel it as her own.

"We're OK," she whispered to the dragon. But then the un-mistakable roar of flames spewing forth came and the forest lit up barely two hundred metres away. Sweat trickled down her back. Heat bit at her face.

"Get up!" Elinta grunted, dragging them to their feet as she jumped to her own. She ran, the men following, their grip unyielding. Her vision swam, the dizziness like a brick to the head, but she ran on. The fire. If it spread. If it cut them off from Zhayra ...

Elinta's foot caught on a rock, and she tilted forward, but Tamir pulled her upright. She didn't waste her breath on thanking him but ran on. The smoke grew thicker, combatting the little light the fires offered. Their coughs doubled. Her chest wheezed. But she didn't slow, didn't even allow it. Not until the bile rose in her throat and she was forced to stop and empty the contents of her stomach by a tree.

"Keep going," Elinta said, her voiced sounding ragged to her own ears.

Nakiah's breaths came in deep, desperate gasps, but the man didn't stop. He didn't complain. Whoever he'd been only this morning was gone. And right then, she was thankful for it.

Thirty minutes into the forest, the trees grew closer together, limiting the light of the Asali to no further than their own feet. The silver and brown branches tangled together in a thin, spindly wall. Elinta had to slow her pace for Tamir and Nakiah. She might still have been able to see, but their vision was severely limited. Elinta had to direct them. Pointing out branches spread across the ground, stray roots, and dangling vines. But still, twigs caught and snatched at their clothes and hair. A cut opened up across Elinta's cheek and seeped blood. Tamir grazed his arm on a tree branch Elinta failed to point out.

The ground spun again.

"Are you OK?" Tamir whispered, shifting his hand to her shoulder as she stopped to lean against a tree. The grating of her skin against the bark grounded her like a lifeline.

"I'm fine," she mumbled, taking a deep breath. But all that did was set her coughing again.

"We haven't seen Vaherin for a while. We should take a break," Nakiah said.

"Only for a moment," Elinta said, closing her eyes. Letting the heat sense take over stopped the spinning. She adjusted the bags on her back. Her shoulder ached from the straps.

Zhayra's stomach clenched tighter as the seconds trickled by.

"We should continue," Tamir whispered barely a minute later. He pushed his hair back from his face. She opened her eyes. Leaves and bits of twigs were now stuck in the tangled mess of his hair, not to mention the ash on his face forming strange patterns as sweat rolled down his skin. She supposed she looked the same.

The roar of fire returned and with it came the heat. It had already been hot under the canopy, but now it was stifling. Within seconds, her shirt was clinging to her back, a torrent pouring down her face and dripping from her nose and chin.

"Move!" she yelled, grabbing both men and shooting forward.

A wall of flame nearly as high as the trees appeared on their right, moving ahead of them at an angle. It would cut them off if they didn't get there first.

"Faster!"

She lengthened her strides, her grip on Tamir and Nakiah like iron as she leapt fallen trees and dodged trunks. Branches whipped at her clothes and skin. Nakiah gasped as one snapped off her and into him. But Elinta only made them run faster. Even as her lungs constricted against the smoke. Zhayra's stomach was twisted, her chest tight as she watched on. What would they do if they couldn't make it?

The wall of flame, a solid red in her extra sense, roared onward, racing them. They were nearly there. If they could just make it through, the flames would continue on behind them, sweeping along at a right-angle to their path.

Tamir tripped.

"Get up!" Nakiah moaned. They hauled him to his feet and straight back into a sprint. "Hurry!"

The flames were closing in. Sweat trickled into Elinta's eyes, but her hands were too busy holding onto the men to wipe them. Her sword had been unceremoniously shoved into Tamir's spare hand. Unable to see, she closed her eyes again and ran purely through the coloured world.

Heat bit at her skin, the fire now only metres from them.

With one final burst of energy, they ran past it, letting the hungry flames sweep behind them.

"Slow down," Nakiah grunted between deep, wheezing breaths.

"Only for a minute," Elinta said, grateful for the man's demand. She dropped them back to a walk, letting Tamir and Nakiah find a grip on her bags again and freeing up her sweaty hands. Elinta rubbed at the stitch in her side. Her wet shirt clung to her skin.

"We should be nearly there, *tarsi*," Tamir said, peering into the trees. But she knew he couldn't see much.

"Only another half hour, I think."

She wasn't entirely sure, but Zhayra's feelings certainly seemed to confirm it. The dragon's stomach had unclenched ever-so-slightly. But the worry was still there. The fear.

A gust of wind blew through the silver-trunked trees, moving some of the heat and smoke for a moment of pure relief. They all gulped down a breath of precious fresh air before the wind settled and the air grew thick again. Their footsteps were the only sounds in the dark night now. What had become of Liyarna and its people?

"Come on," Elinta said, her voice ragged from the smoke. She pulled them back into a jog, her feet dragging but moving.

Zhayra's dim white form came into view only fifteen minutes later, tucked under the thickest part of the canopy. Air rushed from Elinta's lungs in relief.

"Hurry," she said, finding a burst of strength and dragging the Asali the last of the way to the dragon's side.

Zhayra grunted in greeting, her relief an echo of Elinta's. There was no time to set up the harness. They helped Nakiah up first, his clothes just as drenched as Elinta's except stained with blood.

"Th—thank you," he stammered as he settled into place. Tears leaked down his grimy cheeks.

"Tamir," Elinta said. She couldn't look at that blood right now, not with the memory it threatened to summon, and gestured instead for him to climb up.

Elinta looked at Zhayra, knowing what she had to ask would be hard with the weight she had to carry. "We'll need to fly adjacent to the clouds."

She'd weighed up the risks. If they flew low and close to the trees, Vaherin would see them if he flew over. But if they were high up—where Zhayra's scales could blend in—he might not think to look above him. Especially if he still didn't know they'd even been in the city. As far as she could tell, Mazen hadn't been there for them. And that was the only reason they'd so far escaped unnoticed.

Zhayra's eyes hardened, and she grunted, blinking once.

Elinta rubbed the dragon's muzzle, letting her pride and thankfulness wash over them. Zhayra nudged her. Nodding, Elinta climbed up and settled behind Tamir, wrapping her arms around his body. She tried to ignore the uncomfortable feel of their soaked clothes meeting and focused instead on staying on the dragon.

Zhayra's wings opened. There was a heavy pause, and the dragon rose into the air. She aimed almost straight for the clouds, faster than Elinta had thought possible with three passengers.

The low layer of clouds, thick blue clumps in her heat vision, drew closer. As the moist air tickled her skin and the dragon levelled out, a gasp escaped Elinta.

"Aesira!"

Tamir stiffened.

"No, no, no," Nakiah moaned.

Zhayra began to turn.

"We can't go back," Nakiah said, his voice a cracked echo of what it used to be.

They could see the mountain even from where they were—already so far from the city—illuminated by the burning forest below. But even as they watched, as though summoned by their attention, a dark shadow zipped through the air and a burst of flames erupted on the mountain.

Tamir's broken gasp confirmed what Elinta already knew in her bones. Aesira's hut burnt brightly on the mountainside as Vaherin swooped back in, breathing another thick river over it. Flames shot into the night sky. It could have been day over Liyarna now, with all the light from the fires.

"*Zetayn eyan pepyan eka ayn air kli nalliyan*," Elinta breathed, the death blessing settling over them like a smothering blanket. Her eyes itched as though to cry, but her body had no more water in it after hours of stifling heat. Zhayra slowly turned around, her own heart aching.

"The sun will burn brightly tomorrow," Nakiah murmured emptily over the fallen city.

When the last of the Calaza finally whipped by under them, Elinta allowed herself her first easy breath since waking. Vaherin hadn't followed them. They'd escaped. Light was already beginning to streak across the paling sky. She switched off the heat sense and allowed herself a moment to breathe. Her muscles were aching from their escape, her lungs from the smoke, and a deep weariness was settling over her. But now wasn't the time to let it take her fully.

"Tell Zhayra we need to find Lorrin," she said to Tamir. He passed the message along to Nakiah.

She'd lost track of how far Lorrin and the rest of the delegation would now be into their trip, and it really depended on how many soldiers were with them and the pace they'd set. But they had to find them and stop them from going to Liyarna. Where Mazen now ruled unchallenged. The thought sent her stomach plummeting again. There was so much death behind them. She just hoped Serren was OK.

Zhayra's course shifted slightly, following whatever signs marked the journey back to Nevira for her. A heaviness sat in the dragon's mind and body, but she kept on, the fire of her fear and anger giving her the strength to push on. Distance was what they needed now. That and to find their friends.

The sky grew brighter as the sun rose, deep streaks of red and orange spreading across the clouds above them. Elinta's breath came as fog on the air, but the sun's warmth spread some heat back into her limbs. Her skin still burned with the memory of the dragon's fire in Liyarna, even as the cool wind shoved against her.

"I'm sorry," Elinta murmured to Tamir. Her voice sounded strained, husky. Her throat was parched.

His shoulders slumped. "Me too."

"We'll fix this," she said. She wouldn't let all those deaths be in vain. She couldn't. So, she used the time to plan.

"There!" Elinta said, letting go of Tamir briefly to point to a distant dark patch near the horizon. They'd had a brief break a few hours after dawn where she thought she might have fallen asleep though her mind had continued to race. Then they'd remounted and continued on. Zhayra's flight had felt laboured for some time now, but the dragon had pushed on. A sense of urgency sat over them all. The shadows had now begun to stretch across the ground, the sun getting closer to the horizon again. Elinta's stomach grumbled.

"I see them," Tamir said, a spark of hope reigniting in his voice. Zhayra had already seen them, a burst of speed pushing them closer to Lorrin and the soldiers. They hadn't travelled nearly as far as she'd thought they would have by now, but then, they were a fairly big group to rally and move each day.

Nakiah stirred. He hadn't said a word since they'd watched Aesira's hut burn. And he'd stared blankly into the distance as they'd rested. The Asali had suffered many losses last night, but she suspected it was the first that would linger with him longest. The blood of it still coated him, long dry but caked into his skin.

Zhayra began to lose height, getting ready to land as they drew closer and closer to the delegation. It seemed they hadn't been spotted yet, but Elinta stared at that group like her life depended on it. She needed to see Lorrin and Niles. To hug them and know they were real and OK. Alive. The day had seemed surreal, a strange dream she might wake up from, right up until that moment.

Features slowly emerged among the group. She could see they were made up of a dozen men and women, all riding horses. They were in the open—thick, brown grasslands behind them, and more in front of them. Then she could make out the three leading the group. General Nash. Niles. Lorrin. Her heart stuttered in relief. Zhayra's soared. They'd made it.

The dragon landed only ten metres from them, sending some of the horses rearing in fright. Elinta slid to the ground and ran, her legs barely holding her up. Their weariness and stiffness threatened to slow her, but it felt like nothing could stop her in that moment. She crossed the distance between their groups in barely a second.

Lorrin was on the ground in a blur, hurrying forward to meet her. She threw herself at him.

"What happened? Are you OK?" he gasped in her ear, returning her fierce embrace. He held her at arm's length, his eyes scanning every bit of her, then flicking behind her to land on Tamir and Nakiah.

Elinta followed his gaze and saw their group as Lorrin surely did. They looked a mess. Nakiah, his tunic stained with dirt, sweat, and blood. His hair wild and his eyes only showing a flicker of life. Tamir wasn't much better. The blood coating Nakiah had spread to him, and to her she knew, during their desperate run through the forest. He had cuts on his face and arms from the tree branches. Dirt and smoke smeared across his face.

Elinta turned back to Lorrin as Tamir helped Nakiah down.

"Liyarna is gone," Elinta said, her voice still hoarse from the smoke she'd inhaled.

"What?" Niles said, stopping beside the prince. General Nash had followed too. The cut on her forehead had healed well in the days they'd been apart. But the woman's blue eyes were heavy as she surveyed Elinta's ragged group.

"Mazen," she said. "He attacked last night. He's king now."

The boys paled. Niles grabbed her and pulled her into his arms.

"You stink," he murmured.

"Thanks," she said, the edge of a laugh slipping into her voice as she pulled back.

Lorrin was scanning her again as though to be sure she was in one piece. At least her clothes were no longer soaked through. She was sure she didn't look as bad as she had while in the forest. A small comfort that the boys weren't seeing the worst of it all. That their fear hadn't run deeper at the sight of them.

"What now?" Niles said, looking between her and Lorrin. His voice was steady, but his eyes revealed his fear.

Lorrin ran a hand through his hair, shaking his head. "I don't know. He could have the whole city behind him now. What's left of it."

Niles handed Elinta a bottle of water and she took several large gulps as the boys took a moment to fully realise their situation. The fact that Mazen now had an army.

"I need to get to Ciar and warn them," Elinta said, her voice a little stronger. "Mazen might try to take the White Mountains, too."

Lorrin's eyes flicked to hers. "I can't go with you," he said, his voice betraying his hatred of the idea. Another journey that he couldn't join her on. More time they'd be parted. "We'll have to go to Culmar. The city needs to be prepared."

"He's right," General Nash said. "The king will need to be warned." The woman had remained calm, steady as she'd heard the news. It was exactly what Elinta needed.

Tamir and Nakiah stopped beside them. "Please take Nakiah with you," Tamir said, his voice as hoarse as her own. "He has nowhere to go."

Lorrin twisted to look back at the soldiers behind him. "We need a change of clothes for this man!"

"Thank you," Nakiah said, looking down at his tunic and arms. He needed to soak in the Afonlin, too.

"Why don't you head over? Someone will help you," General Nash said gently.

Nakiah nodded and stumbled toward the group.

"His wife," Elinta said softly. Understanding lit in their eyes.

"Where's Serren?" Niles said, looking behind them as though expecting to see the woman.

"She stayed behind. She will be OK," Tamir said, his voice tight. Elinta watched him, wondering how he wasn't a wreck knowing his wife was in Liyarna and Aesira was dead.

He turned to Elinta. "I will not be able to join you in the White Mountains either. There is another group of our people who must be warned."

Another? Why didn't he mention them before? "Of course."

"A horse would be of great help," Tamir said to Lorrin.

The prince called out another instruction to the men behind them. Elinta handed the water bottle to Tamir.

"I'll go with Elinta," Niles said. "I'll be Nevira's representative."

"Good idea." General Nash nodded. "Do you think they will help us?"

"I think they're more likely to than Liyarna were," Elinta said. "Maybe even more now that Mazen's taken over."

A soldier led a horse over, tentatively handing the reins to Tamir. "There's food and water for two days," he grunted.

"Thank you."

The soldier quickly rejoined the other men, glancing questioningly back at their group as he went.

Tamir handed the water bottle back. "I will leave immediately."

He slipped into the saddle, wincing. It seemed even his muscles were stiff from their escape and the long flight after. She looked up at him, worried after all they'd just been through about him going alone.

"I can send someone with you?" Lorrin asked, apparently thinking along the same lines.

Tamir paused, then finally shook his head. "These people have been separated for a long time. I am not even sure how they will respond to me, and I—I have ties there."

"Very well," Lorrin said. His parents would not have let the man go by himself but, thankfully, the prince was not his parents. General Nash said nothing to remind him of their opinions either.

Elinta opened her mouth to say the parting blessing, but the words seemed caught in her throat. Tamir held her eyes, understanding lighting in his own. He nodded and turned the horse north. He glanced over his shoulder.

"I'll be in Bradfin, the upper northwest." Then he pushed the horse into a trot.

"Lorrin," Elinta said, shaking herself. She didn't have any time to waste. "I need a moment with you."

General Nash and Niles exchanged a look, but Elinta wasn't entirely sure what it was. The general nodded and returned to the soldiers while Niles went to say hello to Zhayra. Lorrin followed Elinta several metres away.

"What is it?" He studied her again. She could see his thoughts racing, fighting for his attention, but he focused on her.

"I—um." She cleared her throat. "I might have a way for us to—to keep in contact while I'm gone." Heat rushed to her cheeks, and she looked away from him. Had Niles and General Nash suspected something of this nature? Not the bond, but the confession it would have with it? Her heart thudded loudly in her chest, and she reminded it sternly that she was not facing danger, but the entire opposite. It just pounded back.

"Really?" Lorrin said. She glanced at him again, only open curiosity on his face now. He had a light dusting of whiskers on his face from travel. It looked good on him.

"Um, yes. But it'll only work with you, I think, and—uh ..." Why couldn't she just spit it out? "You won't be able to initiate it at all, and I don't know if it's two-way, but at the least I'll be able to check on you. If you're OK with that," she said in a gush, totally avoiding *how* she'd be able to do it. She just hoped she'd be able to pull it off. It seemed clear to her from Aesira's story that the feelings didn't have to be reciprocated, so that wouldn't be a barrier at least.

"How?" Lorrin said.

Elinta's eyes widened. "Uh, well, Aesira said we could open a bond with people that … people that are special to us."

A small smile tilted his lips. "Like what's between you and Zhayra?"

"But it won't be open all the time."

"Yes," Lorrin said, holding her eyes. "I don't like the idea of parting again, but this, this could work."

Elinta smiled, the heat returning to her cheeks again. "Good. OK. Good."

"Elinta," Lorrin said, and the look he gave her told her he hadn't missed what she'd said. "You're special to me, too."

Her mouth opened and closed.

Lorrin saved her. "Why don't you check in nightly?"

"You'll know it's me when your ears pop," she said, not trusting her mouth to say anything more. But now wasn't the time, anyway. Even if a strange feeling of relief had settled over her.

"We should get going," he said, some of the urgency slipping back into his tone. Perhaps he'd had the same realisation as her. That there were still things bigger than them happening right now. "I'm glad you're OK."

They crossed to Niles and Zhayra. Elinta still had her bags slung over her shoulders—another part of her that ached—but she lowered the one with the harness to the ground. She had time to set it up while they finished catching up.

"Who else made it out?" Niles asked.

"I don't know," Elinta said.

"But what about MG? Did she get out?" Niles asked, turning from Zhayra.

"No," Elinta said quietly as she pulled out the dragon's harness. Her shoulders strained with the effort. "Piran, Aisla, Maaka. They're all gone too."

They said nothing, but the silence spoke for them. The weight that seemed to settle on their shoulders, the sweat beading on their faces, said it all.

"What else?" Lorrin said, reading her as her brother used to.

Elinta set about slipping the harness in place. There were a few things they needed to know. And none of it was good. She tried to think of the best way to deliver it all. But there was no way to soften the blow.

"He has the other *illayas* sword," she said, not looking up from her work. "And ... he has the *ngaran* with at least one other dragon."

The air escaped Niles's lungs in a whoosh. Tamir's reaction had been much the same when she'd told him about the dragons.

"He—how?" Lorrin said, his face paling several shades. She knew it wasn't the sword he was questioning.

Elinta shook her head. "I don't know, but Aesira said it could be possible to do."

Lorrin grabbed one of the straps to help her as she climbed up Zhayra's leg.

"Does it change anything?" he asked, somehow managing to keep his voice even and controlled.

"No ... not really. He'll just have more eyes around."

He nodded grimly. More eyes and more fire at his disposal.

Elinta slipped the last strap into place, then tied the empty bag to it.

"I'll grab my bag and some extra food," Niles called up, hurrying back to his horse.

Lorrin took her hand as she jumped down to join him on the ground.

"Be careful," he murmured. "Don't forget to check in."

She mustered a smile. "If all goes well, we'll have Ciar to help us now." And maybe they'd also have ... No, she'd think about them later. She still had to convince Zhayra to go.

Niles appeared next to Lorrin and handed her some bread. "Are we ready?"

"Yes," Elinta said, hugging Lorrin. Her heart ached at separating their little group again. The knowledge that anything could happen to him, and she wouldn't be there.

The prince and Niles gripped arms.

"Don't cause any trouble without me," Niles said.

"I wouldn't dream of it."

Elinta jumped up first and clipped herself into the harness while Lorrin said goodbye to Zhayra.

"Alright, come on up," she called down to Niles. Her stomach grumbled again, reminding her of the bread Niles had given her. She'd eat it on the way.

Niles grinned, though it looked somewhat forced as he stared up at her. "Er, OK."

He followed her example, climbing onto Zhayra's bent leg, then jumping to pull himself onto her back. "She's not going to fly rough, is she?"

"No," Elinta said, deciding not to tell him about the tickle in Zhayra's stomach. "She'll be good."

"OK." He broke off into a yell as Zhayra leapt into the sky, and soon his laughter was echoing over Lorrin and the soldiers they left behind.

CHAPTER SEVEN

"THIS IS FANTASTIC!" NILES said into Elinta's ear. His grip on her was as tight as ever, but the joy in his voice was genuine. And it was infectious.

Elinta grinned. "Don't say that too loud. She might decide to do some trick flying."

"Oh, uh," Niles said, his grip tightening. "Please don't do that!" he yelled over the wind at the dragon.

Zhayra's stomach tickled, but she just continued on at an even level and pace. Elinta regretted that the dragon hadn't had a chance to have a proper rest after their flight from Liyarna, but there wasn't any time to waste. So Zhayra couldn't expend any energy on scaring Niles half to death with her flying. At least there were only a couple more hours until nightfall.

"I know we're in a rush, but can we stop at the next water source? You really stink."

Elinta thumped her fist against his knee, pressed against her thigh.

"Ow! It's just the truth."

"How did things go in Nevira?" Elinta asked to distract him, but she quietly agreed. She desperately needed to wash.

Elinta felt him shrug before he said, "Lots of people from the city decided to stay. Aldon and Mira would have gotten to Culmar today. They went ahead of the main group."

"Did your father go with them?"

He laughed. "Yeah. He's pretty adamant about staying near them." His tone sobered. "I don't think anyone really thought something like that could happen to Nevira."

"No," Elinta said. *Or Liyarna.*

With dusk already in the air, they stopped for the night by the Afonlin. Elinta jumped straight into the river (clothes and all) to scrub the grime and blood from her skin and hair. She lingered in the water, letting herself sink deep beneath it, hoping the water would wash away more than just the dirt. After, Elinta changed into some fresh clothes behind Zhayra—who had curled up as soon as they'd landed and gone straight to sleep—while Niles bustled around their little camp.

Elinta and Niles shared a small meal from his pack. He did his best to keep the mood light, but Elinta's mind was still in Liyarna and all that had happened.

"Things'll get better," he said, nudging her knee with his own when she didn't react to his last joke.

"Yeah," she said, finally looking at his face. The firelight flickered in his lively brown eyes. She was beyond thankful he'd offered to come with them. She didn't want to be alone right now.

"So how are we going to find Ciar?" Niles said, sitting back. "Didn't you say they moved around a lot?"

Elinta nodded. Ciar had told her that they'd come to her if she ever returned since finding them would be a problem for her. She just hoped they *could* find her. "I guess we'll go back to the Eggslaying cave and wait."

Niles frowned. "Isn't that where you got hurt?"

"Yes." Elinta's hand trailed to the scars on her thigh. "Hopefully, the mountain cat's gone now."

"I'd offer to evict it, but maybe we could just send Zhayra in," Niles said.

Elinta laughed. "I don't know; I'd like to see you try."

Niles grinned and slung an arm around her shoulders. "I really think the *Zearla lurai* should do it. I hear she's got all kinds of cool powers and stuff."

"Powers?"

"Yeah," Niles said. "Weird stuff like different vision and the like."

"Weird?" She shoved out from under him, ruffling his messy blond hair so it stood up straight.

"Oi!"

Elinta's laugh died on her lips, though, at the memory of another young face with blond hair. One who had pulled her close like that only days before she left Nevira. One she'd never see again. His birthday would have been soon now. Perhaps even tomorrow.

"I'm going to sleep," she said, standing.

Niles's face sobered as he caught the change in her mood. "El," he said, reaching for her hand, "things'll be OK, you'll see."

Under the shelter of Zhayra's wing, Elinta closed her eyes and pictured Lorrin. She thought of his eyes, dark blue with specks of lighter colour around the pupils. She imagined the way he looked at her with unspoken words lingering in them. And in the darkness, stars twinkled to life in her vision though her eyes were still closed. They were almost ... blurred. It was as though she wore glasses that needed to be cleaned. But something told her it wasn't Lorrin's vision that caused it, but the bond itself. An echo, Aesira had called this ability. The image jolted and winked in and out as Lorrin blinked fiercely. She smiled. He'd never experienced that unexplained heaviness in his eyes before that signalled a dragon looking through them. The blinking paused, and a hand appeared in front of his eyes. With a thumbs up. Elinta tentatively reached out to his ears, and the world around him sounded in her own. The night was surprisingly quiet there with only the drone of crickets and the crackle of a fire to fill it. But, yet again, the sound wasn't quite right. It had a slight tinny edge to it.

"Is that you?" Lorrin's voice whispered. "Everything's fine here. Aunt Jaida and I will be in Culmar late tomorrow night. The men are following behind us. I hope you're OK."

Her heart warmed at hearing his voice, even so far away. Elinta caught herself about to reply. He couldn't hear her, but he was fine. He was safe. But he'd left the soldiers behind to get to Culmar quicker. If anything happened on the way back ... She sighed and pulled away, letting his sight and hearing fade.

The White Mountains came into view only a few hours after they left camp. But for a long time, they never seemed to draw any closer, staying as a smudge on the horizon until suddenly they loomed in front of them in the evening light.

Elinta stared at the mountains, marvelling at the way a landscape could remain unchanging over months when the world could change so drastically overnight. The tall peaks before her seemed identical to her memories from that day she and Zhayra had landed there after fleeing Kethmere. The same snow-covered peaks, the same forest spread across their bases. Elinta pulled her jumper tighter to herself, feeling the ghost of the cold waiting for them. She and Niles had rugged up that morning, preparing for the biting temperature of those mountains.

"Ready?" Elinta said.

"My nose is already cold," Niles grumbled in her ear.

Zhayra grunted, tilted in the air, and aimed straight for the massive Eggslaying cave. Elinta, still using dragonsight, saw it before Niles did. Her stomach clenched—not at the memory of the mountain cat, but at the shattered shells inside. At what they meant and everything that had happened since.

The dragon landed in front of the cave, her wings smoothly tucking into her sides as she crouched. A swirl of snow rose up to meet them. Elinta shivered.

"Finally," Niles groaned, slipping to the ground. His legs wobbled, drawing a smile to Elinta's lips as she dismounted next to him, sinking up to her ankles in the snow. Her own legs were steady now and no longer ached after flying though they were still stiff from her run through the Calaza.

Elinta turned to Zhayra, feeling the sadness return to the dragon as her eyes wandered over the landscape. "Do you want to go in?"

Zhayra stared at the cave, then finally blinked once.

"Do you—do you mind if I stay here?" Elinta asked. She had too much heaviness in her heart already. Mazen taking over Liyarna, Aesira and Blaine's deaths ... She couldn't take any more. She didn't want to see the damage King Cenric had caused again unless the dragon needed her. Feeling Zhayra's distress was enough for her right now.

Zhayra blinked twice and slipped into the cave, her long tail leaving a trail in the snow before disappearing inside.

Niles watched her go. "Is she OK?"

"Yeah, I think so."

"Well—" Niles held his arms close to his body, glancing around, "—I guess we'll set up camp here." He sat down where he was, sinking a few inches into the snow. There were no rocks to sit on, no fallen logs or branches since there were no trees up this high. There was nothing except the cave and the snow. He grimaced. "I hope they don't take long to find us."

Elinta turned in place, looking out over the mountain and the forest below them. The world all seemed distant from up here, covered in the long afternoon shadows. It was easy to see how quickly the Asali here could become disconnected from the world. She hadn't really appreciated how beautiful it was up here the last time she'd come.

Niles's footsteps crunched in the snow beside her. "Not a bad view, huh?"

Guilt settled in her stomach. She shouldn't be enjoying the scenery. Not with Mazen out there. There was always something for her to practice or train now.

Elinta turned to Niles, drawing her sword as she did. "Up for some sparring?"

"Definitely!"

Niles had his sword out in an instant, stepping back to raise it and cock an eyebrow.

"Ready?"

In response, Elinta leapt forward, sloshing thorough the snow, to slash toward his leg.

Niles stumbled back, having to lift his feet up higher to move, but easily blocked her blow. He stabbed out in return. She blocked, kicking at his legs. Back and forth it went, each trying to land a blow with the flat of their blades while trying not to slip in the heavy snow around them. Zhayra's heart was heavy, but Elinta tried not to focus on it as she fought. Snow quickly soaked through her pants, even up as high as her knees, as their movements sent it flying.

Zhayra emerged from the cave as they finally broke apart by some unsaid mutual agreement. Elinta's breath came in heavy puffs and sweat beaded on her freezing skin while Niles's breath was equally laboured. His nose was red in the cold.

"Nice!" he said, grinning as he ran a hand through his hair. "I've never trained in the snow."

"It's different," Elinta said, stooping to brush snowflakes from her wet pants.

Zhayra settled into a crouch beside them, and after removing the harness from her back, Elinta set about getting Niles and herself some dinner. Niles's supplies were dwindling, and she pulled out the last piece of bread he had left. They had no butter, cheese, or spread to go on it, but luckily it was heavily flavoured. She broke the bread in half and handed a piece to Niles. Hopefully, Ciar's people would find them soon. She didn't want to be around Niles if they had to skip an entire meal.

Sitting on Zhayra's foot, as she took a bite, Elinta reflected on their trip. Where she had been nervous about meeting the Liyarnan Asali, Elinta felt at peace as she waited for Ciar to find them. Well, as at peace as she could be given the circumstances. But she didn't worry about what she would say to them or how they would react. She was confident that Ciar, at least, would understand the consequences of what had happened since she'd last been to the mountains.

"Oi," Niles said, looking down at her from where he stood beside her and Zhayra. "What's going on in that head of yours?"

"Nothing, just thinking about the Asali."

"I'm sorry about Mazen's grandmother," he said after a moment.

"Me too." She looked back at her food. "I don't want to lose anyone else."

"Hey," he said, tilting her head up, "we won't. We'll be ready next time."

He flicked her nose.

"Hey!" She rubbed at the spot.

Niles grinned. "Come on, hurry up and finish your food—or give it to me. We'll train again. I like it out here."

When it grew too dark to train, Elinta and Niles decided to move closer to the cliff-face the cave was built into. With the rock at their backs to serve as a windbreak, they would be marginally warmer. But with no trees up here, they had no fire for light or warmth.

Zhayra had curled up against the cliff, catching up on the sleep she'd missed. But Elinta, though she was exhausted, wasn't ready to sleep yet. Blaine had visited her dreams the last few nights, and now she knew he'd be joined by Aesira, Piran, Aisla, and Maaka. She couldn't face them yet. And she couldn't face the idea that others might soon join them.

Niles said nothing as he sat on his pack beside her, resting his back against the rockface, his hands on his knees. He looked about as ready to sleep as she was.

Zhayra's head snapped up and Elinta glanced around, straining for what the dragon had heard.

"Elinta!"

Elinta and Niles jumped to their feet as a tall, glowing figure appeared rounding the cliff-face. A spear was in his hand, and he wore a fur jacket much like her own.

Elinta squinted, the strength of Zhayra's eyes making it easier to make out his features in the gathering dark. "Illar?"

The tall Asali stopped in front of them, his grin showing his perfectly straight teeth. He looked exactly as he had when they'd collected *rellaesi* together.

"It is good to see you again, *Zearla lurai,*" he said, glancing between her and Zhayra. "I see much has changed since we last saw you."

"Yes," Elinta said, gesturing at her eyes. "This is Niles. Niles, this is Illar."

Illar smiled again. "*Layzun.*"

"Thanks. It's good to see you, mate. We were thinking we might have to camp here tonight."

"Come, if we do not leave now, we may have to." Illar pulled a wooden torch from inside his jumper, lighting it with a strike of flint. He led them further up the mountain, Zhayra following slowly in their footsteps.

"I am sorry it took so long to get to you," Illar said, guiding them around an outcropping of rock. Elinta grabbed Niles's hand to help him, knowing that with just the flickering fire to help his eyes, he couldn't see as well as she could. Luckily, the wind had calmed, and the flame was relatively steady. He gave her an appreciative nod.

"I'm glad you found us. I wouldn't have known where to start," Elinta said.

Illar laughed lightly. "The mountains are vast."

The night was thick when they finally came to a series of small caves in the mountainside. Firelight flickered from inside a few of them. The entrances were small; they would have to turn sideways to enter whichever one Ciar was now inside. Elinta turned to Zhayra.

"We could be awhile," she said. There was a lot to go over, and it couldn't wait. Not even until morning.

Zhayra grunted and turned to find a place to sleep outside amongst the snow. Elinta watched her go a little jealously. Despite her avoidance of sleep, she wished she could enjoy it as Zhayra did. But at least the dragon would be well-rested. There was still so much more to do.

Illar slipped into the cave on the far right, having to duck to fit in. Elinta followed, with Niles bringing up the rear. Her sword scraped on the grey rock as she passed through.

"Elinta, welcome!" Ciar sat at a small fire in the centre of the small cave. His wife Raisa and their son Eiran were the only others in the cave. Where the Asali had all shared one massive cavern the last time she'd seen them, it seemed they had now spread out among the small caves. At least they would have some privacy while they talked tonight.

"Hello," Elinta said, managing to bring a warm smile to her lips. It was good to see Ciar again, the first person she had seen after leaving the village full of people who had tried to kill her and Zhayra. His presence was strangely comforting, and she felt something within her relax. A very welcome surprise.

"Come, join us," Ciar said, his deep voice ringing around the cave. He'd let his hair grow a few more inches, the thick, dark curls sitting around his ears.

"Is Zhayra here?" Eiran asked, jumping to his feet. The boy had shot up in the months that had passed. He looked more like his father, too, but his eyes were still an exact mirror of Raisa's. So white as to almost match the sclera.

"She's outside. Why don't you go and say hello?" Elinta said, exchanging a glance with Raisa. Eiran didn't need to hear what she had to say.

The woman frowned.

"Eiran, go see if you can stay with Laira's family tonight. Elinta has much to tell us."

The boy nodded before running from the cave.

"I will take my leave as well," Illar said, glancing around the cave. His eyes landed on Elinta. "It is good to see you again." Illar disappeared through the opening.

"This is Niles," Elinta said to Ciar and Raisa. "He's a friend of mine and Lorrin's."

"Welcome," Ciar said, then turned back to her, a smile touching his lips. "You are still with the prince?"

"Yes."

Raisa placed a hand on Ciar's arm when he opened his mouth to speak again. "Why don't you come and sit? Are you hungry?"

"Are we ever!" Niles said, hurrying to sit by the fire. Ciar and Raisa had covered the stone floor with a thin fur to stop the cold seeping up into them; it was this that Niles sat on. Elinta shook her head at her friend and joined him. The warmth of the fire kissed the bare skin on her face.

"Please," she said.

While Raisa sourced some food for them from their stores at the back of the small cave, Elinta realised just how much she had to tell them. They didn't even know that Mazen was alive. She'd have to start at the beginning, right from when she'd left them.

So, as Raisa handed her a hunk of bread and some meat, Elinta launched into her story, beginning with arriving in Nevira with the prince.

Hours passed as she and Niles brought them up to speed with all that had happened. Ciar and Raisa grew more worried the longer she spoke. When Elinta had finished telling them of the events in Liyarna only days ago, a heavy silence fell.

Raisa reached out and took Elinta's hand. "I am sorry for your brother, Elinta, but my heart is glad that his love was not lost to you as you thought."

Elinta squeezed the woman's hand but shoved away the pain and emotion her words awoke. Blaine's love was lost to her now even if she hadn't lost it in life.

Ciar shifted. Elinta glanced at him, expecting him to tell her they needed time, at least the night to speak about all they had heard. Liyarna had needed even more than that and they'd still said no. "We will join you in Culmar."

His words rang around the little cave.

"You—you will?

Ciar and Raisa exchanged a glance before they both nodded.

"We don't recognise Mazen as king," Raisa said, her unnervingly white eyes turning fierce.

"It will take us time," Ciar said, "to prepare for the journey. It will be three weeks before we could reach Culmar."

Three weeks. It was actually fairly quick given the length of the journey on foot, but so much could happen in that time.

"Three weeks is better than not at all," Niles said, filling the silence for her. "We'll need all the help we can get."

The Asali nodded, firelight flickering over their glowing faces.

"It's getting late. Perhaps we should continue this in the morning? You have both had a long journey." Raisa looked between them, a tinge of concern on her face. She'd tied her long hair back sometime during Elinta's story, but a few strands came loose with the movement.

"Yes," Elinta said, standing. As she'd filled them in on everything, she hadn't realised just how tired she was. Luckily, the fire had dried her pants as she'd sat talking and she was now quite warm.

"You are welcome to stay with us tonight," Ciar said, "there is plenty of room."

Elinta looked uncertainly at Niles. She'd meant to join Zhayra outside, though it would be cold and the snow would likely melt into her clothes again. But she didn't like to sleep without the dragon when they were together. Especially since she usually slept better, too.

"Go on," he said, gesturing with his head.

"I'll sleep with Zhayra tonight," Elinta said. After saying good-night, Elinta slipped out into the night, taking a fur blanket with her.

Zhayra had settled to her right, away from the cluster of caves inhabited by the Asali. The dragon was curled on her side, her eyes shut, and her breathing even. The moonlight glinted off her scales, but Elinta probably still wouldn't have seen her without her dragonsight. She'd forgotten how well she blended in with the landscape here.

Elinta pushed through the snow and laid her blanket on the ground by Zhayra's curled torso. As she lay down, the dragon grunted and spread her wing over her, tucking her head lower to stop the cold air from reaching her. Zhayra's eyes didn't even open as she moved. Elinta stroked the tired dragon's scales. She still had so much more flying ahead of her. And then who knew after that? Maybe they'd had the last of their restful days and hadn't even known it. She couldn't even remember the last normal day she'd lived through.

Eyes already growing heavy, Elinta decided a quick check on Lorrin's emotions would be enough to tell her if he was safe. He might have already made it to Culmar. She could have checked in the morning to see if he had, but she didn't want to go outside of the agreement she'd made with him. Check-ins at night only. She yawned. Emotions tonight. A proper check tomorrow night.

Picturing herself reaching out to him, Elinta tried to feel for his chest, his stomach, his heart, the places where she felt the most emotion from Zhayra. If Lorrin was already asleep, would she feel anything from him? She kept reaching out, working in the same way she might if she were to reach for his eyes.

His emotions slammed into her like a brick wall.

Elinta gasped, jolting upright. "Lorrin!"

His chest was heavy, aching, his throat thick. Anguish. Deep, unrelenting anguish.

Zhayra pulled back with a grunt, turning her head to fix an amber eye on her.

"Something's wrong with Lorrin," Elinta said, her heart in her mouth. Turning to rest her back against the dragon, Elinta closed her eyes and fought to control the fears that threatened to rise. She reached out to Lorrin, reached for his eyes, dreading what she'd find.

Elinta's vision cleared, and with Lorrin's tear-blurred eyes, she stared down at the body of King Aldon.

CHAPTER
EIGHT

"**N**o," Elinta whispered as Lorrin looked down on the ashen face of his father. Elinta looked along with him. The tears made it feel like she was looking through a dirty window, worse than this tentative bond usually was. She knew that no amount of blinking would clear it. But that was OK, she didn't want to see it properly.

King Aldon was lying on a stone table, all but his head covered by a white sheet. Lorrin must have moved it to see the body. She couldn't see whatever had caused his death, though a bruise had formed on his face, and a cut had been cleaned on his forehead. The king's eyes were closed, and no trace of pain twisted his features. He looked younger, lying there. But he was gone. She'd known instantly.

Lorrin jolted, his eyes rising to look at his warped reflection in a window across from him. The night was dark in the port city though a few lights blinked in the distance, some reflecting off the black ocean. Lorrin was still in his riding clothes, covered in dust, as though he'd only just arrived in Culmar. He must have ridden hard and fast to get there. His lips moved.

Gasping, Elinta hurried to tap into his ears, her own emotions threatening to sabotage the attempt.

"—two nights ago. The same time as the attack on Liyarna." Lorrin's voice reached her. It was thick, heavy in a way she hadn't heard before. And he sounded exhausted. "My mother's fine. She wasn't—wasn't with him. Tell Niles his father is OK, too."

"Lorrin," she whispered, her arms aching to reach out and hold him. But he couldn't even hear her.

She watched his throat bob in the reflection. His eyes were red from the tears she looked through along with him.

"Don't come back," he said. "You're needed there. I'll—we'll be OK."

His eyes flickered back down to his father. Someone had placed his crown on his head. "It was quick," he said, his voice strengthening a little. His hands gripped the edge of the table so tightly his knuckles had turned white. Except one was bloody, as though he'd punched something. Repeatedly. "But he fought hard. He killed one of them before they got him."

"I—" Elinta said, cutting herself off and feeling her own tears well in her eyes. She couldn't tell him how sorry she was. How much she hurt for him. She felt a tear roll down her own cheek.

Elinta stayed connected to him for a few more minutes, hoping her presence would offer some small comfort, and with no choice but to stare down at the body with him. She didn't want to leave him there alone with his father, but she had to pull back. She had to tell Niles.

It was with some relief that Elinta severed her connection to Lorrin's emotions, eyes, and ears. Though his emotions didn't affect her own, knowing the pain he felt hurt her nearly more than she could bear. Her own grief was still too raw. Zhayra's large amber eye was peering at her as Elinta cracked open her own eyes, no longer connected to the prince who was so far away.

"His father is dead," Elinta whispered.

Zhayra keened loud and long, an expression of her own love for Lorrin. Another tear slipped down Elinta's cheek.

"Elinta?" Niles's tired voice reached her, a note of fear in it.

Zhayra pulled back her wing so Elinta could jump to her feet. She ran to Niles, a sleepy figure stumbling from the entrance of Ciar's cave.

"What's wrong?" he said as she crashed into him, wrapping her arms around him.

"The king's dead," she breathed against his shoulder.

She felt his body stiffen.

"Lorrin?"

"He's fine. It happened before they got to Culmar. When Mazen attacked Liyarna. Mira and your father are fine, too." She pulled back, glancing over his shoulder to see Ciar and Raisa directly behind him. Their glowing faces were pale.

"We've got to get back there," Niles said, pulling away from her, all trace of sleep gone from his eyes.

Elinta nodded, her mind racing. "We'll have to stop and get Tamir."

She wiped the tears from her face, her mind already working out everything they had to do to get back to Lorrin.

Niles nodded. "Let's go."

"No," Ciar said, stepping forward. "You all need some sleep. Zhayra especially. Please stay for the night."

Elinta paused; it hurt to even consider it.

Though Lorrin had told her not to come, she wasn't needed among the White Mountains anymore. Ciar had already agreed to help them. But there was one more thing that called for her attention. One more place she knew deep down she should go. She shoved the idea away. One thing at a time. They needed to find Tamir first and learn if he'd managed to convince the desert Asali to help them. Who knew how long that would even take?

"He still needs us to do this." Elinta took and squeezed Niles's hand. "We could be in Culmar in two days."

Niles's mouth opened and closed, his eyes betraying the anguish he felt for his friend's loss. His shoulder's slumped. "OK."

"We will have some food ready for you in the morning," Raisa said, breaking their silence.

"Please try to sleep," Ciar said. "We will follow after you as soon as we can."

Niles ran a hand down his own face before he turned back into the cave.

Elinta joined Zhayra again, pressing into the dragon's warm body, but it was nearly dawn before sleep finally overtook her racing mind. King Aldon's face had now joined the others.

Elinta was already awake when Niles came to wake her and Zhayra. His hair was a mess and he had heavy bags under his eyes, which she was sure were a mirror of her own. Raisa and Ciar had breakfast ready for them. They ate as quickly as they could without making themselves sick. Elinta hardly tasted the warm bread as it went down. The king's body lingered before her eyes: his and Blaine's.

Ciar filled their bags with food and water, carrying them out to Zhayra while Elinta and Niles worked together in silence on the harness. Snowflakes fell lightly around them. One landed on Elinta's neck, melting and sending a streak of freezing water down her back.

The sun had barely peeked over the horizon when they'd finished. None of the other Asali were to be seen in the dim morning light. It was eerily quiet; not even the snowflakes made a sound as they fell. It seemed fitting. Even the mountain seemed to feel their grief. Elinta glanced around at their small group, feeling like they were the only ones on the whole mountain range.

"Here," Ciar said, handing Elinta her satchel and Niles his pack. "We will see you in Culmar in three weeks, less if we can."

"Thank you," Elinta said.

Raisa pulled Elinta into her arms. "It was good to see you again, even under such circumstances. Please give our sympathies to King Lorrin."

Elinta drew back in shock. *King Lorrin.*

Niles merely nodded as she turned her wide eyes on him. Elinta found herself wishing he'd crack a joke to lighten the mood.

"Thank you for everything," Niles said.

Mounting Zhayra, Elinta called down the blessing to her friends before they were left behind in a swirl of snow.

They flew hard and fast to the Bradfin desert, but it was late afternoon before they found the small community of Asali Tamir had gone to find. Still, Elinta hardly remembered most of the journey. Niles had done his best to lighten the mood—a fact she was beyond grateful for—but she could tell his thoughts were also in Culmar.

Small animal hide tents dotted the desert landscape below them, set around the only source of water Elinta had spotted for kilometres. The small oasis seemed to sparkle in the late sunlight, its cool, clear waters inviting even from the air. A figure crouched beside it turned to watch as Zhayra landed on its bank, sending orange sand rolling across the ground from her wing beats.

"*Layzun,*" the man said after a moment, his voice deep, and his skin tanned from the harsh sun. His glowing eyes flickered over them.

"*Layzun.*" Elinta dismounted beside Niles and stripped off some of her many layers. Sweat already trickled down her face and back. It would be a wonder if she didn't get sick from all the temperature changes that she'd experienced in the past few days. *"I'm looking for Tamir Aylan."*

The man tilted his head, glancing between the three of them again in clear confusion. But he pointed over his shoulder to one of the larger tents among the group.

"Thank you."

Zhayra stayed by the oasis, dipping her large mouth in to scoop up water. Niles and Elinta practically ran to the brown tent the man had indicated, kicking up sand as they went. Whatever intentions they may have had about being diplomatic or careful around this new group had vanished at the thought of getting home to Lorrin sooner.

"Tamir?" Elinta called, rounding the A-frame shape to find the open flap. The scent of herbs and spices washed over her as she stood waiting for her eyes to adjust to the change in lighting.

"Tarsi?" Tamir looked up from where he sat cross-legged on the material floor of the tent. The herbs she could smell were drying on a line hanging from the back wall, though she couldn't identify any of them. A bowl of food was in Tamir's lap, and an older woman with long brown hair sat across from him. Her eyes were the same dark grey as Tamir's. He frowned, looking over her.

"We need to go," Niles said, peering around Elinta's shoulder.

"What has happened?"

Elinta glanced at the woman sitting quietly beside Tamir, unsure whether to share what had happened in Culmar. Would the woman even understand in their language? Her expression was curious, but it gave nothing else away.

"It is alright," Tamir said, putting his food aside and standing. He had changed into a long tan tunic, matching the style of the one the man by the oasis wore. "This is Rieka, the leader of these people."

"Who is she to you?" Elinta said, looking between them. She cringed internally at her lack of delicacy, but she really couldn't bring herself to try. They needed to get back to Culmar.

"She is my mother's sister," Tamir said, stepping forward, his face becoming increasingly worried. "What is wrong, Elinta?"

"King Aldon is dead," Elinta said. "Mazen's people attacked his party on the road at the same time he attacked Liyarna."

"*Inna ayn nai rai?*" the woman asked, smoothing out her red tunic as she joined them in the entryway. She looked between them in concern. Elinta glanced at the woman, but she didn't have the discipline to try to translate what needed to be said.

So Tamir hurriedly explained the situation to his aunt in Asalin. Her eyes widened, pulling the wrinkles tight around them.

"How did it go here?" Niles asked. "Will they help us?"

"I believe they will, but," Tamir paused, "I need more time here. I only arrived last night."

"Then we should go," Niles said. "If you don't need us?"

Tamir nodded, looking between them. A frown crinkled his brow as he took in their urgency.

The ground shook a little as Zhayra came to a stop behind them, leaning her long neck around to peer inside the tent. The sun shone brightly off her scales.

Reika's eyes widened even further. "*Zearla!*" she said in wonder.

Zhayra grunted, her own impatience a tight ball in her stomach.

"Are you sure you can't come now?" Elinta asked. If Tamir didn't come with them now, it would take him a week, perhaps more, to get to Culmar with the horse Lorrin had provided.

"We will need all the help we can get against Mazen."

Elinta smiled gratefully, but his words drew to mind the other place she had been avoiding thinking about. Her head felt like it was going to spin. She'd been moving too fast for too long now, not giving herself a proper moment to rest. She took a deep breath, forcing herself to calm.

"We'll see you in Culmar," she finally said.

Niles tugged her out of the tent, gesturing for her to climb Zhayra's back first. He settled in place behind her seconds later, and the dragon shot into the air. A cluster of the desert Asali had gathered among the tents to watch them leave. Tamir's farewell echoed after them.

That night, Elinta stared long at Zhayra from her spot by the crackling fire. Tamir's words reverberated through her head. *We'll need all the help we can get.*

Zhayra grumbled, feeling the knots in Elinta's stomach.

"We need to go there, Zhayra."

The dragon grumbled again, her own stomach clenching at the idea. It was enough to tell her that Zhayra had been thinking along the same lines as her. Perhaps for some time.

"Go where?" Niles asked. The bags under his eyes had deepened, but he was alert as he looked between them. "What are you talking about?"

"We need to talk to the dragons."

Niles nearly dropped his food. "But—but I thought she couldn't go back?"

Elinta slowly shook her head. "She can. She just doesn't want to risk Mazen being there. But he's in Liyarna now."

Zhayra grumbled again, but her nerves were steeling.

Niles slowly nodded.

"You should go. Tomorrow."

"But it'll take you two more days to walk to Culmar." They were only a few hours from Lake Lusinata, the place where she and Zhayra had once swum together. But Niles would have to spend at least one more night on the road before he'd arrive in Culmar, before he'd see Lorrin, if she left him now.

"Yeah," he said, "but the dragons would level the playing field. We could stop Mazen."

Elinta sighed. "I was hoping you'd tell me it could wait just a little longer. I don't know what we'll face there."

"You know, I couldn't tell?" He winked. "Lor will understand."

She'd already checked in on him, tentatively reaching out for his emotions first, unsure if she wanted to look through his eyes again. But there hadn't been any attacks in Culmar, though the prince's emotions were still sorrowful. When she'd finally accessed his eyes, she'd found him talking with General Nash, General Sonnen, Shae, and Queen Mira. They were planning the defence of the city, including building walls around the borders. He hadn't said anything to give away that he knew she was there, but his feelings had lifted slightly. Lorrin had been at the head of the table. He'd already begun to assume his new duties, just days after his father's death.

Elinta sighed again, mirrored by Zhayra. "Alright, we'll drop you a little closer in the morning and then go."

"Give him a hug for me," Elinta said, pulling Niles in for a hug of his own.

"Wait, is this my hug or his hug, then?"

"Yours," Elinta said, pushing him away.

"Be careful, El." He glanced at Zhayra, "And you, beasty."

Zhayra grunted, a lightness tickling her chest at the nickname.

"You, too. I don't know how long we'll be." Elinta settled on Zhayra's back, clipping into the harness. "Stay out of trouble."

Niles just nodded.

Elinta stared down at him for a moment, too many thoughts and feelings swirling around in her head.

"Go on," Niles said, the look in his eyes telling her he understood it all. "Get going and we'll see you soon."

They shot back into the air, leaving Niles just a little closer to the city. He'd arrive late that night if he hurried, and she knew he would. Elinta couldn't help but watch him as they flew away. She wished they didn't have to separate, but she also wished he could be with Lorrin even sooner.

Zhayra's nerves hadn't settled overnight. Elinta knew from the core memories belonging to the dragon that she'd accessed that this would be the first time she'd been home since Mazen had killed her mother. And it would be the first time she would open herself back up to them. For months, Zhayra had kept herself separate from her people, closed off to their senses. But now, the heir was finally returning home.

They paused at the southern edge of the continent, landing on the white beach to look out over the clear blue water. Zhayra's memory of the flight over did little to tell Elinta how long the journey might be. She'd flown through a storm, battered by the wind and rain, and chased by Vaherin, but it had been day when she'd left and night when she'd crashed in the forest outside Kethmere. She breathed in the sea air deeply.

"Ready?" Elinta asked, looking up into one of Zhayra's large amber eyes.

Zhayra blinked once and lowered her bulk back into a crouch for Elinta to mount her again. It was time.

CHAPTER
NINE

E LINTA RELISHED THE FLIGHT over the sea, drinking in the
time she had with Zhayra in peace. Would this be the last
they would find together before things with Mazen were finished? The waves rolled by under them, a much calmer version of
the sea that Zhayra had last seen. The sun reflected off the water,
sending beams of rainbow light up at them. Fish swam under the
waves, oblivious to the danger above them. But anxiety continued
to eat at Elinta.

What would they find at the dragon isles? Mazen had been
joined by dragons in the attack at Nevira. Though, some had
returned home upon seeing Zhayra. Would they be there? What
had Mazen told them to convince them to join him that could be

so easily undone by Zhayra's presence? She just hoped whatever had happened between them, it would sway them to her cause.

Elinta sighed. Maybe she hadn't found as much peace out here as she'd thought.

"We'll be OK, Zhayra. I'll be with you," she called over the wind.

The dragon grunted, the nerves in her chest loosening for a second before curling once more.

Elinta stroked Zhayra's smooth scales. How much of this trip could she influence, or would it all be up to the dragon?

Elinta scanned the horizon, not really expecting to see anything. "Wait ..." she mumbled. They couldn't be nearly there already?

Land had appeared in the distance, growing closer and closer with every passing second. The first streaks of the sunset had only just begun to appear across the sky, and they were already there.

Zhayra's wing beats quickened, contentment fighting her anxiety as she aimed straight for it.

Elinta gaped at the islands highlighted in the oranges, pinks, and reds of a summer sunset. The clear blue water like a frame around them. The features grew clearer as they drew closer.

There were three islands, and the sight of them drew Zhayra's memory of them to Elinta's mind. One long and skinny, the other two were like splotches on the water. Sheer, rocky cliff-faces bordered each of them. She knew it was the same all the way around them. The islands were said to be impenetrable to humans, and Zhayra's memories had confirmed this. But the memory hardly compared to seeing them in real life.

"Zhayra," Elinta said, stunned, "they're beautiful."

The dragon's stomach lifted. But reality crashed back down on them both as a winged form rose from one island, flying to another. In fact, as she looked, more and more figures seemed to be moving around the islands: flying in circles above them, moving from one to another, or flying out over the ocean. Two dragons, one blue and one green, flew together, rising in the air, spiralling around each other, twisting and turning like some kind of dance Elinta didn't understand. Elinta's gut churned at the sight. This was it.

No one challenged Zhayra as they drew closer, but Elinta wasn't sure if it was because they still couldn't sense her or if they weren't worried about her approaching figure. It wasn't until they flew past a yellow dragon that any of them seemed to notice them at all. Elinta twisted in her seat to watch the yellow turn around to follow them, a grunt of surprise escaping it. But no aggression showed in its body language—it was interest lighting in its eyes. Elinta turned to face in front of them again just as a small green dragon joined them. A youngling. Elinta's heart soared at the sight of its small body. She grinned and waved. The youngling's eyes widened, and it pulled away. Even though Zhayra herself was proof that the dragons had reproduced since leaving Eldras, seeing a small dragon was something else. It eased something inside of her she hadn't realised had been there.

Zhayra seemed to be aiming for a particular spot to land. It was a large flat area of a brown-red rock. Long cracks ran through it. Dragons tilted up their heads to watch as they landed on the smallest of the three islands. Elinta waited, her eyes scanning the dragons, the landscape, unsure what to do in the seconds that followed. She felt unbelievably small amongst them.

Something shifted in the atmosphere, and Elinta knew it could only mean one thing. Zhayra had reopened herself to her people.

The yellow dragon landed beside them, a keen escaping its chest. It was larger than Zhayra, with thicker but shorter horns on its head. A male, Elinta guessed, comparing its appearance to how Vaherin had looked. But the others that slowly appeared around them ... Elinta couldn't tell. Two greens landed nearby, a blue walked out onto the rock, while a maroon—Elinta's heart stuttered at the sight, but then she realised it was too small to be Vaherin—flew up over a cliff-face to their right that looked out over the sea. Over a dozen landed in their rock-clearing, but Elinta was sure others watched on, likely through the senses of the ones around them now. Some grunted, some keened, others remained silent. Awe settled inside Elinta at the sight of so many dragons. She caught a glimpse of another youngling in the distance, but a large blue dragon beside it seemed to be keeping it from coming any closer. Elinta drank them all in.

Zhayra shuffled uncomfortably, her claws scratching at the dirt.

Elinta slid from her back and, feeling the eyes of every dragon on her, walked around to Zhayra's face, taking her head in her hands. The dragon needed her in that moment. Needed her to give her that last push. "Show them what happened, Zhayra."

Only the queen could force her senses on the other dragons, but Zhayra's memories had revealed that the dragons could still share their senses with each other. She wasn't sure how, but perhaps it was offered to them in a way, and the dragon could accept or decline, she guessed. It was only now that she realised that she didn't know nearly as much about the dragons as she'd thought. What she knew came from being a *Zearla lurai*, but there was much that it still couldn't tell her.

Zhayra blinked once, lifted her head, and looked around at their audience. Elinta twisted, following the dragon's gaze, and waited. Minutes trickled by. The shift in their emotions when it came—though Elinta could only feel Zhayra's—was unmissable.

The dragons shuffled uncomfortably in place. The yellow who'd followed them drew back his lips and growled. Others did the same, showing reactions of anger and hurt, but two ... two flew away.

"Where are they going?" Elinta said to Zhayra, but the dragon just looked at her.

Zhayra's heart squeezed, and fire rose in her throat. Disappointment.

"What's going on? Will they help us?" Had it been long enough for them to have already decided? "Zhayra?"

Zhayra held her eyes, and her own slowly steeled as her lip began to twitch. The dragon faced the others, her eyes raking over them, pulled back her head, and roared. It was not like the roars Elinta had heard from her before, those being from happiness or worry. This one was full of anger. Of challenge. Elinta slapped her hands over her ears, recoiling from the dragon as her roar sounded over them.

The islands were silent in the wake of Zhayra's challenge. No one moved. Not one of them.

Elinta's ears rang.

"Well?" Elinta finally said, breaking whatever had settled over the dragons.

They shuffled uncomfortably, refusing to meet Zhayra's eye. With a low growl, another turned and fled.

Elinta looked between Zhayra and the dragons, desperation slamming into her even as she felt the utter disappointment settling over Zhayra. Elinta had left Lorrin alone to grieve for this. In the hope that these dragons would help them stop Mazen from killing anyone else. And now, even after seeing what Vaherin and Mazen had done, even after the challenge the heir to their throne had set, they were going to turn their backs on her. On Zhayra. And they'd decided in mere seconds.

"What are you all doing? Can't you see how dangerous he is?" Elinta shouted, stepping out of Zhayra's shadow. All eyes turned to her and she stumbled for a moment under their gazes. She forced herself on, anger overpowering her nerves. "He killed your queen! And now her successor is asking for your help."

A grumble went through the group.

"It's no use, Elinta Ferran. They won't help anyone now."

Elinta's blood froze as his voice swept over them. She turned around mechanically, joltingly, to see Mazen walking toward them from her right. His black hair impeccable, his maroon eyes glinting. His dragonscale armour covered every inch of him except his face and hands. A figure from her nightmares. Vaherin looked down on them from a nearby grassy cliff-face, his horns glinting in the light. The tension in the air had skyrocketed.

Zhayra growled, leaping toward Mazen before he'd even come to a stop. The dragons jumped into motion, their own growls echoing over them. A blue landed in between Zhayra and Mazen, spreading its wings and blocking her path.

Mazen's low laugh drifted over to them. His words carried the accent Elinta had only ever heard in Asali children. "As you can see, the dragons seem to have no wish for further bloodshed."

"What are you doing here?" Elinta said through gritted teeth. Her heart hammered in her chest, her blood racing as the image of Blaine lying dead in Nevira threatened to overtake her.

"The same as you," he said, calmly stepping around the blue dragon.

Zhayra twitched, but another growl from the blue—and no doubt some other warning in the emotions of those surrounding them that Elinta couldn't sense—stopped her from attacking.

"I came here to ask for help again," Mazen spread his hands, his eyes darkening, "but they wouldn't hear of it. I admit, I hadn't counted on them losing their need for vengeance."

He—he came for help? After everything he'd done at Nevira? Elinta clenched her fists, letting her nails dig into her palms in an effort to ground herself. "You're lucky they're here."

Mazen tilted his head, looking over her with a slight frown. "You may have the bond, but you're no different from the rest of your kind. Weak. But I am surprised you didn't meet me at the fortress. I waited for you."

Elinta's hand reached for the reassurance of her sword's hilt though she didn't dare draw it in front of the dragons. She ignored what he said about the deal he'd offered.

"Why did you do all this? Liyarna? You could have just stayed there from the beginning! Ascended to the throne naturally and educated the humans of the time! You could have stopped all this. Why did you even leave?" The words spilled out of her, questions she'd long needed to know the answers to.

Mazen's slitted eyes flickered briefly up to Vaherin before fixing on her again. He laughed softly. "The same foolish words as my father." He stepped away from them, going so far as to turn his back on Zhayra before facing them again. "You would have had us make peace with the men who slaughtered their eggs." He looked around the dragon isles, his eyes sweeping over the dragons. His maroon eyes, so hard and dead ... had grown watery. "Should I have sat down with Bada and turned a blind eye to all he and his brother had done, Elinta Ferran? While he wiped away their history as he'd wiped away their home? Should I have embraced him as a friend?"

Elinta slowly shook her head, his words hitting home. He had a point, but there was a simple solution. "But what about his son? His grandchildren and their children? You could have talked to any one of them."

Mazen smiled, but it didn't reach his eyes—back to their empty state. "I doubt you truly believe that. Your people are fickle, no more than children who cannot be trusted even to rule over themselves. Your entire history is proof enough. Even after uniting under one crown, you still found ways to draw blood." He laughed. "It doesn't make sense to leave you to your own devices! Especially when your royal bloodline is so polluted. No, Elinta. You deserve no mercy because you gave none."

The words reverberated over her. *Polluted.* Elinta reached out for Lorrin's emotions, feeling the thickness in his throat even as she felt the fire in Zhayra's belly. Lorrin was not what Mazen said. Had never been and would never be.

"I guess I know why you're doing this then," Elinta said, daring to look away and make eye contact with a few of the dragons. They all looked away from her. "But you're wrong. We're going to stop you, and things *are* going to change."

Mazen's laugh was unexpectantly real and even slightly—unfairly—pleasant. "You really do believe that," he said. His brow furrowed, his strange eyes scanning her again as though she were a puzzle he couldn't understand.

Zhayra growled in warning, but Mazen didn't even look at her.

"You're not going to win this, because I cannot lose."

Elinta gaped at him, the fire in her veins still churning, but a strange understanding had settled over her. He made sense to her now even though he was wrong, had chosen the wrong path. He had been bonded to a dragon when the worst event of their entire history had happened. Had Mazen been building up to this all this time? He'd killed so many, even his own grandmother, because he didn't believe true peace would ever come. Or maybe this was his version of it.

Mazen tilted his head, watching her thoughts play out across her face. "Perhaps you could have joined me if things were different," he said. "Come, Vaherin. We'll leave Elinta and Zhayra to their peace talks." He didn't raise his voice nor even look away from them, but Vaherin heard his words, likely through Mazen's own ears, and launched himself off the cliff.

Elinta couldn't help herself; she stumbled back a step as he landed in front of them before she could brace herself. Zhayra stepped back, not in fear, but to place herself beside Elinta as Vaherin surveyed them with his large amber eyes. They were the same colour as Zhayra's, but so very different. His eyes were as cold as Mazen's, and Elinta didn't need any connection to his emotions to notice the anger radiating off him.

The blue dragon had continued to position itself strategically as they'd all moved around, making sure it was close enough to stop any fight from breaking out. The other dragons stood at the ready, too. But Mazen showed no interest in them. He barely even acknowledged them.

He mounted Vaherin smoothly, making even Tamir's graceful movements seem jolted. Another reminder of Mazen's abilities and experience. Elinta stared up at them.

"Vaherin," Elinta said quietly, the words slipping out of her. "This isn't right."

His lip curled back, and he breathed a low growl over her. Zhayra echoed it, her wing spreading out above Elinta protectively.

Without another word, dragon and Asali disappeared into the sky.

Elinta tried to follow, dragging her sword from its scabbard and jumping toward Zhayra, but the blue dragon stopped her. The circle of dragons around them quickly closed, low rumbles of displeasure echoing over her.

Zhayra roared once more. The dragons flinched but didn't move away.

"You heard what he's done! What he's planning to do," Elinta cried. "He has to be stopped."

The blue dragon turned his eyes on her, understanding and frustration shining through, but he didn't budge. Elinta's shoulders slumped, and she slid her sword back into its sheath.

"We'll leave in the morning."

Two dragons—the blue that had stopped Zhayra from attacking Vaherin and a small green one—stood watch over Elinta and Zhayra that night. Apparently, they didn't want to risk them leaving to follow Mazen even now. Or at least, that was Elinta's guess. Elinta lay beside Zhayra's head, staring up at the stars, her thoughts moving too quickly to grab. Her heart had eventually settled after their encounter with Mazen, but she could feel the echo of the fear and anger sitting in her muscles and coursing through her blood. Elinta sighed.

"I should check on Lorrin," Elinta said, still looking at the stars even as a soft breeze blew across her face. She never tired of how beautiful they looked through dragonsight. Nor the calm they seemed to press into her.

Zhayra grunted.

"... can you feel him when I reach out?"

Zhayra blinked twice.

"Really?" Elinta rolled onto her side, propping herself up on one arm so she could face the dragon properly. Zhayra's eyes stood out in the dim light of the moon. Her scales glinted with a silver light.

Zhayra grunted.

"Strange." So many things about the bond didn't work how she'd thought they would.

"What am I going to tell him when we get back?" she murmured. Ciar was three weeks away, Liyarna was under Mazen's control, and the dragons wouldn't help. She fought the growing fear gnawing at her.

Zhayra's stomach twisted.

"We can try again tomorrow, I guess," Elinta said, dropping her arm and rolling onto her back again. "Before we go." Elinta told herself that over and over until some of her fear began to lessen.

The two dragons watching over them shifted, but neither made a sound.

Elinta sighed again. "I'll be quick," she said even as she reached out to Lorrin's eyes.

Lorrin was asleep. At least, she guessed he must have been because all she could see was darkness. A blank image in her mind.

His emotions were flat too, though she could still feel them, so she knew he was OK. Alive. Elinta pulled away and stared back up at the stars again. If only there was some way she could have spoken to Lorrin. Talking everything through with him would have helped her sort out her mess of feelings. But their tentative bond, which she opened each time, did indeed seem to only work one-way. She was a silent observer, there, but not really.

Zhayra shifted her head closer to Elinta, her warm breath coming in bursts against her arm. "We'll work this out," Elinta said, rubbing her hand along the dragon's muzzle. "We'll be fine."

Elinta was nudged awake in the cold dawn by a large, green snout.

"I'm awake," she groaned, rolling over and batting at the dragon, her mind not yet awake. Zhayra released her own groan, but the nudging continued.

"OK!" Elinta sat up, glancing around them in the early morning light. They'd slept in the same rocky clearing that Zhayra had landed in yesterday, having been left alone by all but the two dragons after Mazen had departed. Not for lack of trying, though. Elinta had attempted to leave the clearing to talk to the others, but their two guardian dragons wouldn't let her move further than the clearing unless she needed to relieve herself. They had even stopped Zhayra from flying to one of the other islands or going in search of food.

Elinta groaned as her stiff muscles pulled with her movements as she stretched. It certainly hadn't been the most comfortable sleep she'd ever had. The green dragon tilted its head, fixing her with its red eye, and grunted rather forcefully.

Zhayra groaned again, shifting her large bulk to a crouch when the blue dragon wouldn't stop nudging her either.

"I guess that means we have to leave now," Elinta said bitterly. She'd planned, *hoped*, to talk to the dragons again now that it was a new day and Mazen was long gone. But it seemed the other

Zearla lurai had been right. They wanted no part in what was going on in Eldras anymore. Not after whatever had happened in Nevira among them. Had they realised they'd been tricked, only to now find out that it had been by the very man who'd killed their queen?

A beam of sunshine broke through the grey clouds, streaking across their little group. Elinta gazed out at the islands, the gentle lapping of the waves against the cliff-face rising to meet her. Dragons were beginning to stir, but they kept a wide berth from her and Zhayra.

"I need some time to get ready," Elinta said to their two guards, pulling her bag toward her.

She ate slowly, washing down the bland bread with a mouthful of water. If there was one thing she was looking forward to about Culmar, besides seeing the boys again, it was the food. Anything other than bread, particularly plain and stale bread, would be a welcome sight.

When she couldn't waste any more time eating, Elinta began to pull out Zhayra's harness. She took her time strapping it to the dragon, too, hoping that something might change among the dragons, and they'd have another chance to convince them. But no others came to see them, and the two guards looked on with disinterest.

"OK." Elinta stepped back at last, turning to the dragons. She tried to sound confident. "We'll leave now. Even though you won't help us, I want you to know when Mazen's gone, you'll be welcome back in Eldras. The new human king is fighting for you."

Her own words bounced around her mind. The new human king.

Zhayra grunted her agreement, holding the eyes of the two dragons for a long moment. But they revealed nothing of how they felt. Even the blue. They just waited for them to go. Sighing,

Elinta climbed up Zhayra's back, tied her legs down and clipped in her belt.

"Alright then, girl," she murmured, fighting her rising fears of what lay before them. Fear seemed to be her constant companion these days.

Zhayra launched into the air, a knot of guilt beginning to form in her stomach, but the blue and green dragons followed a full length behind them.

Elinta frowned over her shoulder at them. "Is this because of us or Mazen?" Elinta called to Zhayra.

The dragon grunted. Both, Elinta supposed that meant. At least the dragons cared whether they made it back to Eldras alive. Zhayra flew around the islands once in a large circle, letting one last roar echo over them, then turned toward the mainland.

CHAPTER
TEN

T HE DRAGONS LEFT THEM once the main continent came
back into view. They hadn't seen or heard a whisper of
Mazen during the flight. He was probably back in Liyarna now,
preparing to attack again. Elinta watched the two dragons for a
moment. The flight would have been a good time to try talking
to them again—if she could have convinced them to help, maybe
they could have talked to the others. But the wind had been too
strong, and the dragons too far away to talk to. They'd maintained
the space between them with strict discipline right up until the
moment they'd peeled away and returned to their home.

Zhayra's guilt had increased as the distance between them and
the islands had grown. Now, as the southern beaches of Eldras

flashed under them, Elinta called for Zhayra to land. She had a feeling she knew what this was about. Or maybe the several things it could be about.

Untying herself from the harness, Elinta dropped to the sand and walked around to look Zhayra in the eye.

Zhayra, the guilt now mixed with a bit of confusion, tilted her head. The sun shimmered off her white scales.

"Don't worry about the dragons." Elinta rubbed Zhayra's muzzle. "I don't think there was any way we could have convinced them. Mazen was right. They don't want to fight anymore. And maybe they shouldn't have to."

Zhayra nudged her softly, but the guilt was still there. She knew, or guessed, that the dragon's thoughts were still on her status. As heir, and potential queen, and all that might entail one day. Elinta rubbed her muzzle again. She didn't want the dragon feeling bad for anything, especially with whatever lay before them.

"Zhayra," she said, thinking of the contentment the dragon had felt as she'd returned to her home, "I stand by what I said in Liyarna. Whatever you want to do after this, I'll be there too ... unless you won't want us together anymore."

Zhayra drew back with a snort, her eyes blinking twice emphatically.

Elinta smiled softly. "I just—if you want to go home, we can do that, or if you want to stay, we can do that too." Her heart ached a little as she said it, but she knew parting with Zhayra would hurt even more. The dragon had become a part of her and losing her now would be losing so much more than just losing a friend or a sister. She felt the need to continue, flashing back to that conversation on the Benhurst mountains above Aesira's hut. "My heart can only go so many ways, Zhayra, but if I have to choose, I choose you. I—I think I understand Mazen a little." She paused, and Zhayra shifted, listening intently. "He chose to go with Vaherin—wherever it is they went—after the Eggslaying because he couldn't bear to be parted either."

Zhayra keened quietly and nudged her with her nose again. Her amber eyes were bright, and the guilt inside her slowly unravelled. Whatever Elinta's future with Lorrin looked like, at least she could always check if he was safe and happy. She knew she'd always be able to open the bond with him. Always. But she'd made a decision in the forest in Kethmere, and again in the White Mountains, and she was going to stick to it. Her and Zhayra. She wasn't going back. She didn't want to.

There was one final bit of guilt twisting at Zhayra's insides, but Elinta wanted none of it left, so she said, "Zhayra, my heart can only go so many ways, but you *are* my heart."

Zhayra leapt forward, a burst of happiness in her chest, knocking Elinta to the sand in her excitement. One large foot landed on either side of her, and the dragon pushed her nose into Elinta.

Elinta laughed. Truly laughed, as she hadn't in weeks. And something shifted in her vision. The dragonsight, which she hadn't switched off since the attack in Liyarna, grew sharper as though she'd been looking through a window without realising it. Zhayra's emotions became clearer.

Elinta gasped, still flat on her back. "What happened?"

Zhayra grunted again, a happy sound, and her tail swished behind her.

Something, *something,* had changed in their bond. Elinta laughed again.

"We should go, girl," Elinta said, though she wished they could linger there longer. She ran her hand along the dragon's cheekbone. "We need to get to Culmar."

Zhayra pulled back, letting Elinta stand. She had to spend several minutes brushing the sand from her skin, clothes, and hair. But the clarity that she saw it all with made the job somewhat fun. Sunlight shone through some of the little granules, while it reflected off others. Elinta stopped and glanced at Zhayra.

"I'm marvelling over sand," she said in disbelief. Zhayra's stomach tickled.

Once they were back in the air, Elinta took a moment to check the other senses. It wasn't just the dragonsight and emotions that had changed. It was everything. The hearing was clearer, sharper. Her heat sense revealed greater contrast between shades even though she couldn't see any further. In fact, none of the senses seemed to reach any further, but the quality of them had grown. Deepened.

Did Vaherin and Mazen have a bond like this? Or was this something else...? She pondered this as they flew. Vaherin hadn't been interested in talking, neither yesterday nor that day in Nevira, but would he listen if Zhayra became the queen? The memory of Zhayra's mother rose in her mind. No, he wouldn't listen to Zhayra, just as he hadn't listened to the yellow queen he'd helped kill. Vaherin was angry. Wait, he was angry right now. She could feel it in his large belly, a fire that smouldered there as though it never truly went out.

"Uh ... Zhayra?"

She could feel Vaherin's emotions. And something told her that wasn't the only sense of his that she could access. But this wasn't something Vaherin had done. There was no way he would open a *ngaran* with her. This, this was Zhayra. The bond hadn't changed, as she'd assumed. *Zhayra* had changed. Elinta pulled back from the maroon dragon's emotions, staring at the back of Zhayra's head.

"Are you the queen now?" Elinta called, feeling a strange disembodiment.

Zhayra's large head twisted around as she flew to look at her, and the dragon blinked once.

"You—you're the queen? You're the queen!" Elinta laughed again.

Zhayra's roar rose up to the meet her.

"Wow—but—wow!"

Elinta did something she'd never done before. She unclipped her belt from the harness and laid along Zhayra's wide back, a huge grin on her face. She watched the clouds flash by above her, feeling more comfortable than she ever had on the dragon.

Had Zhayra merely had to accept her role as queen to become it? She'd long wondered how the dragon could be the heir, but not queen, when there was no one else to take her place. Maybe she'd just been too afraid. And their time on the beach had been what she needed to finally accept her place. To finally *decide* to be the queen.

Elinta laughed again, her body rising and falling in time with Zhayra's wing beats.

It was no use going back to the dragon islands now, though. The dragons had been afraid, some had been angry at the idea of joining them. She couldn't force them to join her, even if some might have agreed now that Zhayra was queen. They'd seen enough violence in Eldras. So, Elinta let go of her worries for a moment and watched the world go by as she laid on the dragon's back and wondered if she could reach out and touch the clouds if Zhayra flew a little higher.

CHAPTER
ELEVEN

L UNCH HAD COME AND gone before Culmar finally came into view. They'd taken a direct line to the port city, journeying straight across the land rather than following the coast. Even though she couldn't see Nevira as they passed near it, Elinta's eyes were drawn toward it. The people there were safe, or as safe as they could be, without her or Lorrin there. But how long would it take them to recover from Mazen?

Culmar spread out before them, a totally different sight from the capital. The docks sprawled along the length of the city, hundreds of small boats moored along the sand and in the shallows, with larger trading vessels anchored further out. Gulls crowded the wooden docks, more than tripling the number of people hurrying about, jumping between the boats and the jetties. The houses closest to the docks were a jumbled mess, just as Elinta remembered them from her brief visit as a child. There were no ordered lines or shapes defining the houses or streets. The buildings were shoved together at odd angles. But the further from the docks the houses and streets were, the cleaner and nicer they became. It was as though those by the sea had been thrown up first, and in a great hurry, before the inhabitants slowly began to spread outward with a little more care.

"We need to find the mayor's house," Elinta called to Zhayra, still looking out at the city. Somewhere down there were Lorrin and Niles. Her spirits rose a little. They'd be in the mayor's house, as King Aldon had decided while still in Nevira. She ignored the thought of the other person somewhere down in the city. That was for another time.

Zhayra flew lower, circling over the city, a mess of wooden and stone buildings of varying colours. The wind dropped at the lower height, revealing the clanging of a warning bell. Elinta jolted, looking around them. But there were no other dragons in the sky, and no boats coming on the waves. The watchtowers were signalling the city of *her* arrival.

Elinta felt Zhayra sigh beneath her, a movement she echoed. One day an alarm wouldn't sound at the sight of a dragon.

"There!" Elinta called, pointing to a building closer to the docks than she'd expected. There was no mistaking it as anything other than the mayor's home. It stood higher than those around it, probably three or four floors in all—it was hard to tell from up here—and bordered by a large metal fence. There was a small courtyard in front of the main entrance to the dark grey stone building, but Elinta could already tell it would prove difficult to land in. Not because of its size, but because there were people standing in the centre staring up at them.

"Let's just hope they move," Elinta called, and Zhayra grunted. There was nowhere else for them to land. Zhayra descended a little more slowly than usual to give the people time to move. And they did. The small group nearly ran to get out of Zhayra's way, some heading inside, some running to the edges of the courtyard. Elinta couldn't help herself. She scanned their faces—most terrified—as Zhayra's body dropped into the courtyard. She was looking for familiar blue eyes or a shock of messy blond hair.

Zhayra's wings folded in. The clanging of the bell stopped. And Lorrin emerged from the mayor's home, not even fighting to keep his pace even. No, he was running. And his limp was gone.

"El!" he called, hurrying forward as she dropped to the ground.

Elinta grinned as he enveloped her in a hug. His familiar scent washed over her, and she breathed him in.

She pulled back. "I'm sorry I couldn't be here."

"You're here now." He pressed his forehead to hers, closing his eyes. "It's good to see you."

He looked over at Zhayra. "And you," he said, smiling.

Elinta studied his face. Despite having looked through those eyes and listened through those ears every day since the last time she'd seen him, she'd hardly actually looked *at* him. Not since that night he'd arrived in Culmar to find his father dead and had looked at his reflection in the window as he'd spoken to her.

His blue eyes still held the marks of grief and a spark of anger she'd not seen before, and bags hung under them, but he was clean and collected. And seemed otherwise healthy though his knuckles were still bruised. A new sword was at his hip now, its sheath similar to the one General Nash and General Sonnen had both had for their special half *illayas*-half steel swords. A scarlet crown flower had been sown into the scabbard. He was king now, Elinta had to remind herself as she looked him over. And what a king he made.

"We need to talk soon," he said, lowering his voice so those around them couldn't hear. Elinta's heart jumped at the look in his eyes. She knew instantly what he meant. The confession she'd made when she'd told him about the bond she could open with him.

"We do," she said, "but it'll have to wait."

He nodded. "Once we've dealt with Mazen."

"Once we've dealt with Mazen."

A throat cleared beside Elinta, and she nearly jumped out of her skin.

"If you're all done with the love-dovey, I would like a hug now."

"Niles!" Elinta grabbed him for a hug.

His arms slipped around her, and she squeezed.

The breath rushed out of his lungs, and he groaned, shoving her away. "OK, OK, I get it. You missed me."

Zhayra nudged Niles's back, grunting.

"Ahh, someone else happy to see me. Hello, beasty."

The dragon pulled back, tilted her head, and blinked twice.

Lorrin and Elinta burst out laughing.

"Hmph!" Niles crossed his arms but grinned at the playful dragon.

"We'd better take this off," Niles said, gesturing at Zhayra's harness.

The three of them stepped forward to undo the straps while Zhayra stood still for them. Soldiers began to move around the courtyard again, sticking as close to the edges as they could, but Zhayra's bulk took up most of the space. One soldier was brave enough to step over her tail, but when it twitched, he nearly jumped out of his skin. Zhayra's stomach tickled, and Elinta realised she was waiting for someone else to try it so she could scare them too.

"Is Tamir back yet?" Elinta asked, stepping back from the dragon.

"No," Lorrin said. "He'll still be another day or two away based on what Niles said."

"And that's only if he left not long after us," Niles added.

The harness now rolled up and inside its bag, Elinta turned to Zhayra. "I don't think you'll be able to stay here." Culmar had even less room for the dragon than Nevira.

Zhayra grumbled.

"There's a grassland out to the west you could go to," Lorrin said. "We've told everyone to stay away from it for you."

Annoyance and gratitude warred in the dragon, but she loosed a thankful grumble.

"I'll check in later," Elinta said.

Zhayra grunted again, then took off back into the air, heading west.

"Come on," Elinta said. "We need to talk."

In the solitude of Lorrin's new room, Elinta filled her two friends in on what had happened during her quick visit with the dragons. They sat on his large bed in a circle, legs folded under them, as though they were gossiping like normal people. Except, of course, they weren't.

Niles sat with mouth agape as she described her chat with Mazen while Lorrin's eyes darkened. But Elinta found, though her trip had been disappointing, that she didn't feel upset recounting their failure. Because it had ended with something else. Something she still didn't quite fully understand but found she didn't need to.

"She's queen now?" Niles said, his mouth dropping back open.

"She is," Elinta said, knowing that Zhayra heard and saw everything passing between them. And approved.

"Wow," Niles said.

"That's amazing," Lorrin said. "So, the senses are different now?"

"A little. I don't really know the full extent yet."

"And Vaherin—" Lorrin frowned "—you really felt his anger?"

Elinta nodded distractedly; something had just occurred to her. There was something else she might be able to access of Vaherin's. Something much more important than his emotions or even his sight.

Elinta opened her mouth to tell the boys her idea, but Lorrin spoke first. "We need to fill in my mother and the advisors. We'll leave out Zhayra being queen and the changes in the bond. They don't need to know that yet." Elinta knew he was thinking less of the generals and more of Shae. There was no telling what trouble the woman might try to stir up if she knew just how important Zhayra really was.

"Let's get it over with then."

"It's a shame the trip didn't go better, but at least you and Zhayra returned safely," Shae said.

Elinta hurried to stop the shock from spreading across her face at Shae's almost kind words. Niles didn't do so well. His eyes widened as he stared at the small woman. Shae didn't notice, her green eyes scanning the others seated at the table. The council had been called in a large room apparently usually used as the mayor's private dining room, though it had been cleared so the large table sitting in its centre was the only thing in the room. Interestingly, the mayor was nowhere to be seen.

Ford seemed to study the woman for a moment before turning his attention away. *We're not the only ones who noticed,* Elinta thought, glancing back at Niles. But if anyone else was surprised by the change in the woman, none of them gave it away.

"This encounter with Mazen is interesting," General Nash said, her blue eyes turning thoughtful. "He respected the dragons' decision, though they didn't agree with him. The fact that he didn't wait to attack you once you'd left is also telling of his acceptance."

"He has some honour left in him," General Sonnen grunted.

Lorrin nodded, glancing at his mother. Queen Mira was silent. She hid her grief well in her body language and facial expressions. She was even dressed perfectly, but her silence gave her away. She'd said nothing other than a quiet greeting when the meeting had been called, and though her voice had seemed strong, Elinta could hear the pain in it. Her heart ached for the queen.

"Only with the dragons, it would seem," Shae said.

Elinta continued to watch the small woman curiously. What had changed for the advisor to suddenly be … perhaps not nice to her, but not antagonistic either? Her light brown hair was tied back in its typical strict bun today, but the usual harshness of her face seemed lessened. The woman glanced at the queen. Had—had the king's death changed Shae too?

"We're back where we started then," General Nash said. "These trips were a waste."

"Almost," Lorrin said, glancing at Elinta, but he didn't mention what else had happened. "But we know where we stand now. And Ciar's people will be here."

"That is a comfort," General Sonnen said. His eyes slipped to Elinta's. "You did well to face Mazen again, kid."

"We didn't fight," Elinta said, but she suspected that wasn't what he'd meant at all. He meant she'd done well to even be in his presence again after what happened to Blaine. Her chest gave another throb. Zhayra's own chest responded to hers. Yes, they had both done well on the islands.

Lorrin glanced at his mother, then at Elinta. Elinta nodded. They'd said everything they'd needed to say.

"That's all for now," Lorrin said, and the room began to disperse. But Shae glanced over her shoulder at Elinta as she left and smiled.

CHAPTER

TWELVE

"**E**LINTA!" FORD CALLED, HURRYING to catch up with her as she left the room and pulling her from her thoughts. She'd been thinking of Vaherin again.

Elinta looked into Ford's eyes, once again seeing not a trace of fear or hate. It was refreshing when so many other people seemed to be filled with it. Many still wouldn't even look into her eyes anymore.

"What is it?" Elinta asked, her brow furrowing. Ford had always been very reserved, quiet. It was odd that he'd called after her. But even so, she bounced on her toes, Vaherin jostling for her attention. It had been hard to push aside her realisation and subsequent excitement to sit through the meeting.

Ford lowered his voice, glancing around to make sure no others would hear. "Did you learn what you needed to from the other *Zearla lurai?*"

"Yes." She wasn't at all surprised that he alone among the people who'd been in the room the day she'd said she needed to go to Liyarna remembered the reason for it. Lorrin had decided not to share the revelation of the other bonds, purely because people might misunderstand exactly what it meant and panic. "Things aren't as bad as I'd feared."

But ... now she had something different in her own bond. Her ability to connect to Vaherin had given her an idea. What she might learn through it.

"I'm sorry, what was that?" Elinta asked, blushing as she realised the historian had spoken again.

"Did Aesira escape Liyarna?" Ford's eyes were drilling into her own.

"No," Elinta whispered, "she's gone." She backtracked. He'd said her *name* that time. "Wait, did you know her?"

"Yes." Ford avoided her eyes, and he seemed to hunch over a little. Was this how the man knew so much about the Asali? He'd been to the Green City.

"Vaherin—" Elinta's eyes widened, her thoughts yanking her far away again at the mention of the dragon. She'd tell him more later— "excuse me, I have to go."

Elinta hurried away. She had to do it and she had to do it right now. Vaherin had been in total agreement with Mazen ever since she'd met him. The anger she'd felt in his body was real and powerful. Elinta knew it was because of the Eggslaying but ... something told her there was more to it. And now she might be able to find out what it was.

Elinta jogged through the mayor's house—if it could even be called that given its size—looking for the room Lorrin had shown her on the way to the council meeting. They'd put one aside for her on the ground floor. Face after face, and door after door whizzed past her.

"Zhayra," Elinta said, her words bouncing in time with her feet, "I'm going to look at his memories."

Zhayra's heart jumped, then settled indicating surprise and then contentment with the idea. Elinta vaguely wondered if Zhayra had peeked into the dragon's past yet. Now that she was queen Vaherin couldn't hide anything from her either. What would Elinta find there?

"Elinta?" Lorrin's voice halted her in her steps. "Are you OK?"

"Yes," she said, twisting around to find the prince (*king*, she mentally corrected herself) hurrying from another room. "I'm just going to my room.... Although, I might be a little lost."

He frowned. "You're in a bit of a hurry."

"Yes." She almost laughed, but she really wanted to get moving. "I think I can see Vaherin's memories."

His blue eyes widened, and he glanced over his shoulder. "I'll be back in a few minutes." He closed the door behind him. Elinta spared a moment of sympathy for whoever he'd just left, since Lorrin had likely only just arrived at the room himself. "It's this way." He led her down the hall.

Elinta watched him from the corner of her eye as they hurried, people stepping out of their way. King. A surge of pride hit her. He was going to be the best ruler this country had seen in a long time.

King Aldon's death was tragic, but it also brought so much hope with it. Hope for Zhayra and the dragons, hope for her.

"Here it is," Lorrin said, stopping outside a familiar door. She looked up and down the hall, cementing its location in her mind. "Do you really think you could see his memories?"

"I think so."

"Do you want me to stay?" he said, glancing over her shoulder back the way they'd come. She thought of whoever it was he'd left behind. Of all the countless things he likely had to do. And the heavy bags under eyes that hadn't quite returned to their usual spark.

"No, it could be hours before I wake up. I'll let you know if I learn anything new."

"OK," he said, a smile tilting his lips as he looked down at her. It drew a smile from her. He squeezed her hand, then strode back up the hall.

Elinta pushed into the room, closing the wooden door behind her.

THUMP!

Elinta spun around, her hand flying to her sword, her heart beating wildly. And found Neva.

"Neva! You're OK!" Elinta frowned at the maid. "Aren't you?"

Neva's face had paled until she was whiter than the sheets on Elinta's new bed. She stood rooted to the spot, a stack of logs scattered at her feet. It was these that she must have dropped when Elinta had entered the room. Neva's green eyes were wide and fixed on her.

"I—I," Neva stuttered. Elinta's confusion deepened. The woman had never had trouble finding words to say before. Then, with another stab of pain to her already bruised and beaten heart, Elinta realised the problem. Neva now knew she was *Zearla lurai*. The woman could hardly meet her white eyes.

Elinta's shoulders dropped. "It's OK," she said, her voice flat. "I'll clean it up. You can go."

A flash of anger lit in Zhayra's throat as she heard the words through Elinta's ears.

Neva glanced uncertainly between her and the logs before hurriedly curtsying and running from the room.

Elinta stared at the door as it slammed shut.

"Neva ..." she whispered.

Elinta shook herself. Now wasn't the time. Elinta didn't even bother to pick up the pile of wood for the empty fireplace but crossed directly to the bed. She unclipped her sword belt, dropping it gently to the ground, and changed into a nightgown since she didn't know how long she'd be asleep for. Her stomach was rumbling, but she was willing to miss dinner for this.

Elinta pulled the covers close around her. She closed her eyes. And thought of Vaherin.

CHAPTER
THIRTEEN

*I*T HAD BEEN CURIOSITY *that led him to the mountains in the southwest. He'd heard stories of a dragon who had bonded with a female shining one long ago. And one with a male before that. He wanted to see one of the forest ones himself. His early years had been spent in the far north of Eldras among his kin. Though he had seen much of the continent, he'd never travelled to see the glowing two-legs in their big city. The ones at his home had arrived just before he'd hatched. He and the other hatchlings had played long with them. But he'd wanted to see these others. To see the people who had convinced the green dragon to share himself with one of them.*

He'd first arrived two weeks ago and had visited several times since. There had been a man. The prince. Still young in their own years, but so much older than him. His iron-grey eyes were bright, intelligent, yet the man, the prince, had never seen the world. He'd instantly liked him.

Now, he was back, and the pull to open to him was stronger than ever. This prince, he wanted to communicate with him, and now he understood that other dragon, the one who'd bonded with the man's own grandmother.

Mazen tilted his head and rested a hand on his muzzle. "What are you thinking?"

He'd know soon enough. He reached out too, not with claw, but with mind and latched onto the man.

Mazen's eyes widened, and a broad smile lit up his features. He bowed his head. "Thank you."

When the vision cleared, time had passed. It had been over ninety years since he'd bonded with Mazen, and they'd been the best years of his life. His wings were now wider and his body broader, and he felt closer to his bonded than ever.

They'd returned to the Ash Mountains to visit his kin for the summer. The day was bright and the sun warm. He'd left in the early morning to fly further up the mountain to look for food, leaving Mazen to his sleep. He'd felt the moment he'd awoken, briefly linking to his eyes to check on him, and feeling the prince do the same. Then he'd continued his flight. The sun shimmering off his maroon scales, scales that his bonded's eyes now matched.

A spike of anger in Mazen's chest caused him to pause, but it was the shimmer of fear curling his stomach that made him turn back. There should be nothing here to make his bonded feel that way. He dove into the man's ears even as he flew.

"—don't understand! What makes you so special?"

He felt his own spark of nerves rise at the unfamiliar voice. There was another two-legged up where the mountain Asali never visited?

"It is not something you can demand," Mazen said, his voice calm but forceful. His bonded's frustration was growing. He forced his wings to go faster, his eyes searching for the first sign of the prince, but he'd flown further than he'd thought.

"Why not? There are many here! Why should you be bonded and not me? We're both princes!"

He felt his wings falter, but he pushed on. Both princes? Was it a human down there demanding the bond?

"I told you," Mazen said, "that's not how this works. It's a bond, given in love and friendship. You have to earn it."

He heard the other man laugh, but it chilled his heart. "You expect me to believe you didn't buy their loyalty? Just give me an egg then."

"No." Mazen's voice was like steel.

Give him an egg! His own rage rumbled into life. How dare he?

"Perhaps, I should just take one."

It happened in the blink of an eye. He rounded a peak, tucking his wings in to cut down the distance he had to travel, the scales of his belly scraping the snow, and found his bonded and the human prince standing by the cliffs. They could have been looking out over the world. Except the human was drawing his sword. And his bonded was unarmed. A roar tore itself from his throat, fear so palpable it blurred the edges of his vision, and he dove straight for the man lunging for his kin.

In a flurry of wings, he slammed into the human and swept him straight off the edge.

"Vaherin!" Mazen's fear reeked. But he felt frozen in the air as he watched the two-leg seem to fall in slow motion. His bonded walked to the edge to watch as the man's body broke on the peak below.

Mazen pressed his face into his cheek scales, shaking with the rage rocking his bones and boiling his insides. The human's death had *only been the beginning. A cataclysm that called the other humans to it. That made them bloodthirsty. Dishonourable.*

"We'll make them pay for it. Don't worry."

He keened, the fire in his chest threatening to go out from his grief. His bonded stroked his cheek. "I'll tell Father everything. He'll understand. It wasn't your fault."

He nudged the prince. He didn't regret killing that human. It had come down to his bonded or a man trying to kill him and steal a dragon egg. There was only one way that was going to end. But what the humans had done because of it ... He watched his bonded leave him on the training field, his step sure and showing nothing of the mess of his emotions.

It was night when Mazen finally returned, but he knew what he was going to say. He'd heard it all. "He won't do anything." Mazen's voice was raw, his eyes rimmed red. Fury and despair raged inside of them both. "All those young," he whispered.

He keened, low and long, the ache in his heart worse than he'd ever felt before, ever thought possible. King Riah knew what had happened, how Prince Tristan had died and why. He'd seen the devastation left by the prince's father and uncle. And yet, he did nothing. Nothing to avenge the young now lost forever. Nothing to avenge the dragons that now fled the continent in droves.

"He's weak." Mazen spat the last word, and he had to agree. What kind of king wouldn't avenge the death of the young and innocent? "He dared to preach forgiveness. Unity. As though the humans could ever be anything other than insects. He knows better than I how they must always fight and kill."

Mazen's maroon eyes darkened, and he stared straight into his eyes. "There's no other way, Vaherin. But I'll only do it if you say it's OK."

He felt his own heart harden. He dipped his head in acceptance, a soft growl slipping through his maw. The king wouldn't help them. But they wouldn't leave it there. They couldn't.

Mazen nodded, drew his illayas dagger and a vial from inside his cloak and stepped toward his scaled foot.

"To unity," his bonded said. He saw the rim of the glass through Mazen's eyes as he raised it to his lips and downed it. But Mazen's eyes never left King Riah, as he too downed his own glass of wine. He felt a drip of satisfaction in his very core as he watched the last drop disappear. Satisfaction reflected in the broken, icy heart of his bonded. He watched and listened on through Mazen.

The king lowered his glass, unaware of the dragon blood now racing through his veins. Ingested and without a wound to reveal it, it wouldn't leave a trace. If he could have smiled as he'd seen his bonded do, he would have. This was the first step. The first step to avenging those young. There was a long road ahead. But in the end, when the dragons had strengthened their numbers, everything would be made right.

"I am proud of you, Mazen," King Riah said, his hands clasped before him on the stone table. "I know how devastated you were at the loss of the eggs. But this is for the best. Our peoples need peace."

"Of course."

Could the king hear the restraint in Mazen's voice the way he could? The anger threatening to break free?

He shifted his bulk, impatience now starting to rise in him as he watched on. It was nearly time for them to go. This was their last night in the Green City for some time. But one day they would return.

"I'll say goodnight now, Father. It's been a big day."

"Yes." King Riah stood, moving around the table to meet Mazen as he too stood. The king embraced his son. "You'll see. All will work out."

Mazen said nothing as he turned around and left his poisoned father to die.

He stared at the young white one, his bulk blocking her way to her mother. His bonded was talking with the queen once again, trying to rally her into taking the revenge they deserved. He'd closed himself off to them all, not wanting to feel their betrayal any more than they would want to feel the anger that had hollowed him out. But the queen could feel it, and he'd felt her recoil.

A strange rush and jump in Mazen's emotions had him twisting his head around before he could remember the young one. Zhayra rushed past him in a blur, bounding off the rocks as she half flew to her mother.

He watched her go. Mazen had done it. He was sure of it. A burst of pride rose in him. His bonded had mentioned the possibility of it before—

"Vaherin!" Mazen's voice was flat.

The white one! He rushed forward, seeing the body of the queen at the feet of his bonded, knowing it meant she had refused yet again but also for the last time, and launched himself after the heir.

The keens of the dragons echoed after him. He just hoped Mazen was quick enough to hide his involvement in the death. Another weak ruler. He roared as he pursued the white dragon, but the fierce wind over the sea blew it back at him. He pushed his wings harder, but the dragon had disappeared into the clouds.

Elinta woke gasping, sweat dripping down her face, and frowned. There was something in her mouth, tearing into the skin in the corners and blocking her air. She was upside down, something digging into her torso. Elinta blinked at the shining figure she was slung over in the darkness.

CHAPTER
FOURTEEN

I T WAS THE ASALI'S shoulder that dug into Elinta's torso. Her mind stuttered, trying to comprehend the shift that had happened while she'd been asleep. She wriggled, unconsciously trying to ease the ache in her stomach from the man's bony shoulder.

"She's awake! Hurry!" the Asali beside her whispered, his dark hair falling around his face.

Elinta's eyes widened, her mind finally catching up and leaving Vaherin's memories far behind. She tugged at the bonds tying her hands behind her back and the ones holding her feet together. They bit deeply into her skin. Panic rushed into her chest even as she tried to push off the man's back to see where she was. There were the logs of wood strewn across the floor. Her room. She was still in the mayor's home. She'd woken before they could move her. The man growled and jolted her as though in warning.

Lorrin! Where was the king? Were Mazen's Asali after him too? She closed her eyes, ignoring the scene around her as she jumped into Lorrin's eyes, her fear rising in her mouth even as the vision cleared. Dimly, she realised the quality of this weaker bond had also improved. Lorrin sat opposite a slumped Niles in an office. Both of them seemed unharmed though Niles had bags under his eyes nearly large enough to match Lorrin's. Neither seemed alarmed. They didn't know what was happening. She struggled, wanting to shout out to them, warn them that they weren't safe. Her fear threatened to overwhelm her. But it was better that they didn't know she was in trouble. If the Asali were here, surely the guards were on their way to protect their new king. She didn't want the two boys to rush here alone. But her emotions continued to rage, and she tried to shove them out of the way as she fought to concentrate.

Lorrin's vision jolted, and he seemed to say something to Niles. They both jumped to their feet, Niles's face paling even as he drew his sword.

"No!" Elinta shouted. Or she tried to, but there was still something in her mouth and it came out muffled.

Niles and Lorrin ran through the door of their room.

"Enough of that." Something tugged at Elinta's hair, and she pulled away from Lorrin's vision in time to see one of the logs Neva had dropped flying toward her face. It slammed into her forehead and blood instantly trickled into her eyes as Elinta felt herself go limp. Bile replaced the fear in her mouth as her vision swam. Zhayra's stomach clenched.

The Asali, his silver eyes glowing as bright as the moonlight in her room, stared deep into Elinta's eyes, still tugging at her hair to keep her head up. *"Do not even think of coming here or the girl dies."*

Zhayra's stomach clenched even tighter, and Elinta felt some kind of shift in the dragon, but she couldn't focus long enough to work out what it was. The Asali released her, and she slumped against the other man's back, the blood now trickling up through her hair and dripping to the floor.

Elinta's vision had blurred, and vaguely she knew that was bad. Her body bounced in time with the movement of the man carrying her. She couldn't concentrate enough to get her limbs working again. But the men didn't seem to be going toward her door, but rather toward the window. Glass crunched under the two Asali's feet, and when her body swayed with the man's movement, she saw another one outside waiting for them. Blood continued to trickle up her face. Bile rose in her throat again and she desperately tried to swallow it down, hanging on enough to her senses that she knew she couldn't empty her stomach with a gag in her mouth. But her mind was swirling as badly as her vision was. Lorrin. She hoped he'd be OK.

"Uppan," one of the Asali whispered. Elinta shook her head, trying to bring the word into focus, trying to translate it as she had been doing so easily before, but she couldn't.

They were halfway through the window, the man carrying her twisted to climb out so that she looked back into the room when she turned her head. The door slammed open and two hazy figures burst into her room.

A voice shouted, tearing apart the night as well as Elinta's aching head, "Put her down!"

Niles ran into the room while Lorrin disappeared back out into the hall. Elinta blinked heavily, wondering if her eyes were playing tricks on her, but he definitely seemed to have left after delivering his demand.

The Asali jumped, landing lightly on the ground outside.

"Oi!"

Niles followed, leaping through the window.

"Ayn kima zali rai," the man carrying her said, pointing at Niles. His voice vibrated through his back. Elinta's head ached. Where was the other man? The one she'd seen waiting for them outside?

The man shifted and suddenly the shoulder supporting her disappeared and the air opened up underneath her. Elinta crashed to the ground, the breath rushing out of her lungs. She lay dazed on the pavement. The sharp clash of steel on steel echoed above her but, with her face pressed to the pathway and blood now trickling into her eyes, Elinta couldn't see what was happening. A loud crash sounded nearby like glass breaking, and there was someone yelling, roaring.

Taking two deep breaths, Elinta pushed herself onto her side, blinking rapidly. Her head! If only she could concentrate. Lorrin's form appeared over her, rage flickering across his face, as he lunged and then parried an attack from one of the Asali. She could hear another set of blades somewhere behind her. Niles and the other Asali.

Elinta wriggled, but the bonds around her wrists and ankles were tight, and the movement sent her stomach pitching again. Zhayra looked on through her eyes, and the feeling made her head worse, but she didn't want the dragon to leave her.

Lorrin appeared before her again, his sword darting toward his opponent like a wasp. The moon and the lights of the building reflected off it. With a flick of his wrist, the Asali's sword flew from his hand and Lorrin jumped forward, bringing his pommel down onto the man's head. He sunk to the ground.

"Elinta!" Lorrin ducked beside her, but Elinta was looking around. There was one more. One other than the one Niles still fought. She grunted, forcing herself to raise her head and gesture around with her chin. Lorrin frowned even as he reached out a hand for the gag in her mouth.

The glowing man appeared behind him.

"Mmph!" Elinta yelled through the gag.

Lorrin spun around, his sword rising just in time to deflect the strike from hitting home in his torso. But it wasn't enough. The blade sunk into his thigh.

Yelling, Lorrin dove back into the fight, but a dark patch was steadily spreading across his leg. It shook beneath him as he fought but held firm.

Elinta struggled to free herself. Free any of the limbs tied so tightly together that they were going numb. But they didn't move even a millimetre. The man was closing in on Lorrin. She struggled to push herself up, grunting, nearly yelling at herself through the gag. She had to do something. Anything.

She got her feet under her, and she swayed, least of all because of the bonds but more from her pounding head, and as though in slow motion, she saw an opening. Elinta threw herself at the Asali. She slammed shoulder first into his legs and they both crashed to the ground. Everything went black.

Elinta's eyes blinked open only seconds later, and she turned dazedly to see Lorrin on top of the Asali, slamming the man's head into the ground. Niles was right beside him.

Everything stopped as though for a breath and then Lorrin was there, pulling Elinta into his arms, his legs supporting her body. Blood from his thigh seeped through her nightgown. But he seemed oblivious to his own injury. Her hands were still tied behind her, squashed under her body.

Lorrin gently pulled the gag from her mouth.

He lightly pressed his hand to her face. "Elinta?"

"I'm OK," she tried to say, but she was pretty sure the words were slurred. Lorrin's face was blurry, swimming, but she could make out the worry there.

Niles crouched beside them, his brown eyes locked on her bleeding head. "I'll get a healer. Don't you dare fall asleep." His hand, warm and sticky, brushed hers, and he disappeared.

Lorrin held her to him, his arms holding her tenderly. The night felt oddly quiet now without the ringing of steel echoing in her ears.

"Are you OK?" she slurred, blinking against the blood drying around her eyes.

"Yes," he said, pulling back to wipe the blood away with his sleeve. "Don't worry about me."

He locked eyes with her and then pressed his sleeve to her head, and she went to smile, but then she frowned. "You shouldn't have come." She was pretty sure it had all come out in one long word.

"Shhh," Lorrin said, his mouth tilting in a smile but the worry in his blue eyes deepened. The moon shone brightly behind him.

"I found someone!" Niles's voice shouted a few minutes later.

"Oh, good," Elinta murmured, thinking of the warmth that stuck her nightgown to her back. Lorrin could use a healer.

"Hey," Lorrin said, "no sleeping."

Had she been sleeping? Elinta frowned up at him. Her head felt like it had swollen to more than double its size. Didn't she deserve just a small nap to ease the ache?

Niles dropped to the ground beside them, and a woman appeared over his shoulder a moment later. Elinta couldn't quite make out the details of her face, her vision unable to focus even at that close distance, but the woman seemed concerned.

"We need to get her inside now."

Lorrin shifted, pulling her tighter against his body, and rose an inch before dropping back to the ground. Elinta groaned.

"I'll take her, Lor," Niles said.

"No, I—"

"Lor."

Another set of rough hands lifted her, and Elinta's eyes began to droop again.

She was in a bed when she woke. The woman from before was standing over her, pressing something to the wound on her head. Niles stood behind the healer, but someone else's hand held hers. Firelight flickered long shadows around the room.

"That's it," the healer said, her voice gentle. "Let's try to keep those eyes open this time."

The skin on her head felt odd. Tight. How long had she been sleeping? Her limbs were no longer bound, and she was fairly sure the healer had already stitched her skin back together.

"Lorrin," she murmured.

The hand in hers tightened.

"I'm here."

"Your leg."

"It's fine," he said.

A loud grumble sounded from outside and Elinta frowned, fairly certain she was hearing things. Zhayra was somewhere outside of the city, beyond furious and equally afraid, judging from the tightness and fire in her body.

"Zhayra's here too," Lorrin said.

"What?" Elinta tried to lift her head, but the healer gently pushed her back down.

"None of that now," the woman said, dressing her head with a bandage.

"Move around too much you might just lose your head, El," Niles said, moving closer to the bed. His hand was pressed to a dark patch on his arm.

Elinta frowned. Attempting to glare at her friend, but the movement pulled at the skin near her wound, and she winced. "My head feels too big to fall off. I might just fall over instead," she grunted, sure her lips stumbled around the words. But Niles and Lorrin both chuckled.

"It does look very big," Niles said, nodding.

"There's no need to tease her," the healer said, her soft voice hardening. "She needs rest."

"Of course," Lorrin said, but Elinta thought she could still hear a chuckle in his words.

"Let's get you two seen to now," the woman said, turning away from Elinta. and Elinta's eyes dropped closed again.

It was still dark when she woke, and her eyes still felt heavy, and her head confused. She blinked at the ceiling, the water in the bay crashing against the sand sounding in her ears. Firelight danced across the ceiling. There was something warm beside her, too. She moved her head barely a couple millimetres before she had to stop, the movement sending pain jolting through her head and neck. But it was enough to see what was beside her. Lorrin.

The new king lay next her, an arm supporting his head. It looked as though he'd been watching her but had fallen asleep quite unexpectantly.

"I thought he'd never sleep," Niles murmured from her other side. He stood over the bed, his blond hair ruffled, and in a clean shirt. A bandage was wrapped around his arm.

"Are you OK?"

"Me?" He smirked. "You're the one with the melon head, remember?"

"Melon head?"

"Zhayra's at the window," Niles said, sitting on the edge of the bed. "I don't think she'll leave until she sees you. Even then ..."

"Tell her I'm OK," Elinta said, her words still strained and hard to keep straight.

Niles glanced away. "You really scared us there."

"I'm sorry," Elinta said, reaching for his hand. Pain shot through her wrist.

He looked back down at her. "Tamir should be back soon, and you'll be up again in no time. Just rest until then, OK?"

Lorrin shifted beside her but didn't wake.

The firelight in the room dimmed and Niles hurried to add more wood to it.

But she didn't see when he came back.

CHAPTER
FIFTEEN

*ARSI.*"

              "Tarsi."

"El?"

Elinta groaned, blinking open her heavy eyes, and found three of her favourite beings leaning over her. A low keen vibrating through the room confirmed that the fourth wasn't far away. Early morning light streaked across the ceiling above them.

Tamir's shoulder length hair had fallen forward as he leaned over her, but he ignored it, pressing his hand to her face. "I was not gone for very long, and look, you have all fallen apart."

Elinta smiled. And Tamir's skin began to glow more brightly, and the now familiar warmth began to flow through her, starting from under his hands and spreading out over her body.

"Niles called me a melon head," she said.

Lorrin turned a frown on his friend. "Melon head?"

"Yeah." He shrugged. "Balloon head just didn't sound as good."

Tamir shook his head, biting his lip as though to hide a smile. "I would not listen to him."

The glow began to die down, and the ache in Elinta's head was gone. She flexed her wrists and ankles. Even the torn skin there had healed.

"Thank you," Elinta said, pushing herself upright. She would never tire of the Asali's healing ability. The heaviness in her head was gone, as was the feeling of having a 'melon head.' Her stomach had settled, and her vision had cleared. She was fine again.

The boys all grinned. Elinta set to work removing the bandage from her head. She'd have to remove the stitches later.

"Lorrin." Tamir gestured for the king to sit on the bed.

Elinta took the moment to study Tamir as he healed Lorrin's leg. He was back in his usual style of clothes, probably having changed out of the tunic he'd worn in the desert once he'd left. But the clothes were dirty and travel worn.

"Did you only just arrive?"

"Yes, I came straight to your room." Tamir smiled gently. Dirt had smudged across his face.

"Thank you," Elinta said again, throwing her bandages to the foot of the bed. Tamir must have ended up leaving not long after she and Niles had seen him.... What did that mean then?

Soon, Lorrin and Niles were both healed and healthy, too. And they all sat on her bed.

Elinta had a hundred questions bouncing around her head, and she wasn't sure which one to choose first. Zhayra grumbled outside, so she thought she'd better make it quick.

"How'd it go with the desert Asali?"

Tamir frowned, pushing his hair back from his face. He looked exhausted now. "They are a different people to the Liyarnans," he said, looking around at them all. "While they have a leader, they lead more in example and suggestion. Punishments are agreed on by the majority. And ... things like this are decided among individuals."

"So," Elinta said, thinking on what he'd said, "is anyone coming?"

Tamir sighed. "One."

"One!" Lorrin and Niles both exclaimed. Elinta merely sighed. Why would no one stand against Mazen? It seemed everyone could agree what he was doing was wrong, but no one would do anything about it. Actions, it seemed, were much harder than words.

"They have distanced themselves from the world in more than just location," Tamir said, his grey eyes darkening. "I thought I had reached them."

"It doesn't matter. We'll work something out." Elinta placed her hand on his shoulder but turned to Lorrin. "Do we know anything about last night?"

Lorrin's face clouded. "They were only after you. I have some men investigating. We'll call a meeting with the council soon."

Elinta nodded, gathering her thoughts. The council meeting would have to wait anyway. Elinta wriggled her legs out from under the covers, finding herself in a fresh nightgown. The healer must have swapped it over before she left. The other one would be ruined.

"I need to see Zhayra."

The boys all jumped to their feet, glancing at her clothing.

"Right."

"We'll see you later."

"She will be pleased."

Lorrin glanced back at her from the doorway, offering her a small smile, his earlier concern gone. Before he could close it, Elinta called out.

"How did you know?"

Lorrin frowned.

"About the attack?"

His expression cleared but then clouded with confusion. "I felt your fear. It was like ... you were pushing it at me. It was still yours, though."

"I pushed it?" Elinta paused, her mind racing. She'd heard of that before in the dragons. Zhayra's mother had pushed her memories of the Eggslaying at the other dragons on their commemoration day. She raised her eyebrows. "It must be because she's queen now."

"That was my guess." Lorrin nodded. "You better hurry. Zhayra's still waiting." He smiled again before he closed the door so she could change.

Elinta sat, smiling after him for a moment as she remembered waking with him beside her. Had he and Niles stayed with her all night?

Shaking herself, Elinta glanced around the room. She wasn't in her room anymore, which meant that the wardrobe in the corner wouldn't have any of her clothes in it. Elinta looked around, trying to decide whether to run down to her own room or borrow something from the small wardrobe, when her eyes landed on a familiar shirt and pair of pants.

"Huh," Elinta said, staring down at her clothes laid out on a small wooden chair. Even her sword was there. Perhaps the boys had fetched them for her.

She quickly swapped out of her clothes, then hurried over to the window, her sword now on her hip. Apparently, she was still on the ground floor, but she could only tell because it seemed Zhayra had to lower her head to peer in through the window.

Though she'd known how worried the dragon had been, Elinta laughed at the amber eye and white scales blocking her view. The sight of the dragon (no matter how little of her she could see) in a human area would never fail to raise her spirits.

"You better move, I'm coming out!" she called, pushing the windowpane up.

Zhayra pulled back with a snort, the tight ball in her chest finally dissipating. Elinta climbed out through the window, which was significantly smaller than the one that had been in her room and landed on the dirty pavement in front of Zhayra. She had a brief moment to glance around, during which she realised that there was no one near Zhayra, when the dragon nearly tackled her.

Zhayra shoved her head into Elinta, causing her to stumble backward into the wall, and she grunted.

Elinta stroked the dragon's muzzle. "I'm sorry you had to wait out here."

Zhayra grunted again, pulling back to look Elinta in the eye. She knew what the dragon wanted because she'd been thinking along the same lines. Last night had been the last she would spend in the mayor's home. From now on, she was staying with Zhayra.

Zhayra blinked once and gestured with her head for Elinta to climb on her back.

Elinta smiled. "Only if you fly nice." She didn't have the harness set up.

Zhayra grunted, blinking once. A flock of gulls rose into the sky behind Zhayra, squawking as they turned as one in mid-air and disappeared into another part of the city. The sight reminded Elinta of the time she'd visited as a child, and one of the gulls had stolen her food. Shaking her head, she climbed onto Zhayra's back.

Once Elinta was in place, her legs gripping the dragon and her fingers digging into her scales, Zhayra gently took off into the sky.

With the salty wind coming off the water and brushing over her face, Elinta finally allowed herself to remember what had happened last night. Her heart hammered at the memory of waking from Vaherin's memories to find herself slung over the Asali's shoulder. Why hadn't it woken her? They'd broken her window to get in the room, tied her up, and carried her and she'd slept right through it all.

She paused. Blaine had had similar trouble waking her on the road back to Nevira as she'd looked into Zhayra's memories. Her stomach coiled. She was vulnerable in those moments, unable to wake until the memories were over. She'd have to be careful in the future.

Zhayra grunted, likely at the nerves in Elinta's gut, and she let her thoughts turn away from her revelation and to the memories themselves. She'd learn more about how the Asali had found her later.

She finally knew what had happened to Prince Tristan. Vaherin had killed him while defending Mazen. Her heart ached at the thought. Had King Cenric known how the prince had died would the Eggslaying still have happened? But it didn't matter because it did happen. And Vaherin and Mazen had gone on to kill King Riah. Had even planned to kill Zhayra's mother if she didn't agree to join them. This was the final piece to the puzzle she'd been struggling to solve in her mind ever since that night she'd met Mazen in the White Palace. She saw him now. Saw him properly. That vibrant, respectful man with eyes like his father was long gone. As was the young, curious dragon. And seeing all the steps and decisions that had led them there filled her with ... relief. She and Zhayra would never have made those decisions.

They would have fought for another option. But it was still scary to realise that she understood. She understood how and why things had happened the way they had.

She just wished they could put all this behind them. Or ignore that Mazen was even a threat. She wanted some peace.

Zhayra turned gracefully, carrying Elinta out over the water. The early morning sun sent the waves into different hues of blues and greens, its influence on the clouds already dissipating.

Elinta stroked Zhayra's scales. "Did you watch them too?"

Zhayra grunted again.

"We'll never be like them."

Zhayra twisted her head around, so Elinta could see one of her eyes, and winked twice. No, they'd never be like Mazen and Vaherin.

They flew over the ocean and the docks, weaving through the air flows and dodging gulls that failed to realise Zhayra was a large predator. One flew so close Elinta could have sworn she felt the air from its wings.

Finally, Elinta was forced to admit they needed to return. They needed to know what had happened last night. How the Asali had found her. She stared at her wrists, where the torn skin had been only hours earlier. And sighed. Yes, she needed to know what had happened. But the thought sent her stomach coiling again.

Zhayra landed back in front of the mayor's house, her large body looking very cramped in the small space.

"I don't know how long we'll be," Elinta said. If only the dragon could fit inside, then she could join her in the meeting, and anything else that might follow. At least the dragon could still watch and listen in.

Zhayra grumbled, but Elinta knew she understood.

Smiling, Elinta twisted back to face the stone building and breathed deeply. Would she ever get fully used to attending these meetings? And as a *Zearla lurai*, no less. It was still so strange knowing that everyone, *everyone*, knew who and what she was. And with her eyes, they always would.

Squaring her shoulders, Elinta hurried into the building. She caught a glimpse of her reflection in the diamond-shaped window in the doorway and paused. The stitches were still in her forehead and there was still a little blood dried in her hair, though it had been wiped from her face. Elinta locked eyes with her reflection. She really did look the part with her white eyes, slitted pupils, and bloodied appearance. Sighing, Elinta rubbed at her head as she hurried inside. Perhaps she should stop by her room to clean it out and remove the stitches. If she could even go in her room anymore.

Elinta found the room easily this time and was surprised to find that it wasn't cordoned off. But then, she supposed there was no need to now. It was all over. She cracked the door open and peered inside, her heart thumping in her chest as though expecting to find a glowing figure waiting for her. But the room was empty. The window had been boarded over with thick wooden planks, and the glass and wood cleaned from the floor. Otherwise, the room looked normal. Shivering, Elinta crossed to the small bathroom, grabbed a cloth, and ran the taps. The bathroom was different from her old one in Nevira: cramped, with just enough room for the sink, toilet, and a small but deep tub. The room was a deep grey. What she'd seen of the mayor's home so far seemed quite at odds with itself. There were wooden floors, floors of large white stones, others with coppery bricks, while the outside was made of dark grey stone. It seemed as though the building had been added to over the years, but each owner had brought a different material. It was a little strange, but the style of decorations were, at least, mostly consistent.

A knock on the door jolted her from her thoughts. Neva, her face pale and eyes slightly red, stood in the entrance to the bathroom. Her hands wrung in the skirt of her pale dress.

"Neva?" Elinta asked, unsure whether her voice would startle the woman into running again.

"Oh, miss!" The young woman ran forward, throwing her arms around Elinta's shoulders.

"... Neva?" Elinta rubbed the maid's shoulders awkwardly. The water continued to run in the sink but the woman's arms, tightly wrapped around her, prevented her from turning it off.

"I was so worried about you," Neva sobbed. "And after I'd run out on you like that! I'm so sorry, miss."

"It's OK, Neva. I understood." And she had. If Elinta had come across someone with a dragon last year, before she'd met Zhayra, she would have freaked too.

Neva pulled back and looked Elinta over.

"Oh, your hair!" She grabbed the cloth from Elinta's hand and gently dabbed at the blood coating her scalp.

Elinta smiled and let the woman work, realising that perhaps Neva needed to help her in order to feel better.

"You're going to need to wash this out."

"I know, but I need to talk to the boys first, and then I think we have another meeting."

Elinta saw the woman's reflection nod in the mirror. "Well, I'll just do my best for now. Are you going to need the healer to take these stitches out?"

"No," Elinta said, looking at them in the reflection. "I can do it."

Neva was quiet for a moment. "I visited you during the night," she said. Her cheeks reddened. "King Lorrin and Niles were both asleep, so I didn't stay, but I dropped off some clothes for you."

Elinta looked down at the clothes she was wearing. It had been Neva? She smiled. "Thank you."

Neva's green eyes met her white ones in the mirror. "The king really cares for you."

Elinta opened her mouth to deny it but found she couldn't. Her lips parted as she noticed in the mirror that a small spark had returned to her eyes. "I care about him too," she whispered.

Elinta knocked tentatively on the door a soldier had pointed her toward. Neva had finished scrubbing at her scalp and had even pulled her hair back in a braid once Elinta had dealt with the stitches resting over the healed cut on her forehead. She'd left the maid only a few minutes ago to go in search of Lorrin and Niles. She'd promised to tell them whatever she'd learnt through Vaherin. And there had been a lot.

"Come in."

Elinta cracked open the door, finding Lorrin sitting behind a desk. Niles was there too, as was General Nash.

"Elinta," Lorrin said, his face brightening. How was it that the sight of him made her want to smile every time?

"I can come back later?" she said, glancing at General Nash. What had they been talking about?

"No need," General Nash said, her blue eyes running over Elinta. "I was just about to leave. It's good to see you're OK."

"Thank you."

General Nash rose from her chair. "I'll see you all in the meeting soon."

Elinta stared after the woman as she crossed to the door. "I'm sorry about your brother," she blurted.

Nash glanced over her shoulder and nodded. How many people had remembered to offer the general their condolences for the late king, too? The woman was here alone, her husband and their twin children still in Nevira. She had Lorrin and Mira, but perhaps not the people she really needed with her while she grieved. The door closed quietly behind her.

Elinta turned back to the boys. "I have a lot to tell you. We'd better find Tamir."

CHAPTER

SIXTEEN

"I 'M AFRAID WHAT WE found is grave news indeed," the soldier said, glancing around at the group. His green, hooded eyes lingered on the empty chair among them. Shae's chair. They were back in the room Lorrin had used for their last meeting and it was already afternoon. General Nash, General Sonnen, Queen Mira—now the Queen Mother—Niles, Tamir, and Ford were all there. Tamir still looked tired from healing her and the boys, but he looked a little better now after cleaning up. And a man Elinta didn't recognise was also there. But he seemed quite comfortable among them and fit in well with his clean silk clothes and well-groomed beard and moustache. She supposed he was probably the mayor. But there was one person missing. Shae had never arrived. Elinta seemed to be the only one surprised by this. What had they all learnt, or at least begun to suspect, while she'd been lying in bed injured or out with Zhayra?

Lorrin sighed. "Please continue."

"We found the body of advisor Shae an hour out of the city."

His words were met with a long silence. The woman was dead?

"The healer placed her time of death not long before the attempted kidnapping." The soldier glanced at Elinta before his eyes darted away. Even he couldn't hold her eyes. "We believe she told them where The Dragon Friend slept. They killed her to cover their tracks."

Zhayra's roar echoed from outside, and the soldier's face paled.

Mira's face fell at the news the soldier had delivered. Ford leaned forward in his seat. He had bags under his eyes and his dark hair was slightly unkept. Unusual for him. But his eyes were bright, attentive.

"How did she know to meet them?"

"Letters," the soldier said, frowning. "We found traces of them in Shae's fireplace. From what we can tell, they'd been in contact for some time.'

"I guess that's why she was nice to me yesterday. She knew what was coming," Elinta said softly. She'd never gotten along with Shae. And had spent most of her time afraid of the woman, who had disliked her from the beginning. But the realisation of what she'd done hurt her more than she'd expected. She'd never in her wildest dreams have thought the woman would sell her out to Mazen. Niles's shoulder brushed against hers.

"Was it quick?" The words were through her lips before she'd thought about them. But would she really have wished a painful death on the woman? Shae had been doing what she'd felt was right for her country. She had seemed to genuinely think handing Elinta over to Mazen would have worked back when the offer was first made. Even if she'd been wrong, Elinta couldn't find any true malice in her heart toward the woman.

The soldier failed to stop his brows from rising. "Yes."

Elinta nodded.

"Thank you, Giles." Lorrin glanced at Elinta, only his eyes showing the anger and pain he felt at what they'd learnt.

The soldier bowed and backed out of the room.

"Cyril," Lorrin said to the man at the table whom Elinta didn't know. "Would you mind giving us a moment? We'll send for you if your presence is required again."

Elinta thought the mayor—she was sure that's who he was—actually looked relieved at being dismissed. His light green eyes flickered to the map of Eldras spread across the table. It was the same one Elinta had seen in General Nash's office just before she'd gone to rescue her family in Bradfin. It even had the sword still attached across the top. The mayor ran a hand over his beard.

"Of course, Your Majesty."

Elinta jolted, hurriedly swallowing the laugh that threatened to slip through her lips at the unexpected sound. The man's voice was so high it reminded her of a mouse's squeak.

Niles nudged her again, cocking his head as though he knew exactly what she was thinking. She flared her eyes at him, a warning that she would strongly deny everything if he called her out, and she turned back to the table as the mayor slipped from the room.

Lorrin sighed. "One thing after another," he muttered. "Did anyone outside of those present know of Mazen's deal?"

General Nash shook her head. "The king didn't want anyone to know for this reason."

Elinta's eyes snapped to the woman as she mentioned her brother, Lorrin's father, but she betrayed none of her grief. Something slid into place inside Elinta. She hadn't realised until now that her own pain had slowly shifted, allowing her to continue working while still feeling the hurt. Looking at General Nash and Lorrin, her spirits lifted. She was proud to be strong like them.

"Good," Lorrin said, breaking through her thoughts, "that leaves us with this." He gestured to the map on the table. Well, Elinta thought, not the map. The sword holding it.

Ford sat forward in interest. Tamir and Niles frowned.

General Sonnen's face remained blank as General Nash stood, unclipping the sword from the map. Thread drifted down onto the table, falling from the tapestry with alarming ease. Yet no one else seemed worried by it. In fact, all eyes were on the sword.

Elinta frowned.

General Nash held the sword out to Elinta.

From the corner of her eye, Elinta could see Ford glancing curiously between the sword and General Nash. She could almost hear his mind working. But Elinta's frown just deepened.

"With Mazen now in possession of a full *illayas* sword, we believe you should have this," General Nash said.

Elinta looked up at the woman, puzzled, but took the weapon. For indeed, it did seem to be a real sword. But she already had her own, given to her by Lorrin. She could feel his eyes on her.

She glanced down at the weapon. The sheath was plain, nothing special or unique about it. The hilt of the weapon was much the same. Bound in a simple, black leather, but a blue shine on the pommel caught her eye. She turned it. A thin circle of illayas had been laid into the pommel.

Elinta fingered it, glancing up to lock eyes with Ford and Tamir. She could see the same thought there. The same disbelieving question.

Elinta gripped the hilt of the sword and slid it silently from the sheath.

Niles was the only one who gasped.

Elinta carefully placed the Eggslaying sword on the table, her hands shaking with the effort not to drop it. Zhayra was the perfect mirror of her disgust.

"I don't want it." The words were through her lips before she really considered them. She stared at the blue sword. She needed it, yes. But could she really bring herself to hold it? To use the sword that King Cenric had used to destroy the eggs and kill their guardian dragon?

Elinta expected Lorrin to speak, or even one of the generals. But it was Tamir who broke the silence.

"You must use this, *tarsi*." Elinta's eyes snapped up to his. His eyes were fixed on the sword, anger and acceptance warring within them. "You cannot hope to face Mazen without an *illayas* weapon of your own."

Ford nodded. "This sword was used for terrible things, but it is not its fault."

"Please, El," Lorrin said. "It is rightfully yours, anyway."

Mira stirred at her son's words but said nothing.

Zhayra's chest loosened, and Elinta sighed, glancing back at the sword.

"Fine," she said, grim acceptance settling into her. They were right. She'd need it if she was to face Mazen. He already had the advantage over her, this would at least put her on the same playing field. "But after this is done, I don't want it."

"In that case, I would like to have the room," Lorrin said. "Just Elinta, Tamir, and Niles should stay."

If the generals hadn't known of Lorrin's request, they did well to hide their surprise. Mira stood first, nodding to Lorrin before slipping from the room like a ghost. Elinta watched her go. The generals followed. Ford was the last to slip from the room, his cloak whirling behind him as the door silently closed.

Elinta stared at Lorrin curiously. What did he have to say that the others couldn't hear?

"I have a request to make of you and Zhayra," Lorrin said. Elinta cocked her head, unsure what it was in his voice she was hearing. It was ... hard. Almost as though he had been steeling himself for this moment, though there was no uncertainty in his body language. She resisted the urge to reach out to his emotions.

He nodded at the sword.

"I want you to coat this in dragon blood."

Elinta blinked, sure that she hadn't heard him right.

"El."

"No," Elinta murmured, then a bit stronger, "no." Her stomach roiled at the suggestion.

Lorrin held her eyes. "You have to."

"No." Elinta shook her head. "No, I won't do it."

Tamir remained silent. But now pure horror and submission battled on his face as he stared at the sword.

Elinta's body tingled at the memory of the poison running through her veins. She saw the moment Mazen had watched his father drink it. Bile rose in her throat.

Lorrin's fists clenched. Niles finally spoke.

"He's right, El," Niles said slowly, his gaze fixed on the table. "Think about it, all you'd have to do is cut him. He'll be doing the same. You know he will."

"That doesn't make it right!" Elinta said, the words bursting out of her. "I'm not doing it. I won't do that to Zhayra, and I won't do it to him. I'm not killing him."

Lorrin's expression shifted. "There's no prison that would hold him."

"I'm. Not. Killing. Him."

Tamir still hadn't said a thing. His face had gone pale.

"Why not?" Lorrin said, his grief and anger raising his voice. "We can't let him keep doing this, El. Last night—" He ran a hand through his hair, his eyes flashing. "All the people he's killed—all the people he *wants* to kill! He doesn't deserve to live."

Elinta shot to her feet, knocking the chair over, as her vision turned red. Her hands slammed into the table. "I WILL NOT BECOME LIKE HIM. AND NEITHER WILL YOU. I AM NOT KILLING HIM."

Lorrin gaped at her, and the anger seemed to drain from him, his body visually deflating. He stood, coming around the table to stand in front of her. His hand brushed her cheek, and she fought back a flinch while struggling with the desire to lean into his touch at the same time. Her mind whirled in confusion.

"You could never be like him," he whispered.

"I won't do it, Lorrin. I won't kill him. I'll hurt him. I'll do whatever it takes to stop him. But I'm not killing him."

"I know." His eyes shone with a silver film. "It's OK."

Tamir spoke up. "If ... if you were to use dragon blood to incapacitate him, I will heal him when the battle is over. You need not kill him."

"No."

"We will find some way to imprison him, regardless. Perhaps now with Zhayra, we may use her fire to make a prison of *illayas*. We can hold him somewhere temporary until then."

Lorrin nodded. "OK," he said, closing his eyes, "we'll—we'll talk to Ciar when he gets here."

Elinta fought the urge to hurry from the room, her breaths still heaving, and forced herself to sit down, to pivot the subject slightly. "What are we doing about Mazen now? Do we even know that he's in Liyarna?"

"We're preparing for his attack," Lorrin said, sitting next to her rather than returning to his seat. "If Ciar gets here first, I'd like to take the battle to Mazen rather than wait."

"What about Vaherin?" Niles asked. "What will we do with him?"

"Zhayra can deal with him. She's queen now. It's her right to decide what will be done," Elinta said, her voice flat. She couldn't hold this against them. She could see the desperation and fear the boys were trying so hard to hide. But ... hearing them ask this of her when she'd struggled with it too, it tore at her heart. Perhaps Mazen did deserve to die for what he'd done. To her. To Blaine. To Nevira, Lorrin's father, and Liyarna. But that wasn't for her to decide or carry out. Not when she knew the cost to her heart would be too great. She didn't need another face to haunt her dreams at night. The tightness in her chest didn't ease.

Silence settled over their group.

"Is there somewhere I can train around here?" Elinta asked, her voice still a little flat as she remembered all the senses she'd decided to learn. But now, she had more cause than ever to get to work on them. She needed to ease some of the pressure off the boys, particularly Lorrin, so that they never asked something like this of her again in their fear.

"We'll find somewhere," Lorrin said softly. "I'm sure the mayor has some rooms not in use."

"When will you start?" Tamir asked.

"Tonight."

CHAPTER
SEVENTEEN

L ORRIN APPROPRIATED MAYOR CYRIL'S ballroom for
their training. It was a much smaller room than the one
at the palace, with simple wooden flooring, bay windows, and a
single chandelier hanging from the ceiling. It was the best room
he could find for their purposes.

Elinta marched out onto the floor. She hesitated only for a
moment before drawing her new sword, the blue colour shined in
the light. Its hilt seemed to fit her hand perfectly. Shoving down
the hate she felt at holding the blade, Elinta turned to face the
boys.

Lorrin had managed to get an hour away from his work to join
them though he still looked exhausted, and his clothes weren't

suited to training. Niles had taken off the grey jacket of his guard's uniform, leaving a white shirt and simple black pants, his sword at his hip, and an eager smile on his face. Tamir also looked ready to fight and had his hair tied back.

"Let's go then," Elinta said.

Niles and Tamir exchanged a glance, silently deciding who would fight her. They both nodded and both stepped forward.

Elinta grinned, closed her eyes, and tapped into the heat sense.

Opening them again, Elinta pushed the colour to the side and nodded. Never would she have thought she'd be thankful for that horrible night running through the Calaza, hardly able to keep from vomiting while the city burned behind her, yet here she was. That night had forced her to find a way to make it work.

Niles held her eyes, a sparkle hiding in them. He cocked an eyebrow. "Ready yet?"

Elinta's only answer was to lunge, sending her sword darting toward his shoulder. He stepped sideways, letting the tip of her sword pass harmlessly by, and sent a fist toward her ribs. Elinta spun aside, just able to bring her blade up in time to deflect a blow by Tamir. She danced backward, letting them spread out, giving herself as much room as she gave them. And perhaps giving her stomach a moment to settle. It seemed jolting movements could still send it roiling.

Lorrin's eyes were fixed on her, but she didn't dare hold them when Niles and Tamir were waiting for a moment of distraction. Tamir dove in again. Niles waited for her to deflect his blow before joining them. Elinta whirled, her breath already coming in puffs, but as she dodged Niles's strike, she felt the slap of Tamir's blade on her leg.

They reset. Niles stepped back, as did Tamir. At her nod, the boys continued.

Elinta had more than one reason to be excited about fighting them both. Not only was it good for her training and her heat vision, but maybe—just maybe she could tap into those extra senses she had when Blaine had died. The ones that had helped her move like never before.

But no matter how she tried, nothing happened. No extra senses clicked. No shifts in her body happened. In fact, as she spun away from the boys, letting her sword cut through the air as she did, her vision tilted, and bile rose in her throat. Pressing a hand to her stomach and gritting her teeth, Elinta jumped back in. There was no time to be sick, to let her dizziness control her. But, as Tamir's blade sliced toward her, a strike she knew he would stop an inch from her skin, Elinta's body swayed and her foot slipped on the polished wooden floor, sending her forward. Tamir's sword slid across the skin over her collarbone.

Horror instantly spread across his face. *"Tarsi!"*

Elinta lowered her sword, letting the tip drop close to the ground and pressed a hand to the wound.

"It's fine," she said, her breaths coming in gasps from exertion. The wound stung, but she could tell that it wasn't nearly as bad as it must have looked to the boys. All three hurried over to her, Lorrin shoving off the wall to cross the room.

Tamir gently pulled her hand back, smudging her blood over his own hand as he did. "I am sorry, *tarsi*."

"It's fine, Tamir," she said. Niles carefully took the sword from her hand. Tamir's face was still lined with tiredness, but she knew the guilt he felt would lessen significantly if he healed her, so she said, "Besides, you can easily heal it."

Tamir nodded, placing his hand on her arm and letting his healing wash over her. The tiredness on his face seemed to deepen as he worked, but he said nothing.

A now familiar warmth spread over her, the brightness of his skin causing her to squint. The light came as a flare of red in her heat sense. A moment passed, and the light dimmed.

"There," Elinta said, running a finger over where the cut had been. She could just see the end of the thin silver scar that had replaced it if she craned her head.

Tamir glanced at her uncertainly. "Perhaps only one should fight you when you are using your heat sense."

"No," Elinta said, taking her sword back from Niles. "I want to fight both of you."

"El," Niles said, glancing between her and Tamir and Lorrin, "it's OK. There's time to work up to it."

"It was your idea to train properly, remember?" Elinta said, glancing at him. "Tamir can always heal me, as you said."

"Oh, no. Lorrin talked me down from that idea. I don't want you to be a pincushion especially when you only just got over being a melon head."

"Why don't you just practice without the heat sense?" Lorrin said placatingly.

Elinta shook her head with a flash of irritation. "Come on, just a few more minutes, and we'll finish. I don't want to leave it at this."

"Very well." Tamir stepped back, getting into position. She felt a little bad for pushing it on him when he was so tired, but she needed to finish well. Lorrin stepped back, too, his eyes not leaving her face. She had the distinct impression that he understood her, understood everything that was running through her mind, all the pressures and fears. He saw her. Whilst she felt that should have made her a little uncomfortable, it didn't.

Niles finally nodded, raising his sword. Elinta dove in.

"You're going to sleep with her tonight, aren't you?" Lorrin's voice echoed in the hallway. Elinta spun around, finding the king striding toward her. Her heart pounded at the sight of him. She glanced at the door to her new room that had just clicked quietly shut behind her.

"Yes," Elinta said, just above a whisper. Flickering firelight from torches along the walls now lit the hallway, with the night now set in. The hall was empty, other than them. She'd intended on sneaking out, but, apparently, she was slightly predictable.

Lorrin stopped in front of her, his face lined with worry. "Don't go out of the city. Please."

Elinta opened her mouth to object, but Lorrin cut her off. "Zhayra can come in. You can stay in the court tonight."

"OK," she said, knowing Zhayra had heard. The dragon had kept a close eye on her throughout the day, but it seemed she wasn't the only one still scared after the attack by the Asali. Elinta's own heart sped up at the memory, but she shoved it away. If she was honest, she didn't really want to leave the city, but she didn't want to stay in her room either. New room or not.

Lorrin's eyes studied hers. "I'm sorry about earlier. About—about killing Mazen and using the dragon blood." He swallowed heavily, his throat bobbing. "I don't want to lose you, El."

Elinta stared up at him, studying his eyes, the lines of his face, the pain he didn't try to hide from her. His pushing had hurt her, scared her. But she understood where it had come from. The last of her anger slipped away.

"I know." Elinta closed the space between them, slipping her arms around him. "We can't be like him. No matter what happens."

As his arms wrapped around her again, she breathed in the scent of him, remembering the night he'd held her close, and they'd danced to a music only he could hear. She knew Niles would have comforted the prince, so would his mother, aunt, and probably even General Sonnen. But she wished she could have been there to hold him after he'd lost his father.

"I'm so sorry," she whispered, sliding her hands up his back and into his hair. She pulled back to look him in the eyes. His thoughts must have followed hers. Silver lined his eyes.

A tear slid down his cheek, and he pressed his forehead to hers. "I wish I'd been there to help him."

"But then you might not be here now," she breathed. "I can't lose you either, Lorrin."

His hand slid to her cheek, his eyes still wet but a light had kindled in them.

"We still need to have that chat."

"We do," she said, slipping her hands from his hair. They may have lingered on his chest before she dropped them to her side. Elinta looked uncertainly at him. For all their intentions of waiting until after Mazen ... maybe it couldn't wait after all.

"Wait," he said when she went to speak. "Let me speak first."

Zhayra pulled away from Elinta's ears, having already left her eyes when Lorrin had invited her to the courtyard.

Elinta nodded, caught in Lorrin's blue eyes. She found herself wanting to reach out to his emotions again, to feel what she saw on display.

"I love you, Elinta."

Her heart stopped, then jolted back into life, heat spreading in her cheeks.

He took her hand, thumb tracing circles. "And I know that you and Zhayra need to be together, whatever that looks like when we've dealt with Mazen."

Elinta listened quietly, unsure where he was going or what exactly she wanted to hear. But then, she'd have said something along those exact lines too, wouldn't she?

"But that won't change my feelings, and whatever you decide, I'll respect it. Though ... you know where my hopes lie," he said, wryly.

A burst of happiness shot through her and Elinta grinned, grabbing the hand that still traced circles on hers. "Zhayra thinks we'll be able to work something out," she said. "She knows I love you and wants us to—what?"

Lorrin was grinning. Grinning bigger and brighter than she'd ever seen before. "Say it again."

Elinta laughed. "I love you."

He placed his other hand on her cheek and pressed a kiss to her forehead. "We'll work it out."

Elinta closed her eyes, letting herself bask in that moment of happiness, letting the rest of her troubles drift away. She opened her eyes, his hand still pressed to her face.

Her cheeks warmed again at the tenderness she saw in Lorrin's eyes.

"Come with me." Elinta dragged him down the dimly lit hall and his chuckle echoed behind them.

"Ready?" Elinta said. Lorrin's arms slipped around her waist, and she felt his heart pounding against her back.

"Ready."

Zhayra's wings unfurled, and she shot up into the starry night. Lorrin's arms tightened for a moment, then released.

Elinta could hardly think with the feeling of Lorrin's arms around her, of his body pressed against hers. Here they were, finally flying together. It seemed almost unfair that he was the last of her friends to fly when he'd been the first to meet her and Zhayra.

Once they were high above the city, the mayor's building so small that it was hardly distinguishable among the sea of houses and shops below them, Zhayra turned to carry them over the dark ocean.

Lorrin's laugh of wonder echoed her own. The dark water was a perfect reflection of the cloud-free sky above them. Thousands of stars shone back at them, their light dancing off Zhayra's pure white scales at every angle. Culmar was behind them, and just the open starry seas before them.

Elinta patted Zhayra's neck. "It's beautiful."

Zhayra grunted, tilting downward to let them glide over the water. She dipped the tip of her wing into the water, sending it streaming behind them, but she could have dipped her wing into the stars themselves for how it looked.

Nearly an hour passed before Lorrin spoke.

"It's nice to get away. Every moment has been about Mazen for so long."

"It has," she said, stunned that he'd voiced something that had weighed on her for a while. There was no peace anymore. "I've forgotten what it's like," she said slowly, "not to be anxious or scared about something."

Lorrin's arms tightened around her waist. "You won't have to be scared ever again once this is over."

"I know." She wondered if he could hear the smile in her voice. She sighed. Peace. That was something she could look forward to. Something she could fight for.

It was nearly dawn before they arrived back at the mayor's house, and Lorrin left her and Zhayra in the courtyard, whispering goodnight, his eyes saying more than his words.

Elinta lay staring at the underside of Zhayra's wing, feeling a little ridiculous with the huge grin on her face, but also not really caring. Lorrin loved her. He understood her situation with Zhayra, and it didn't change anything.

Zhayra grunted and Elinta rolled onto her stomach to catch her eye.

"Thank you for last night."

Zhayra grunted again.

"You know, I think it's time we tried something a little extreme with training," Elinta said, her stomach contorting at the idea that had come to her after their flight last night.

Zhayra pulled back, bringing her wing in as she did so that Elinta was exposed to the morning, and stared down at her.

"You'll see," Elinta said, sitting up so she could press her hand into her clenching belly. She was absolutely going to regret this. But first, she had to find the boys.

Elinta sat at the dining table between Niles and Tamir. The hall was bustling with people reaching for mugs of coffee, bowls of porridge, plates of eggs, fruit, and pieces of bread. But one person seemed to be missing.

"Where's Lorrin?"

"Work," Niles grunted around a mouthful of eggs. He looked as though he'd simply rolled out of bed and come straight to the dining hall. He probably had, knowing his love of food. "Had to get up early, too."

Elinta glanced away guiltily. Had he gotten any sleep last night?

Niles's eyes narrowed. "What's that look?"

Tamir glanced up from his coffee.

"What look?"

"I don't know," Niles said slowly, his fork halfway to his mouth.

Elinta hurriedly changed the subject before Niles could work it out and give her a talk about courting his best friend. She hadn't forgotten that night in Shae's office as they'd listened to the council meeting.

"I'm going to be out for a while today. I don't know how long, so don't worry if I'm not back for lunch."

Niles's eyes narrowed further. "You better be taking food with you, young lady."

Elinta laughed. "I'll take some bread."

But in truth, she wasn't sure whether she would eat later. The very thought of her plan was making it impossible for her to down any breakfast. What would it be like come lunch time?

Tamir frowned, lowering his cup. "You are pale again, *tarsi*. What are you planning?"

"Something a little reckless. With the senses," she hurriedly added at the look they both gave her.

"I see," Tamir said, taking a sip of his coffee. "Please be careful. You have been more reckless than usual lately."

"What?"

Niles nodded. "Last night was intense."

"Oh," Elinta said, thinking back to their training. She grimaced. "Yeah, it was a little. I'm sorry. I just ... I just want to make sure I'm ready."

"You will be." Niles reached out and squeezed her hand.

"Right." Elinta stood, taking a deep breath. "See you later."

"This was a really stupid idea."

Elinta stared at her hand on the clip holding her to Zhayra, frozen.

Zhayra twisted her neck, letting them glide through the air so that she could see Elinta.

"A really, really stupid idea."

Zhayra grumbled, looking between Elinta's face and her hand on the clip. She'd already untied her legs from the harness, though even that had required her getting over a moment of doubt.

"This better work," Elinta said.

Zhayra returned to looking straight ahead, beating her wings twice to maintain their low height over the sea as Elinta had instructed.

The beginnings of the idea had come to her while flying with Lorrin, and then again after yet another dream of Mazen. Moments before they'd clashed in the air above Nevira, Mazen had been standing easily, impossibly, on Vaherin's back. He'd been using some of the senses. He had to have been to achieve that feat of balance.

But it was the echo of Aesira's words in her mind that had cemented the idea. *Often, great emotional stress can help in accessing the senses.* The woman had gone on to say not to rely on this, but Elinta couldn't think of any other way to access the two senses she wanted the most: equilibrioception and proprioception. Balance and a deeper awareness of her body. Maybe forcing it could help her work out how to access them easier the next time. That was her hope, anyway.

"Ready?"

Zhayra's response was a low, uncertain grumble.

Gritting her teeth, Elinta undid the buckle. Before she could change her mind, she shoved her feet under her and slowly straightened, spreading her arms out to either side of her. Elinta wobbled dangerously, but Zhayra was already flying the smoothest she possibly could.

Elinta took a deep, steadying breath, focusing on maintaining her balance.

Sea mist sprayed in her face, but Elinta didn't dare close her eyes as she once again wobbled. Barely two seconds in, she dropped into a crouch, gripping the harness strap tightly.

"This was a very bad idea," Elinta muttered, but she forced herself to stand again. She kept her eyes forward and her arms stretched out. Her stomach was tied into a knot, her chest aching with nerves. Surely, surely, it would click soon.

Zhayra flapped her wings again to keep them going, and Elinta dropped to grab the harness again. When they evened out, she mentally berated herself. That could have been the moment she'd needed. If only she hadn't crouched.

"Zhayra," Elinta shouted, still wobbling. "Use your wings again."

The dragon obliged. Elinta rose, went down, and then on the next beat of Zhayra's wings she tilted, her arms swinging out to find her equilibrium.

She toppled straight off the dragon and face first into the sea.

"Right," Elinta said, wiping a stream of water from her face fifteen minutes later. "Ready?"

Zhayra grunted again, droplets of water shining on her scales in the sunlight.

Once again, Elinta unclipped herself from the harness and shoved her feet under her.

They glided for nearly two minutes, Elinta's stomach still in her throat. But she forced herself to focus.

"Alright," Elinta called. "Flap again."

She braced herself.

Zhayra flapped her wings. Once. Twice. Three times. Elinta tumbled off, her stomach catching the brunt of the fall this time.

"Again," Elinta said, flicking her sopping hair from her face as she forced her feet under her. Her shoes slid slightly, then held against Zhayra's scales.

Zhayra took them a little higher and kept her wings spread to either side.

Elinta looked down, the fall now a little nastier. At this height, she wouldn't break anything, but it would hurt quite a lot if she slipped.

Elinta spread her feet a little further apart, and relaxed her body, trying to ride the slight dips and rises, the slight gusts of wind, and odd spray of seawater.

How had Mazen done it? Standing so confidently while Vaherin beat his wings to keep them in one place?

Zhayra's own emotions were a contrast to Elinta's as she glided along. Her chest was light, her stomach even tickling occasionally. She seemed to find the whole idea somewhat funny though she was proud of it. Elinta mentally shrugged. If she had been in Zhayra's situation, she supposed it wouldn't have seemed so bad.

Elinta glanced down again. How long had they been flying? She paused. Had something changed without her even noticing?

"Is the flight smoother?" Elinta called.

Zhayra grunted, paused, and grunted again, an equivalent of blinking twice Elinta supposed.

But ... she looked around. It seemed easier. When had she last fought to keep her balance?

She hesitantly lowered her arms, a tentative grin spreading across her face.

Elinta didn't wobble.

"Zhayra! Flap your wings!"

Zhayra's chest lifted. She beat her wings.

Elinta rode the wing beats with ease. She chuckled uncertainly.

"I think it worked," she muttered. But how? She didn't feel any different. There hadn't been a moment where the senses had seemed to click on.

She spread her arms and laughed.

"It worked!"

Zhayra roared, twisted her neck around and fixed her eye on Elinta.

"No, no, no," Elinta said, trying to sit down again, but she wasn't quick enough. The dragon had lowered her height without Elinta noticing, so that they were hardly above the water. Now, Zhayra pitched to the side and sent Elinta tumbling into the crystal-clear waves.

The dragon dove into the water beside her, her chest nearly bursting.

❦❦❦

After another morning of trying to access the two new senses—which had taken her even longer than before—Elinta decided to wander into the market by the docks for some lunch despite her sodden clothes weighing her down. Salt from the water had dried on her skin, leaving it with a strange stiffness, but she didn't mind. Zhayra followed along behind her. They carved a path through the crowds, people hurrying out of their way. The market was bustling, people of all ages, heights, and skin tones jostling among the stalls, those nearest to Elinta turning to watch as she and the dragon passed. The salty and fishy scent of the docks wafted over them, clinging to Elinta's nose and mixing with the scent of baked goods sold within some of the stalls.

Zhayra kept her tail straight and still as they walked, careful not to knock down any people or stalls. But most people steered well clear of the dragon. A couple even turned on their heels and ran. But Elinta wanted the people to see them, to see Zhayra as she was. A caring, intelligent creature who wished no harm on Culmar. Plus, it had been years since Elinta had been in the city. The last time she'd been—with her father and Blaine—she'd come to the very same market, and Elinta didn't want to face the memory by herself. Not when she had neither of those people with her now. Her stomach jolted. What if her father was here today looking for food or horses? What would he do if he saw her?

Zhayra nudged her gently from behind, jolting her from her thoughts.

"Thanks," she murmured. Elinta dropped back to walk beside the dragon's head, shoving a piece of wet hair from her face. "What do you think?"

Zhayra grunted, looking around them. Elinta grinned, watching the dragon as they walked through the market with a feeling of surrealness. Though most people gave them a wide berth, some staring with wonder, some with open hatred, the fact that they were there, they were walking in the middle of a city, was a dream come true.

Elinta stopped in front of a stall selling fresh pastries. The smells sent her mouth watering.

She pointed to a steaming pastie, the label stating it was full of vegetables and chicken. "I'll have one of those, please."

The baker, a short, stubby, and cleanshaven man, nodded nervously. His face was pale, his eyes flickering between her and Zhayra. The man's son stood behind him, his eyes glued to Zhayra as well. Except it wasn't fear she saw in them. Something about him reminded Elinta of Eiran and Laira, innocent children without the taint of fear and anger on them. Her heart warmed a little.

"Would you like to say hello?" she asked the teenage boy. His blond hair fell over his eyes as he looked at her. He held her eyes like so few had ever done. Her white, slitted eyes.

The baker jolted, glancing between her and his son as he grabbed the pastie Elinta had indicated. The boy nodded, a hesitant grin spreading across his face. He slipped out from behind the stall and stopped a metre from Zhayra.

"Hello," he said, his voice surprisingly deep for his age.

Zhayra tilted her head and grunted softly.

The boy smiled. "Can I pat her?" he said, turning to Elinta.

"Ask her," she said, fishing a coin from her pocket for the pastie.

"Oh!" the boy turned back to Zhayra. "Can I pat you?"

Zhayra lowered her head, and the boy tentatively reached out and stroked the smooth scales of her muzzle. A crowd had begun to form, and gasps spread through the group at the movement. A man at the back watched on with a scowl, his dark eyes betraying his hatred. The baker numbly took the coin from Elinta's hand, still looking at his son.

"You can say hello, too," she said to the man.

The baker looked at her, then at his son. "I—I don't know."

"Come on, Father," the boy said, twisting around. He grinned at them, revealing crooked teeth.

"Alright." He stepped out from behind the stall, wiping his hands on his apron, and Elinta physically saw him brace himself as he crossed the distance to the boy and Zhayra. But when he got there, he stretched out his large hand and stroked her.

Murmurs arose from the crowd surrounding them, more and more people joining them by the second. The front row, a group of middle-aged women with scarves covering their heads to protect them from the summer sun, had bunched together, nervously whispering to each other, wonder and fear warring in their eyes. But the man with the dark eyes was now scowling and leant over to whisper to the man beside him. There was something in their faces that set Elinta's nerves on edge. Another man joined them, and then another, and their angry murmurs reached her. One of the men shoved forward through the crowd.

Time to go, Elinta decided, grabbing her pastie. She jumped up onto Zhayra's back, strapping her legs in. Without another word, Zhayra shot into the air, throwing great gusts at the baker and his son, but huge smiles spread across their faces as they watched her fly away.

CHAPTER

EIGHTEEN

"Y OU AND ZHAYRA WERE in the city yesterday?" Lorrin grunted, sending his sword darting toward Elinta's leg. She danced backward. "Yes."

"How did it go?" he asked, following after her. Sweat beaded on his forehead, a detail she couldn't see in the heat vision.

"Fine." She shrugged, but something in her voice made him pause.

"Did you see him?" Lorrin let the point of his sword drop, his eyes widening with concern.

"No," Elinta said, stepping back and thinking of her father. She hadn't seen him at all since arriving in Culmar, and she doubted he would have hung around to see her if he had been in the market, too. "There were just some men that looked like trouble. We left before anything could happen."

Lorrin nodded, but his eyes studied her face. "Do you want to see him?"

Elinta's eyebrows rose. "I—I don't know. Not right now." Besides ... it wasn't really her choice. He didn't want her anymore. Before Lorrin could respond, Elinta darted forward slapping the flat of her blade on his chest.

"Cheat." Lorrin grinned.

"Did I cheat or were you just not paying attention?"

Lorrin shook his head, diving back into the fight. She made it half an hour into their training session before her stomach rose and her vision jolted. Lorrin made her switch off the heat sense just as Tamir arrived. Niles was on guard duty and couldn't meet them tonight.

"I am sorry I am late," Tamir said. "Ford and I lost track of time."

"It's alright," Elinta said. She'd been surprised at first to learn how quickly Ford and Tamir had seemed to become friends, but she realised it shouldn't have come as a shock. Both men were historians. With Ford having a large amount of knowledge of the Asali for a human and Tamir openly curious about their own more recent past, it made sense that they'd connect.

"Tell me about your training over the sea," Tamir said, crossing the room. His eyes landed on the Eggslaying sword in Elinta's hand, but none of the disgust she still felt showed in them. Did Tamir really agree with her having it? She focused on his question.

Elinta had spent yet another day over the ocean, trying to force the equilibrioception and proprioception to work. Aesira's words still echoed in her mind, but she needed to work out *how* to switch it on first.

"It's coming along," Elinta said. "I only fell in twice today, but I'm getting a little better at balancing without them. It's sort of hard to tell sometimes whether I've turned them on or not."

"Might you be able to switch them on now?"

Elinta paused, wiping at the sweat on her face with her sleeve. "I could try."

But, though she tried as hard as she could, Elinta couldn't do it. She still needed that extra boost of fear and adrenaline, something that was becoming harder and harder with each flight over the sea.

"Never mind," Lorrin said. "You'll get it soon."

"I hope so," Elinta said. It looked like she had another day over the ocean ahead of her.

Lorrin walked Elinta back to her room. They strode down the strange halls side by side, seamlessly passing over from wooden hallway with picture frames to grey stone hallway with stuffed animals dotted throughout it.

"Has there been any word from Ciar or Harlan?" Elinta asked, used to the strangeness of the mayor's home now. And though she knew Lorrin would keep her informed, she couldn't help but feel a little out of the loop after her days out training. Even though she didn't really want to be waiting around the mayor's home, she still needed to know what was going on.

"Nothing more," Lorrin said. "Harlan gave his word he would come, but I don't know when he could get here. And Ciar could still be another two weeks. It could all be too late, depending on when Mazen makes his move."

He ran a hand through his hair. "If only we knew what he was up to."

Elinta nodded. "I could try to look through Vaherin?"

Lorrin shook his head. "I don't think that's a good idea. If they realise it's you, we could force them into something drastic."

She'd already offered once before, and Lorrin's response was along the same lines then. He had a point, but the idea of knowing what they were doing was beyond tempting. It would ease the mounting anxiety she felt every time she thought of them.

"More drastic, you mean."

"Yeah." Anger flickered in Lorrin's eyes, but then disappeared as he let out a long sigh.

Elinta stepped in front of him, pulling them to a stop. She could hear the worry in his voice. "We'll work this all out. Together."

He smiled, gently taking her hand.

A soldier passed them, nodding as he did. "Your Majesty."

Lorrin's gaze was fixed on the man's back as he walked down the hall. A shadow seemed to fall over his face. "I still haven't gotten used to being called Your Majesty."

"You're doing a great job, Lorrin. I'm so proud of you." She paused, taking a leaf from Niles's book. "Your Majesty, sir."

"While you were at the dragons' islands, Niles spent a whole day ending every sentence like that."

"I know." Elinta winked. "He told me the other day."

He held her eyes. "Thank you, Elinta."

Elinta frowned. "What for?"

"Everything," he said, squeezing her hand.

"I should be the one thanking you," she said, shaking her head. "You've done so much for me and Zhayra."

He smiled. "I'm happy to do it."

They continued walking, her door coming into sight. "I'll see you in the morning," Lorrin said. His eyes drifted down to her lips, but he gave her hand another squeeze and left her by the door.

Elinta slipped into her room, changing into some more comfortable clothes. Neva had left her a knot of sweet bread with a chocolate centre on the bedside table. Smiling, Elinta took the bread with her. She didn't see the maid as much now that she wasn't using her room to sleep in anymore, but Neva had made every effort since that night the Asali had attacked. And though Elinta had more than forgiven her, she knew the maid still felt guilty for being afraid of her.

The night air caressed her face as she emerged into the courtyard. Zhayra was already there, her large bulk taking up most of the space. But it was late in the night and the only other person was a guard by the gate. Elinta waved to him, then crawled under Zhayra's wing to eat her bread.

🔥🔥🔥

Elinta woke to the sun shining brightly through the membrane of Zhayra's wing. Days had passed since her training session with Lorrin, and still no word of Mazen had reached them. They continued to prepare the city, with the makeshift walls being thrown up on the western, northern, and southern borders nearly complete, patrols in the streets doubled, and the men stationed at the watch towers tripled. Each day, a trickle of civilians left the city, but Lorrin had decreed that all healthy men of fighting age were to stay and help prepare. They'd expected, even asked, people to leave, but it was the trickle of people coming in that had surprised them. Men from Nevira and even some of the smaller villages nearby had begun to arrive, carrying old swords, spears, and axes. Whatever weapons or tools they had found, they'd taken with them and reported to the mayor's house. To King Lorrin. Lorrin didn't know what to do with them, so he'd assigned them to join the Culmar men in preparing the city and building defences. Then they were to be integrated into the ranks of the soldiers.

Elinta didn't like the idea of civilians being involved in the fight, but if Ciar's people and Harlan's troops didn't arrive, then they'd need all the help they could get in stopping Mazen's Asali. Then she'd be free to focus on stopping Mazen, however that would look.

She sighed, staring at the underside of Zhayra's wing. She stood by what she'd said to Lorrin and the boys. Elinta wasn't going to kill Mazen. That was one of the reasons why she'd been training so much. But would it be enough? Would it ever be enough?

"Miss?"

Elinta frowned. "Neva?"

"Oh, you are there!" Neva's muffled voice said.

Zhayra shifted, letting Elinta slip out from under her wing. Neva stood in the entrance to the mayor's house, a tray of food in her arms.

"I thought you might be hungry."

"Thank you, Neva." Elinta moved to meet her at the door, but Neva crossed the distance to her instead. Elinta watched in surprise. Though Neva had been kind to her, she hadn't expected the maid to ever grow comfortable enough to be near Zhayra. But the young woman did just that, stopping in front of her.

Her eyes flicked between her and Zhayra, but the dragon had drifted back off to sleep. Elinta still marvelled at Zhayra's ability to sleep so easily.

Neva's eyes rounded. "It's so big."

Elinta laughed, taking the tray from Neva and sitting down. She gestured for the woman to sit with her on the cold stone of the courtyard.

"Her name's Zhayra," Elinta said, handing Neva a slice of toast and jam.

"She's whiter than the clouds," Neva said, her green eyes still fixed on the dragon. "King Lorrin said you've been with her all this time. I can't imagine."

It was about half the number of words she'd have normally expected from the maid, but she supposed the woman was still trying to process everything. Elinta nodded. "I can't imagine being without her anymore."

Neva nibbled at her toast. "How did it happen?"

"She crashed in a storm while escaping from Vaherin. The dragon with Mazen," she added.

"Oh," Neva said, tucking a loose strand of her dark hair back behind her ear. "Do you really have to fight him, miss? I really don't think you should."

Her heart tightened at Neva's words. How many times had she wished for things to be different? How long had it taken her to accept her place? She couldn't leave Lorrin, Niles, and all the humans to suffer at Mazen's hands. Not when she could do something about it.

"I'm the only one who can," Elinta finally whispered.

"Let's have a look to the north," Elinta called over the wind.

Zhayra tilted easily in the air, carrying her away from the western border of the city. They'd offered to take a quick look at the work along the city's borders for Lorrin. Though he had soldiers and workers reporting in, Elinta and Zhayra could gain a different perspective from the air and fill him in on everything in one go.

The western border looked good. Still, she couldn't help but feel that it wasn't enough. Walls could help them fight the Asali, Liyarnan, and full supporters alike, and the troughs of water they'd set up would help with the dragon fire. But ... what was it really against the dragons? Even though the dragons, as a whole, had refused to fight, Mazen still had at least three others with him. The ones she'd seen in Nevira—at least one of which was bonded to him. Did that mean she and Zhayra would have to take care of Mazen, Vaherin, and the other dragons?

Elinta rubbed Zhayra's scales. Part of her wished the battle would start soon, but the other wished it would never come. She didn't know how much more waiting she could take, though. Her nerves had been steadily eating away at her insides for so long, it was a wonder she hadn't disappeared entirely.

Zhayra's wings stopped beating and she glided through the air. They'd reached the northern border.

Lorrin had set men to work building another watch tower where the men could fire arrows down onto the Asali on the other side of the wall. The room at the top of the tower was nearly complete. But one strike from Vaherin would send it shattering onto the street below. Maybe she should have gone back to the dragons and forced them to fight. She sighed. She couldn't think like that. They were doing what they could. And the dragons wouldn't have been able to fight the Asali on the ground once they were in the city without hurting her own people.

Elinta scanned the wall. It looked good, especially considering how quickly it had been erected. At just over three metres tall and a patchwork of stone and wood, the wall seemed solid enough. It would help to funnel the Asali into the middle where a small gap had been left. Just like in the western wall. Anything to help the humans get the upper hand.

"Look's good, hey, girl?" Elinta called.

Zhayra grunted her agreement, but Elinta knew the dragon could feel her mess of emotions. "Let's head back," Elinta said, and moments later, Zhayra drifted back out over the city, toward the mayor's home.

General Sonnen and General Nash met her in the courtyard.

"How's it looking, kid?" General Sonnen said, watching her climb down. He had his usual uniform on, closely matching Niles's except for the blue lapels on his shoulder that signified his rank. His arm was no longer in a sling. Indeed, his injuries seemed fully recovered now.

General Nash wore the same uniform, her blonde hair braided back from her face.

"Good. I just wish there was more we could do," Elinta said.

General Nash looked out over the city. "I'll be glad when your friends from the mountains get here."

"Me too," Elinta said.

"There's another meeting tomorrow," General Sonnen said. "You'll want to be there."

Elinta frowned, her heart jumping. "Bad news?"

General Sonnen shook his head. "More planning."

She nodded.

"We've got to go, Reynard." General Nash glanced over her shoulder at the man who'd just appeared in the doorway trying to get their attention. "There's always something to do. We'll see you tomorrow, Elinta."

She waved as they ducked inside, the other man following in their wake.

Elinta twisted to look at Zhayra. "I'm going to get some lunch. Then I've got training with Niles. We managed to carve out some time."

Zhayra blinked and took off back into the air, arching in mid-flight so that she could return to the grass field.

Elinta was on her way to the dining hall when she glimpsed long dark brown hair and a black regal dress through the crack in a door to a side room. Mira. Elinta stopped in her tracks. She hadn't spoken to Lorrin's mother in ... so long she couldn't remember. Her heart constricted. She should see her. And at the very least offer her condolences. Elinta nodded to herself. And she would at least know whether the queen wished to stay away from her now.

She tried to ready herself for whatever words the queen might utter.

Elinta backtracked and gently knocked on the door as she pushed it open. Mira was seated in a chair by a window overlooking the docks. The sight reminded her so much of their time in the tea rooms in Nevira that a tentative smile tugged at her lips. The queen turned.

"Elinta?"

"Hello," she said, her voice coming out quietly. She hurried inside, closing the door gently behind her.

Mira's eyes swept over her, taking in Elinta's sword, her eyes. "Is everything alright?"

"Yes," Elinta said, crossing the room to stand beside her. The queen didn't rise. Sorrow was heavy on her shoulders, in her eyes, in a way the woman had never revealed before. "I haven't had a chance to speak with you in so long, and I—I wanted to say I'm so sorry about your husband."

Mira was silent, her throat bobbing. "Thank you," she said at last, her voice carrying only the barest hint of a tremor. "I suppose you needn't be afraid anymore."

"He did what he thought was right. I can't begrudge him that, Mira. He was a good man."

"He was." A silent tear fell down the queen's cheek, and Elinta tentatively held one of her delicate hands, the only comfort she knew how to give.

"Lorrin will make a great king," Queen Mira said, her voice thick but proud.

"He already is."

Elinta scanned the dining hall, but none of the boys were there. She supposed they must have all been busy. Even Tamir had countless meetings scheduled, informing the soldiers on the best tactics to fight the Asali and stay alive. Even if she hadn't been spending her days out over the ocean, she probably still wouldn't have seen any of them. But Elinta's eyes snagged on a familiar form. Ford. She grabbed a bowl of the hot stew served for the day and slid onto the bench opposite the historian.

"Elinta," Ford greeted. Whatever burden he'd shouldered recently seemed to have diminished a little, she thought, looking over him. But that same heaviness that she saw in Lorrin's eyes and in her own reflection still sat over him.

"I wanted to thank you for befriending Tamir," Elinta said. "People don't seem to know what to do with an Asali."

Ford smiled. "He's a good man. But it was he who befriended me."

"Do you like Culmar?" Elinta ventured, unsure what to say. All her conversations with Ford had been about the dragons, or some history connected to them. She liked the man, though, and would never forget what he'd done for her.

"It certainly has a distinct smell," Ford said.

Elinta laughed. "The docks are a bit strong," she said, thinking of the rotten fish scent that clung to the weathered wood in the area.

"Tamir tells me you've been practicing the senses."

"Yes." She sighed. She still couldn't tap into the two new senses without emotional stress. As it was, Zhayra had needed to increase their height as they flew over the sea in their training sessions so that Elinta would become more distressed. It still wasn't entirely working. "I can't quite get two of them. Aesira said I shouldn't rely on my emotions to turn them on, but I just can't get it without being scared or nervous. And even then, it's hard."

Something flickered in Ford's dark eyes at the mention of Aesira. "She was right, but I think she would understand what you are trying to do."

Elinta stared at the man. There were so many questions surrounding him, but there were too many other things she needed to keep her mind on. She didn't have the time or energy to unravel this man, no matter how curious he made her. All she needed to know was that she trusted him, and so did the boys.

"You were amazing in Nevira," Elinta said. "Niles and I are training soon. Could you join us? I'm sure there's a thing or two you could show us."

Ford's lips twitched. "I've seen you fight as well, Elinta. But perhaps I can swing by."

"We'll be in the ballroom in an hour."

Ford's eyebrows rose at that.

"It was the only place we could find," she said.

They finished their meals in companionable silence, then Elinta went to her room to change.

"Do you think he'll come?" Elinta asked, stomping her foot forward as she stabbed at Niles's chest. He deflected her blow, spinning inside her guard to lightly touch the back of his hand to her face.

He grinned. "Maybe."

Elinta scowled at his colourful form as he stepped back to reset their positions. She'd been fighting with her eyes closed to change it up a little.

"You'll get forehead wrinkles," he said, wagging a finger at her.

She laughed, diving forward as she did. He met her blow again, his sword swinging down to slash at her shirt. She stepped back, sending her sword slicing toward his chest at the same time. The tip passed within millimetres of him. A successful hit by their rules. Elinta opened her eyes, grinning.

Niles frowned, playfully kicking out at her.

"Uh, uh! You'll get wrinkles," Elinta puffed, blocking another blow.

A gentle knock sounded on the door, and by unsaid agreement, the two lowered their swords. Elinta ran across the room, her bare feet slapping on the smooth wooden floor. They'd learnt only seconds into their first training session in the room not to wear their shoes.

Elinta pulled the door open, and Ford slipped inside.

"Ah, come to beat us with a book, my good man?" Niles called, bringing Elinta a glass of water as he sipped from his own. He grinned, shaking Ford's hand once Elinta had taken her drink.

"Something like that," Ford said, his eyes scanning the room.

It was a large room and empty aside from the new dummy Lorrin had had made for them. The dummy made the chandelier hanging from the ceiling seem quite out of place though. "This is a good space."

"It is. You might want to take your shoes off," Elinta said, gesturing at his feet. "The floor's slippery."

"I'll keep that in mind," Ford said, following them into the centre of the room. He'd taken off his dark green cloak, revealing the twin daggers at his hip.

Niles rubbed his hands together. "So, what's the plan?"

"I would be happy to work on your close-quarters technique if you would like as Tamir has been doing with the soldiers. He mentioned he hadn't had the chance with you yet."

Elinta nodded, thinking back to the times she'd tried the tactic when fighting the Asali before. She'd seen Ford doing much the same thing in Nevira, but he'd been more successful than her.

"That would be great."

"Alright!" Niles said, pumping his fist.

Ford strode across the room, gesturing for them to follow. He stopped in front of the dummy. "Elinta, you first."

Ford spent the next hour showing them both different techniques for staying in low and close, slashing with the length of their blades rather than stabbing. He demonstrated each set of moves, using his knives as he spun effortlessly around the straw man. Ford didn't once lose his usual quietness, but Elinta felt as though she was seeing a different side to the man. A side many didn't see.

Elinta's thighs were aching from crouching by the time they stepped back from the dummy, but she couldn't deny the sense of confidence Ford had given her.

"Well done, both of you," he said, nodding.

"Thank you for coming by," Elinta said, walking across the room with him and Niles.

"Of course," Ford said. "Keep practicing. You're both brilliant fighters. It won't take long to master."

"Thanks, mate." Niles shook Ford's hand again, and the historian slipped from the room.

"He really is quite the mysterious fellow."

CHAPTER
NINETEEN

E LINTA HURRIED DOWN THE hall. She was late for the meeting with Lorrin and the generals in Cyril's private dining room. She'd spent another morning with Zhayra over the ocean trying to access the senses and had come back soaked once again. Elinta had needed a bath to heat her bones after that, the ocean water surprisingly cold even for the end of summer. She straightened her shirt, lengthening her strides.

Elinta turned into the last corridor, the door coming into view. A soldier stood at attention to its right. He nodded as she pushed into the room. She didn't miss the way his eyes tracked her even though his head didn't move.

"Elinta, there you are," General Nash said, looking up from a stack of papers in front of her.

"Sorry I'm late," she said, hurrying to take a seat at the wooden table.

Elinta scanned the faces at the long table. Everyone she'd have expected, even Ford, was there. Mayor Cyril had joined them again, wearing a dark purple jacket today even though he still seemed uncomfortable at being included—glancing around at the other occupants as though waiting for one of them to tell him he wasn't welcome. And Mira, her face completely composed, sat to Lorrin's left. No sign of the sorrow she'd revealed the day Elinta had spoken to her.

Anger flared in Elinta's stomach as she looked between Mira and Lorrin. Mazen had caused so much pain and suffering in the short time he'd been active again. She had to stop him. Had to end things.

"I've called this meeting to nail down some details in both of our plans: for either an attack here or one in Liyarna," Lorrin said, looking around the group. "I believe it's been ten days since Ciar promised to join us. Is that right?"

Elinta and Niles both nodded. Elinta had kept careful track of each day that drew Ciar and his people closer to them.

"Ciar promised three weeks, less if they could."

Lorrin nodded. "So, let's work with three weeks, and hope for less."

Everyone at the table agreed.

"We've called in all of Culmar's reserves, and the civilians in training are doing well," General Nash said, "but I think a push for recruits would benefit us. We'll need everyone we can get."

Lorrin's eyes turned thoughtful. Elinta could almost read his thoughts. He was worried about the civilians getting hurt but weighing that up against the fact that they would probably be injured in the battle even if they didn't fight, and likely killed afterward if Mazen won anyway. It really came down to how and when they would be injured, rather than if. A grim reality.

"I'll leave that to you," Lorrin finally said.

General Nash nodded, making a note on the paper in front of her.

"How are the walls going?" Lorrin asked.

"Finished," General Sonnen grunted.

Elinta nodded. It was a true feat to have finished them so quickly, but many had volunteered to help those who'd been assigned the job. The walls didn't stretch around the whole of the city, that would have taken months, but rather would help control the movements of Mazen's Asali. The western side had the longest wall, with the small gap in the middle that she'd seen just days ago with the northern wall.

"And the watchtowers?"

"Fully stocked, Your Majesty," General Sonnen said. "With the extra arrows being made, we've enough to last weeks."

"I doubt this battle will last that long, so we can be sure our archers won't run out. And if we have the chance to march on Liyarna once our allies arrive? How long will it take to have the supplies ready?" Lorrin asked.

General Nash and General Sonnen exchanged a long look. "Three days," General Nash said. "We have some supplies ready to go, but we can't prepare without knowing *if* we'll be going."

"Get what you can ready, but nothing that will hinder us here." Lorrin glanced at the map of Eldras still spread on the table. "I don't like the idea of fighting Mazen on his own turf. The grasslands here," he pointed to a spot about halfway between Nevira and Culmar, "are the best place to meet him. Do you think he'll come, Tamir?"

"Yes," Tamir said, his dark grey eyes lingered on the marking of Liyarna on the map. "I do not think he cares where the battle takes place. He will be confident."

General Nash shifted, glancing at Mira. "There is one more thing we need to discuss, Lorrin. Your coronation."

Lorrin held up a hand. "That'll have to wait. I—" He frowned, glancing out of their small window.

Elinta followed his gaze. A shadow had fallen across the western window, large enough that Elinta wondered if a late summer storm was coming in. But distant yells in the city quickly sent the thought from her mind. They were not the warning calls of a storm in a seaside city. Elinta's heart dropped, her blood running cold. A feeling reflected in Zhayra. She waited on a precipice, waiting to hear what was happening. Which way she would tip.

The soldier Elinta had passed at the door to the room burst inside. His face drained of colour.

"There are dragons over the city, Your Majesty," he puffed, all signs of composure gone. As though to echo his words, the alarm bells began to ring. They seemed to bounce around Elinta's very bones.

The generals shot to their feet, Tamir and Ford exchanged worried glances, but Lorrin stood calmly. Once again, Elinta felt pride rush through her at the sight of him leading.

"How many?"

"Three, Your Majesty," the man said, glancing at the window. But there was nothing to be seen outside. No signs beyond the shadows and the bells.

"Are they attacking?"

"They—no." The man frowned.

Lorrin was silent for a moment, but Elinta didn't watch him. Instead, she dived into Zhayra's eyes, her heart thundering in her chest with fear for the dragon. Through Zhayra she could see the bustling docks and the city beyond them. The dragon was flying over the ocean again, but she was low to the water and moving so fast it passed as a blur under her.

"General Nash, please make sure the soldiers assigned to the walls are gathering. General Sonnen, I need you here to receive reports from the heads of the units." Lorrin's voice sounded in her ears, but Elinta continued to watch Zhayra.

Relief began to spread through her as the dragon drew closer to the city. Zhayra wasn't going after the other dragons—wherever they were—but returning to the mayor's home from a flight over the sea.

Elinta heard chairs scrape at the table, likely the generals leaving, but still she didn't pull back from the dragon's eyes.

Zhayra glanced up. The green dragon they'd seen over Nevira, the one bonded to Mazen, flew lazily over the city to Zhayra's right. Could Mazen see the city even now? Was Mazen watching Zhayra?

"Elinta?" Lorrin's voice sounded much closer than before.

"One moment," she said, her voice sounding surprisingly strained to her ears.

The boats moored offshore rushed under Zhayra, then the docks, and the dragon finally slowed enough that she was able to come to a brief stop over the courtyard to allow the frantic soldiers and servants time to move out of her way. She landed lightly on the grey stone.

Elinta breathed her first easy breath since she'd checked on the dragon and pulled back.

The room had significantly emptied with the two generals, Mira, and Cyril gone. Those left were staring at her.

"Zhayra was out of the city," Elinta said by way of explanation. "She's in the courtyard now."

"Good," Ford and Lorrin said at the same time.

"You'd better go down to her. We'll keep you updated. I want the rest of you with me. Farrell, have our armour brought here."

"No," Elinta said. "Zhayra and I should go and talk to the dragons. They might listen now."

The guard, Farrell, had paused in the doorway. Lorrin waved him on.

Ford frowned, looking around the table. "Why would now be different?"

Elinta took a deep breath. "Zhayra is the queen."

Ford's eyes widened. "The queen," he said with wonder.

Elinta's eyes were fixed on Lorrin. She didn't want to go against him, but she would if he said no. She needed to try this.

"OK, just—just please wear your armour," Lorrin said, his blue eyes locking on her.

"I will."

Farrell returned twenty minutes later, but in the time he'd been gone, there had been a steady stream of men and women reporting to Lorrin. General Sonnen had already begun sending messengers, though General Nash was still on her way to the western wall.

"The eastern towers report no movement over the ocean, Your Majesty," a thin, lean man with a long moustache said, bowing as he spoke.

"Good," Lorrin said, taking his armour from Farrell. "Tell them I want word every thirty minutes unless something changes, but I doubt we'll be attacked from the east."

The man bowed again and left. Word had already arrived that no Asali had been seen in the north, west, or south. It seemed the dragons were only there to keep an eye on them for now, while Mazen did ... whatever it was he was planning. The bells had been called off.

Three young boys had returned with Farrell, each carrying armour for Niles, Tamir, and Ford. But Neva had arrived with Elinta's.

"Here you go, miss," the maid said, placing the bag containing the *illayas* armour on the table.

"Thank you, Neva." Elinta took off her sword belt and grabbed the jerkin, lined with *illayas* at the bottom, from the pile. Once that was in place over her shirt, Neva helped her into the breastplate, clipping it in place from the back. Then came the greaves.

Done, she slipped her belt and sword into place outside of her armour, Elinta tried not to think about the last time she'd worn her armour. About the blood that had covered it. She gave Neva a nod.

"Be careful, miss."

"You too," she said. "Stay inside." Elinta grabbed the maid and pulled her in for a hug. Neva returned the gesture fiercely before hurrying from the room.

Elinta turned to face the rest of the room.

"I won't be long."

Zhayra was still in the courtyard when Elinta emerged through the front doors. Men, women, soldiers, and servants squished past the dragon's large body, hurrying to and from the mayor's building. Zhayra glanced around her, her tail wrapped tight around her body in an effort to give the people more room.

"It's time to go," Elinta said, hurrying to the dragon's side. Zhayra had been listening to the meeting even while Elinta had been looking through her eyes over the ocean, so she knew what Elinta was planning. Elinta didn't allow herself a moment to think too much about what they were doing. How it could go wrong.

Grunting, Zhayra lowered herself further for Elinta to climb onto her back. Once she was in place, her legs tied and her belt clipped in, Zhayra rose slowly into the air.

Elinta kept her sword in her sheath as they flew toward the green dragon. Zhayra kept her pace slow, relaxed, the complete opposite of an attack. The wind caressed Elinta's face, and she took in deep, steadying breaths.

But the green dragon didn't stop its circling. It didn't even let Zhayra get close to it. Every time they drew within ten metres of it, the dragon abruptly changed course. The fourth time it happened, Elinta asked Zhayra to stop following it.

"She doesn't want to talk," Elinta said. "But maybe we don't need to. Can you send her your memory of Mazen killing your mother?" Elinta looked across the city at the two other dragons, both a deep navy blue, circling in the south and west. They were the same ones who'd been over Nevira. And, she guessed, they hadn't been at the islands when she and Zhayra had visited. "Send it to all of them."

Zhayra grunted, her chest tightening a little. Did sending a memory mean she had to watch it too?

"It's OK." Elinta stroked Zhayra's neck.

Elinta waited in silence, the beating of Zhayra's wings the only sound so high up above the city. Her eyes were fixed on the green dragon, waiting for a sign that it had seen the memory.

A shudder seemed to ripple along the dragon's body and a keen burst from its mouth. It stopped in mid-air, locking its red eyes with Zhayra's amber ones. Then it turned from the city, flying out over the sea before turning south.

Elinta gaped after it. "It's—it's going home?"

Zhayra snorted. It wasn't at all what she had been hoping for, but it was better than the dragon staying where Mazen could use it. Elinta twisted to see where the blue dragons were. They hadn't stopped circling but, as she watched, widened their circles to cover what the other dragon had left abandoned. It seemed the blue dragons didn't care what Mazen had done. Only what he could do.

CHAPTER
TWENTY

"**M**ARCHING OUT TO MEET Mazen is no longer an option," General Sonnen said, looking around the room.

Night had now fallen, and still there had been no sign of Mazen, Vaherin, or the Asali fighting for them. The green dragon had not returned, but the two blues continued their circling.

"I agree," Lorrin said. "I doubt these dragons will let us leave. Have we heard from the scouts yet? Do we know where Mazen is?"

General Nash shook her head. "I doubt they are even alive, Your Majesty," she said heavily. "We should have known the dragons were coming, but no messages arrived to warn us."

Lorrin sighed. "So, we're blind."

General Nash nodded reluctantly.

"If you want to march out to meet him," Elinta said, her mind racing, "Zhayra and I could distract the dragons."

Lorrin frowned. "How?"

"We'll lead them away. Give everyone a chance to leave."

"The civilians would be safe, but we wouldn't be in any better of a position," General Sonnen grunted.

"No, we wouldn't," Lorrin murmured.

No one said anything as Lorrin continued to think. Elinta could practically see the thoughts whirling around his mind again. If Elinta couldn't keep the dragons distracted ... would the dragons attack? And if they did meet Mazen in battle on the field, would the dragons be able to pick them off more easily?

If only they'd had more time for Ciar to arrive. It all depended on how long it had taken for the Asali to prepare. They could arrive any time within the next ten days, but as Lorrin had said earlier, they had to plan as though it wouldn't be until the tenth day.

"Is your estimate still three days to march out?" Lorrin finally asked General Nash.

"Yes."

Lorrin shook his head. "We'll make our stand here. Culmar is our best chance for defence. But I want some more men sent out to find Mazen and his troops. I want to know exactly how long we have until he gets here. If the men get safely past the dragons, we'll continue evacuations for the remaining women and children."

General Sonnen nodded. He'd been in charge of stopping the evacuations earlier in the day when the dragons had first arrived. "I'll arrange the scouts, and I have a man who can see to getting the families ready."

"I need to make a final check of our defences," General Nash said. "I'll get the group of volunteers ready to help put out any fires."

"I can brief the scouts on what to expect from the dragons," Ford offered.

Tamir sat forward. "I will come also. We will give them a better chance of getting through."

"Very well."

Everyone dispersed. Elinta watched as Tamir and Ford left, side by side. It was strange to witness the two friends, knowing that though Ford looked older than Tamir, the Asali was actually over a thousand years older. She smiled at the intrusive thought. When she looked up as the last person disappeared through the door, Elinta was alone with Lorrin.

"Do you think it will be enough?" Lorrin murmured, his words echoing in the room.

Elinta stood from her seat, taking the one Lorrin's aunt had just occupied to his right. "It has to be."

Lorrin took her hand, his rough thumb drawing circles.

"You're doing amazing," Elinta said. "This is the best we can do. We'll make it work."

"I wish so much of this didn't rely on you," he said, his blue eyes flickering between her own white ones. "I wish I could fight with you."

Elinta forced a smile. "We all have a part to play."

"I hope those men get through," he said, looking out the window at the night sky.

"Things are finally coming to an end," Elinta murmured, following his gaze.

Lorrin's eyes jumped to hers, widening.

"We'll just make sure we come out the other side," Elinta said.

Elinta and Lorrin shared a late meal with Niles and Tamir when they all returned. Niles had been checking on the soldiers assigned to the mayor's house. Tamir reported that the dragons over the city had not altered course as three scouts had slipped through the walls. It seemed they'd been successful. Perhaps the green dragon leaving had been more of a blessing than Elinta had initially thought.

But they didn't talk about the dragons, or Mazen, or the Asali, as they ate their meal. They just enjoyed each other's company, knowing that it would likely be the last time they would have together until the battle was done. Lorrin had asked the guard watching the door that he only be disturbed in an emergency.

They laughed and joked, Niles leading the way, as only he could, to lighten the mood. Zhayra listened and watched from the courtyard, the lack of space or privacy preventing them from joining her. But the dragon was there—in Elinta.

They laughed long into the night, but Elinta was lighter than ever when she finally crawled under Zhayra's wing and closed her eyes.

"Miss! Miss!" Neva's voice pierced through Elinta's tired brain.

She groaned.

"Miss! Oh, miss, you must wake up."

Elinta cracked her eyes open, confused for a moment as she stared up at the underside of Zhayra's wing, the maid's words lingering in her mind.

"Neva?" Elinta said. The maid hadn't woken Elinta since she'd moved out of her room.

The dragon's wing pulled back to reveal Neva, her face deathly pale, her hands clutched over her heart. The bag containing Elinta's armour was at her feet.

"What is it?" Elinta jumped to her feet.

Neva bit her lip, drawing a pinch of colour to her white face. "Mazen's here."

"What?" Elinta hurried forward, pulling the bag toward her. The soft lighting and cool air revealed it to be dawn. She'd slept for five hours. "Where? When?"

"They only just arrived. The scouts never returned. King Lorrin says we didn't know they were coming until the watch towers saw them."

"Help me put this on," Elinta said, already tugging her jerkin over her head. She glanced around the courtyard, wondering at how she could have slept through the commotion of Mazen's arrival, but it seemed not everyone knew yet. There were hardly any people out, but the longer she looked, the more began to appear.

Neva hurried forward, her hands shaking as she grabbed the breastplate and then the greaves.

"How many are with him?"

Neva shook her head. "Does it matter? They are stronger and faster."

"Neva!" Elinta said, letting her voice turn harsh. She'd never heard the woman speak that way.

"I heard one of the soldiers say they more than match our numbers. And then there's the dragons ..."

Elinta stared at the woman. Neva was, unfortunately, right. The average human soldier did not equal one Asali. And if Mazen's army was as big as, or even bigger, than the one in Culmar ... She scanned the area around them that had filled up within seconds. Soldiers and messenger boys were now running around, some hardly managing not to collide on their errands. What they needed now was time. Time to make sure everyone was prepared to fight.

Elinta turned to the maid and grabbed her by the shoulders. "Neva, tell Lorrin I'm going to buy everyone some time."

"What are you going to do?"

"Something stupid."

Neva gaped at her.

"Go."

Nodding, the woman picked up her skirts and ran back inside the building.

"You can't come with me," Elinta said, turning to Zhayra, hating the very idea of going alone.

The dragon growled, her lip curling.

"We can't risk flying out there. If those dragons think we're attacking, we could start the battle before Lorrin's ready."

Zhayra growled again, looking down at her feet.

"No," Elinta said. "They'll see you walking, too."

The dragon shoved her head forward, looking into Elinta's eyes.

"I'll be careful. I'm just going to talk to him. Besides, he would have attacked by now. He's waiting for me." Somehow, she knew it was true. Something about the way he'd talked to her previously, especially at the dragon islands, told her. Something in Mazen wanted to be heard and understood.

Zhayra keened, nudging her.

"I'll be quick. Don't fight the dragons without me." She glanced back at the entrance to the building. "I better go. I doubt Lorrin will like this any more than you do."

CHAPTER
TWENTY-ONE

E LINTA RAN THROUGH THE winding streets, her hand gripping the hilt of her sword to stop the weapon bouncing
against her leg. The streets were full of men and women running
to their posts, but there were still civilians in the city. How many
hadn't left when they'd had the chance?

Elinta was already tuned into dragonsight, but now she focused herself and used the strength of Zhayra's ears. Sounds
assaulted her. The thumping of footsteps. Chainmail clinking
together. Already ragged breaths of men and women. The beats
of the dragons' wings, now flying lower. The waves pounding
at the docks behind her, the few boats left moored slamming

into the wooden posts tying them in place. And the panicked breathing of the innocent.

She ran on, her eyes fixed west. That's where he would have come from. She jumped out of the way as a man ran from a building, a leather jerkin only half pulled over his head.

"Sorry!" he yelled as he too ran off into the maze that was Culmar.

The western towers came into view, standing out above the buildings. Men were already at their posts inside, the tips of their arrows peeking over the rails and through the windows.

Nearly there.

When the patchwork wall came into sight, Elinta forced herself to drop back to a walk. She didn't want the men to think she was scared, panicked, because of her breathing. And she didn't want Mazen to know she'd run all the way there to see him.

"Elinta?" General Sonnen's gruff voice called from somewhere to her right, but Elinta didn't acknowledge him. He'd try to stop her, too. But she needed to hear whatever it was Mazen had to tell her. If only to buy time.

She stepped up to the wall and peered through the gap left to funnel the Asali.

Mazen stood alone, his troops several hundred metres behind him. Lines and lines of them, stretching away. His mouth cocked into a grin as his eyes locked on her. His mouth moved, but she was too far away to hear even with the strength of Zhayra's ears. He seemed to realise it, too. Mazen raised his sword for her to see, then lowered it to the ground. He strode forward another ten metres, leaving his weapon behind.

Elinta nodded. She let her sword belt drop to the ground. Then sent her satchel after it.

"What are you doing, kid?"

Elinta stepped out into the open. Murmurs rose from behind her.

"Elinta!" General Sonnen called.

She glanced over her shoulder at the undercurrent of concern in his words. She held his eyes and nodded once before taking another step out.

On the other side of the wall, she hesitated. What *did* Mazen want her to hear ... and should Lorrin hear it, too? She'd managed to push her emotions at him only last week, could she figure out how to shove her hearing at him now?

Elinta slowly crossed the space between her and Mazen, trying to buy herself time without being obvious. She tried to picture Lorrin, wherever he now was, and herself physically pushing the sounds around her at him. But nothing seemed to happen. *Would I even know if I did it?* Yes, surely there would be some feeling of confirmation, some echo of the bond working in her. Perhaps her ears would even pop as they had done when Zhayra had tuned in to her ears on her run over.

She continued forward. Perhaps if she tried to picture him beside her, experiencing everything she did? Her next step hesitated, but she forced herself on. Lorrin wasn't there. Not beside her and not in her senses.

As the distance between Elinta and Mazen slowly evaporated, she was forced to give up her attempt. She'd just have to relay it all to Lorrin later, if she made it back.

Mazen smiled as she stopped barely two metres across from him. It was a smile she could have admired if it hadn't contained his anger, barely hidden, around the edges. For a moment, she saw Vaherin's memory of him. A young man, respectful and eager to learn and see the world. A man she perhaps could have called a friend. But the image flickered and disappeared as he spoke.

"It's good to see you, Elinta," he said, his lyrical accent floating through the air. Once again, he was clad in his scale armour, something she had never seen him without, at least in person. But it looked as impeccable as ever. It was as though it hadn't already been through a battle.

"I can't say the same for you," Elinta said, her voice steady. All she had to do was keep him distracted. Whatever time she could buy for Lorrin to prepare.

He laughed, his eyes slipping over her shoulder to survey the city behind her before returning to her. "Tell me, I'm curious did things go with the dragons how I expected?"

Elinta shrugged. "I'd never force them to fight, not by a lie or any other means. It seems the same can't be said of you. Though I noticed you're missing a dragon." She gestured above them to where the green dragon had been circling yesterday.

Mazen's maroon eyes narrowed. "No matter. This is over, with or without her." He tilted his head, his slit eyes studying her. "It's too late for you, but you could still give the people trapped in the city a chance. If you give up now."

Elinta copied his head tilt, slowly scanning him. "No."

The man who had not spared his own father would do nothing to save the innocents in the city, but she had to try something. "Let the women and children go. They have nothing to do with this."

His face darkened and he stepped forward. She held her ground, even as she felt Zhayra's chest tighten at his movement.

"Why should I?" Mazen said, his voice as cold as death. "Your people did not spare a nesting dragon or the eggs she guarded. Why should I offer what you never did?"

His eyes slipped over her shoulder again. "Your prince is coming."

Mazen lunged.

Though she didn't turn, Elinta's guard had dropped just as her heart had at the thought that Lorrin might be leaving the temporary safety of the city. Mazen had the upper hand, crossing the distance between them in barely a second. He spun her around, wrenched her arms behind her back, and grabbed her hair, pulling her head back. She cried out as her scalp pulled tight.

"Look at them," he murmured in her ear, his breath tickling her skin. Men peered around the edges of the gap she'd passed through. Lorrin and General Sonnen stood in the open space. "I offered you mercy. More than your king ever gave to the dragons."

"That wasn't—" she broke off into a muffled cry of pain as he tugged at her hair. Several strands pulled free. Fire rose in Zhayra's chest, but Elinta silently begged the dragon not to move, not to come.

"You're going to lose, and the humans left behind will finally be in their rightful place."

Mazen shoved her away, sending her sprawling in the dirt. She spun around, struggling to stand as she did.

"I have one last gift for you."

He raised his hand in the air, and two Asali emerged from the ranks, dragging a struggling woman between them.

"Serren?" Elinta gasped.

The Asali released her, shoving Serren toward them.

"Come," Mazen called.

Serren pushed her filthy brown hair over her shoulder and walked right up to Mazen. Elinta stared at the woman. A trickle of blood had dried along her delicate face, stretching from under the hair near her forehead all the way down to her jaw, which was bruised a deep blue. Her left eye was swollen. Bruises littered her bare arms and legs, but Serren showed no sign of the pain or discomfit she must have felt. Her eyes were strong, her back straight.

"Tell Tamir I will grant him the chance to die with his *ngaparta*, but nothing more." Mazen held Elinta's eyes. "There will be no more war after today, Elinta. Only peace."

Mazen spun on his heel, and strode back to the Asali ranks, picking up his sword as he went.

"Serren," Elinta murmured.

"I will be fine," she said, glancing over her shoulder. "We must get inside the city."

"Right." Elinta grabbed Serren's hand and pivoted, hurrying back to the wall. She picked up her belongings as they reached them, releasing Serren's hand so she could slip her sword back into place.

Lorrin hurried them back through the gap, pulling them away from the open space and into safety. Serren winced at the movement but said nothing.

"Are you alright?" Lorrin asked the woman, looking her over. "I've sent for Tamir."

At the mention of her husband, a smile tilted Serren's lips. "I will be more than alright then."

"I'm so sorry," Elinta said, her eyes trailing over the woman's injuries. No mortal wounds, but still painful enough.

Serren took her hand. "I am not sorry for staying. Only that our people have betrayed so much to him."

Before Elinta could ask what else Mazen knew, Tamir's voice rose above the clamour of the soldiers preparing for war.

"Serren?"

Elinta turned to see him pushing through the crowd, closely followed by Ford. Anger and devastation tore through Tamir's eyes as they landed on the bruised and bloodied form of his wife. He crossed the remaining distance in a sprint.

"Serren!" He gathered her tenderly into his arms, running his hands over her face and arms as he looked her over. His healing glow quickly spread, and the bruises began to fade, and the cuts began to seal. Serren kissed him, whispering something only he could hear against his lips.

Lorrin's hand brushed Elinta's and she turned, wondering what she'd see on his face.

"You scared me there," he said quietly, looking back out through the gap to where she'd stood moments before with Mazen.

"I was trying to buy you time," she said, jokingly glaring at him. "I—" she broke off as she glanced at Serren. Ford had stopped beside them, and the woman, now healed, was embracing him. Elinta frowned.

"I doubt he'll wait much longer," Lorrin said, breaking Elinta's train of thought.

"He will not," Serren said, catching the last of their conversation and walking over. Tamir was glued to her side, Ford just behind them. "I would like to join you, but I will need a spear."

Tamir said nothing to object, his hand clutching hers, their *illayas* bracelets touching.

Lorrin called to a soldier nearby to source one for her.

At that same moment, a dragon roared in the distance, and the two over the city echoed it. Elinta watched as the men around them paled, their voices dropping off until a heavy silence settled over them.

"Lorrin!" Niles called, standing halfway up the wooden ladder to the closest watch tower. He pointed over the wall. Elinta hadn't noticed when he'd joined their group, but she didn't linger on the thought, following his gaze.

Elinta and Lorrin stepped up to a small peep hole left in the wall and looked out over Mazen's army. They'd begun to move.

CHAPTER
TWENTY-TWO

E LINTA GAPED, HER HAND clutching Lorrin's, searching for comfort, as the Asali army began a slow steady march toward them. There had to be hundreds of them. Hundreds of men and women who could move faster, who had more experience, than any of the men defending the city.

"I have to get to Zhayra," she whispered. Zhayra had continued to watch and listen to everything through Elinta. She just hoped the dragon was right where she'd left her. At the mayor's home.

Elinta twisted in place to lock eyes with Lorrin. "I have something for you."

She slipped her hand into her satchel, her fingers recoiling at the touch of the cold metal within, but she gripped the hilt firmly and pulled out Mazen's dagger. Lorrin's eyes widened.

"I want you to have it for the battle," she said, pushing it into his hand. "Then we'll destroy it after."

He nodded, pushing it through his sword belt.

And that was all there was time for.

"Your Majesty!"

Lorrin's head whipped around as General Sonnen approached. "A group has already entered the city."

"What? How?"

Sonnen shook his head. "They slipped in through a weak spot in the north. We lost a dozen men."

"I want two squads sent after them."

Even as he spoke, the roar of flames reached them from deep in the city.

Elinta felt the blood drain from her face, the memory of Liyarna burning slipping before her enhanced eyes.

Niles, Ford, Tamir, and Serren stepped up behind her.

"We will get you to Zhayra," Serren said.

"We need to move now," Lorrin said. "General Sonnen, once we get Elinta to Zhayra, I'll come back. You're in charge here."

The general nodded, his eyes lingering on his son's as he clasped hands with Niles. And their small group was off, each with their weapons in hand.

Their way was clear for the first few blocks of the sprawling city, with the two blues in the east and south, and Vaherin still nowhere to be seen. Civilians and soldiers raced through the streets, some carrying buckets of water as they hurried to the fires already sprouting in the city. But soon it became clear that more than a small group of Asali had slipped through their defences in the north while Elinta had been distracted with Mazen.

A dozen Asali appeared ahead of them, running to their right when they came to a halt at the sight of Elinta and Lorrin. The group altered their course, running straight down the narrow alley for them. Ford and Tamir stepped forward in perfect sync to meet the first of the Asali. Elinta watched in awe as they weaved and struck together, whirling around one another, their movements a perfect balance. It was like watching Niles and Lorrin fight together, but infinitely better. But there was no time to watch and wonder at the men, as two Asali slipped past them. Serren struck, her spear darting out, the tip burying into the bone of a knee before she brought the other end around to slam into the man's head. Lorrin and Niles shoved forward, driving the next of the Asali back, gaining precious ground. Serren continued to send her spear through gaps in their line, striking viciously and without remorse. One Asali remained. She turned on her heels and ran.

A quick check was done to make sure everyone was OK, and then they pushed on, stepping over the bodies of the wounded and unconscious. Elinta had no idea if any were dead. She didn't let herself wonder.

Around the next corner, a Culmaran family ran from a building. The mother clutched her two small children tightly to her body as they ran. The whites of her eyes showed as she glanced around.

"Get to the mayor's house," Lorrin called to them. There was no escaping the city now. The woman nodded, frantic tears running down her face as she ushered her young daughters on.

An Asali dove into their group's path from Elinta's left. She stumbled back, narrowly avoiding the knife the man wielded. Lorrin's sword darted in, and as the Asali deflected, Elinta dove toward them, dropping low and sticking close as she'd practiced with Ford. She sliced her *illayas* sword across the back of the

Asali's legs. As the man wobbled, she sent the hilt into his head. He crumpled.

Elinta and Lorrin exchanged a silent nod, and they lead the group on.

"Where are Vaherin and Mazen?" Lorrin shouted over the clammer, his voice bouncing in time with his feet.

"I don't know," Elinta said, glancing up at his words. Mazen had not followed them and Elinta didn't dare check through Vaherin's eyes when it was so dangerous on the streets.

From the corner of her vision, Elinta saw a dragon swooping down on the city to the north, reaching down with its claws to strike at a watchtower. She didn't watch the moment it connected but pushed herself harder.

The mayor's large home came into view, and they slowed their pace. There had been no sign of Asali for some time, and perhaps they hadn't reached this far into the city yet and the other defences had held for now. But they weren't going to risk a trap.

"Slowly," Ford warned as they drew closer still.

They crept forward, peering around. The mayor's home seemed quiet. Lorrin and the generals were no longer inside, and so there were no longer any messengers running to or from it.

Lorrin drew them to a halt. "Ford, Tamir, Serren, you three wait here. Make sure no one comes up behind us. Niles and I will get Elinta to Zhayra."

The three nodded. Elinta looked over them, "I'll see you all soon. *Zetayn nalliyan ayn palla kli ayn karn mai ris.*" She ran on before they could respond, the boys on her tail.

"Zhayra!" Elinta yelled as they reached the courtyard. The dragon was waiting for them, her harness ready. Elinta didn't bother asking the boys who'd done it. Elinta smiled as she locked eyes with the dragon, relief seeping into her bones at the sight of her.

Then, Elinta's blood turned to ice.

The heavy beats of wings on air. Familiar beats. Her chest tightened, her mind already showing her Blaine's body on the ground. She was unable to do anything. See anything.

"No!" Tamir cried from behind them, breaking through the fear holding her.

Elinta glanced up, to see Vaherin's large maroon form sweeping down upon them, his maw opening. Mazen grinned and—Zhayra jumped upon her and the boys, Lorrin's arm dragging her down to the ground as the dragon's white wings spread over them like a cocoon. The immense roar of flames covered them as the fire slammed into Zhayra's fireproof scales and membrane. Elinta gripped Lorrin's hand, Niles's own on her shoulder. She clenched her jaw, swallowing the scream that had threatened to escape in the moment before Zhayra had covered them. She counted the seconds. One. Two. Three. Four. Then the fire stopped, and she heard Mazen's dark chuckle as Vaherin's wing beats receded.

Zhayra's wings pulled back, and the dragon peered down at them.

"Are you OK?" Elinta gasped, throwing her arms around the dragon's muzzle.

Zhayra snorted, her heart in her throat.

A hand settled on her shoulder, and she turned to see Lorrin's pale face. "We have to get back to the wall."

Elinta gulped. "Be careful," she said, throwing her arms around him and then Niles.

"We'll see you soon," Niles said with a wink, though his face had drained of colour too.

"Don't you dare hang around if the dragons turn up at the wall," Elinta said, looking at them both.

Niles saluted, and with one final look her way, the two ran back toward the waiting figures of Tamir, Ford, and Serren. Elinta jumped onto Zhayra's back, quickly clipping her belt in place with shaking hands.

Zhayra leapt into the air. The wind tugged hard at Elinta's hair, but the braid she'd put in her hair the night before held, with only a few blonde strands breaking free. She'd have to thank Neva for showing her a better braid, one that stopped her hair from impeding her vision.

As Zhayra levelled out, Elinta called to her. "Head back toward the west wall. Let's see if there's anything we can do to stop the Asali getting in." Then they could turn their focus to the dragons. Zhayra shot across the city, low and fast. The buildings passed in a blur. As they reached the wall, Zhayra altered her flight, pushing them higher to get a better view. The Asali were against the wall now, the two armies locked together at the gap. How many of those Asali were innocent? Forced to fight by their new king and his followers?

There was nothing they could do now to stop them from getting in. But Elinta decided to use some of Mazen's tactics.

"Burn the ground behind them," Elinta called over the din below them. Fear could be an effective offense, too.

Zhayra grunted, puzzled, but then the feeling eased as the dragon seemed to understand Elinta's thoughts. She swooped low, shooting fire down behind Mazen's army, scorching the ground and lighting the trees on fire.

Startled shouts rose up in the second between Zhayra's breaths, then the fire began again, drowning out all sound.

They'd laid a wall of fire two-hundred metres long when Vaherin and Mazen came for them, a mere red streak in the sky.

"Zhayra!"

But Zhayra had seen them and had stopped her river of flame, turning them around to meet Vaherin. But the impact never came. The green dragon who had left them the previous day, the one who had bonded to Mazen, had returned and was flying so fast Elinta's eyes could barely track it. It came to a halt in front of them, putting itself between Elinta and Mazen. A deep growl reverberated around its chest.

Elinta gawped at it. The same surprise, mixed with pride, had settled over Zhayra.

Elinta reached out as though with a hand and grabbed Vaherin's emotions, flinching at the rage that boiled inside him.

"Vaherin!" Elinta yelled, wondering if he would even hear her. "Stop this. Please!"

Vaherin lunged. His jaws aiming straight for the green dragon's neck. He found his mark, the green dragon screeching in pain even as it clawed at Vaherin's chest and face, leaving a deep carving across his snout. Then Vaherin jerked his head, and the dragon fell silent. As the dragon's body went limp, he opened his mouth and the green dragon fell to the ground, narrowly missing the back line of Asali. It all happened within seconds.

"Move!" Elinta yelled. But Zhayra was ahead of her. Before the green dragon's body had even hit the ground, Zhayra was shooting through the air, putting space between her and Vaherin.

Elinta looked around wildly, her mind racing. "Let's lead them away. Go to the sea!"

Zhayra didn't respond, but immediately turned and shot toward the ocean. Vaherin's stomach jolted in surprise. And then they were after them. Elinta pulled back from the maroon dragon, no longer wanting to know what he felt. She gasped.

"Zhayra! I've got it!" She laughed in disbelief. Of all the times to have an epiphany, this was surely the worst. But connecting to Vaherin had given her an idea. *The* idea. For weeks she'd tried to work out how to solve the problem of their races communicating, and an idea had lurked on the edges of her mind. She hadn't thought about it since before Liyarna was attacked with everything going on ... but it seemed her mind had merely needed space from the issue.

Zearla lurai ambassadors. She laughed again, but Vaherin loosed a roar so loud she jumped in her seat. Elinta shook her head, sending the thought from her mind, and lowered herself on Zhayra's back, letting the wind shoot over her. Now was definitely not the time to think about it any further.

The city whizzed by and already Elinta could see soldiers and Asali clashing within the streets. One of the blues flew low, breathing fire over the city. They should have gone after one of the dragons instead of going for the wall. But she was doing all she could now to help the city from the air. Within minutes they were over the docks, the gulls rising in a panic under them, circling as they looked for a place to flee to. As soon as the crystal blue ocean appeared under them, Elinta called to Zhayra.

"This is it!" This was where they'd make their stand.

CHAPTER
TWENTY-THREE

V AHERIN WAS RACING TOWARD them, the sun glinting off his long horns. Mazen grinned as the distance closed. But Elinta wanted one last chance to talk to Vaherin, and so did Zhayra.

"Now, Zhayra," she said.

Zhayra pushed Vaherin's own memories back at him.

The maroon dragon came to a shuddering halt, his body tipping dangerously as the memory of what he'd done to Tristan slammed into him.

"It wasn't your fault," Elinta called, reaching for his emotions again. "What happened with Tristan—you were just protecting

Mazen. What Tristan did was wrong, the Eggslaying was wrong, but so is this. Enough blood has been spilled. We can fix this."

Mazen's eyes darkened as he looked between Zhayra and Vaherin. "She's the queen now, isn't she?"

His words carried to her enhanced ears. Elinta gave a firm nod but didn't turn her attention away from Vaherin. Her heart sank at what she felt within him. That rage and hurt still roared in his chest, and a determination had settled over him.

"You're a fool, Elinta, if you think we can be swayed now. If you know what happened with Prince Tristan, then you know you are not the first to try to make us stop. We're finishing this."

Vaherin growled his approval.

Mazen twisted in his seat to look behind him. "But maybe we won't start with you after all. You had your chance to buy mercy," he said, a dark grin turning up his lips. "We'll start with your friends."

Elinta followed his eyes to see them locked on one of the blue dragons. Elinta felt her heart stop. "No," she whispered as the dragon began to dive.

Too far away to do anything, Elinta jumped into Lorrin's eyes, her fear sending her heart hammering against her chest again. Bile rose in her throat as she watched. As Lorrin seemed to hear the beats of the dragon's wings draw closer, saw him turn as if in slow motion, to see a dark blue figure sweeping from the skies, the sun glinting off its exposed talons. And she saw it snatch up the blond-haired, brown-eyed figure beside him.

"No!" Elinta gasped.

Lorrin's eyes were glued to the figure of his best friend being carried away as he sprinted after them helplessly. Niles was being carried toward her and Mazen's distant figures.

Elinta was back in her own eyes in a heartbeat, her mind taking a moment to adjust to the change in angle. She watched the blue dragon soaring toward them, Niles clutched in its claws.

The blue dragon swooped by and threw—*threw* Niles to Vaherin, who snatched him up in his own large claws.

"Stop it!" Elinta screamed, as Niles body jolted to a stop when Vaherin caught him. She could have sworn she'd heard something break inside his body, even across the huge distance between them. Niles's legs dangled limply below him, hanging freely over the docks. For Mazen hadn't followed them completely over the ocean. Not that it would matter at that height.

Mazen's smile widened. The blue dragon flew back over the city, diving once more to wreak havoc upon the poorer districts. But Elinta didn't watch. Her eyes were glued to the shining eyes of her friend, to the blood seeping from his shoulders where Vaherin's claws had sunk deep into his flesh.

"It's going to be OK," she called, knowing he couldn't hear her, not without the enhanced hearing that only she and Mazen had. "Please," she begged, locking eyes with Mazen, not daring to tell Zhayra to move closer for fear Vaherin would drop Niles. "Please, don't do this."

Mazen opened his mouth, but stopped, glancing down with an amused expression as though he could see Niles. Niles was speaking.

"El, it's OK. It's OK. I wouldn't change any of it," he said, a cocky grin tilting his lips. But she could see it in his eyes. The realisation that he wouldn't be going any further than this. That he wouldn't be *allowed* to go any further.

"No," she said, shaking her head. She wasn't going to let this happen. Wasn't going to lose him, too. "You're going to be OK. You're going to be fine." She couldn't give over Zhayra. But surely there was something else. Something else she could offer Mazen.

"I've never been so proud of you. Never."

"Stop," she cried. "Stop! I'll do anything. Please."

Mazen said nothing, content to watch her fighting to know what to do. But she was immobile. Frozen in fear.

"You're going to change the world. I won't be there to see it, but knowing is enough." Niles's grin widened. His blood dripped onto the docks below as his skin slowly paled.

"Niles," she sobbed.

An urgency seemed to enter his rasping voice. "It'll be strange without my good looks around. But Lo—"

"How dull. Vaherin?"

"NO!"

Vaherin's claws twitched. And Niles's scream tore through her, ripped her heart in two, as the talons dug deeper. They found their mark, his blood running, streaming, now. Then the scream ended. An unearthly silence fell even though Elinta was sure she was still screaming, sure that Zhayra had roared even as she launched herself forward. Then Vaherin's claws released. Niles's body seemed to hang, untethered and limp in the air, and then he began to fall.

Zhayra dove after him, both of them knowing, knowing it was already too late, but she couldn't leave him. Couldn't let his body break on the docks below. But a flash of maroon came from their left and slammed into them from above, shoving Zhayra off path. The tip of Vaherin's wing crashed into Elinta's shoulder, and something within it popped, something came loose. She screamed as pain ripped down her arm.

Sobbing, Elinta was forced to tear her gaze from Niles's body as Zhayra fought to balance herself in a flurry of wings. Vaherin swept away, coming back around in a large half-circle. Elinta drew her weapon, her hands shaking, not letting her eyes slip down. Down to *him*. Already on the rotting wood of the docks.

Mazen's eyes darkened as they fixed on her blue blade, his face twisting uglily.

Vaherin growled, flashing his teeth.

Elinta forced her left hand to grip the harness, gritting her teeth as her shoulder protested, and held her sword ready as Vaherin charged toward them.

Zhayra led them further over the ocean, grief and rage like a knife in the dragon's chest, before twisting to meet Vaherin in mid-air.

Their bodies slammed together, their scales rubbing and tearing, their claws viciously vying for a grip on the other, for a weak spot to tear into. Their growls filled Elinta's ears even as their jaws snapped for each other. Mazen was out of her reach, but Elinta sent the tip of the Eggslaying sword at Vaherin, catching a rogue claw and breaking off the very tip.

They broke apart for a moment, Elinta's breath coming in her ears. Zhayra's chest heaving. Zhayra lunged back in, her teeth snapping for Vaherin's throat, but the dragon dodged, shooting above them. Elinta flattened against Zhayra's scales, wary of his claws clipping her as they had over Nevira.

Vaherin rose, Zhayra followed him with her gaze. He seemed to pause in the air as he reached his peak, then flipped, Mazen hanging on easily, and shot back toward them, his wings tucked against his body.

Growling, Zhayra watched his free-fall. Elinta clung to the dragon, her shoulder aching, her tears still dripping down her cheeks. Thirty metres. Twenty. Ten. Elinta bit her tongue as the urge to yell at Zhayra to move nearly overtook her.

Then Zhayra shot to the side, twisting as she did to bare her claws, letting them rake along Vaherin's side as he zipped past. Only one of her claws found its mark, carving a long line through his flesh.

Mazen wordlessly roared even as Vaherin spread his wings to stop their fall. Zhayra sped after them, a trickle of crimson pushed up her neck by the force of the wind.

Elinta watched the stream, a knot settling into her stomach. Could they beat Vaherin and Mazen? They'd landed one lucky blow, but ... She shook her head. They didn't have a choice. They had to win. And if they did, maybe the other dragons would leave. They'd stand a chance of surviving this day.

Zhayra continued to race after them, Vaherin's tail flailing wildly behind him, the tip catching Zhayra's snout. She snorted, shaking her head, then snapped at his tail. But he'd pulled too far ahead, twisting in the air so that their bodies slammed together once more. Elinta's body jolted as the dragons came together again and again. She hadn't tied her legs down, but the buckle of the harness held firm. She waited for an opening, waited for a chance to strike at Mazen or Vaherin but none came. Mazen was likewise hindered.

Vaherin swiped at Zhayra's face, his claw catching her cheek and sending several scales falling into the ocean below. Zhayra roared, breaking away from the larger dragon, shooting up into the air.

"Are you OK?" Elinta yelled. She'd been trying to turn on the balance senses, but nothing was happening. All that work over the ocean, and she still couldn't turn it on at will.

Zhayra grunted, her chest full of fiery anger, her breaths coming in short bursts. How long could the dragon keep doing this? How long before she grew tired?

A flock of gulls screeched from her right, twisting in mid-air to avoid slamming into Zhayra. Vaherin was hot on their heels.

"Try to get me an opportunity to fight them," she called. "You don't have to do this all on your own."

Zhayra grunted once more, and turned to meet Vaherin again, coming down on him with her teeth bared and her vicious claws reaching for him.

He ducked away, coming up and around her claws to strike at her side. Elinta stabbed at his jaw, the tip of her sword sinking into his flesh before his teeth could find their mark. He keened, reeling backward, but brought his tail around to crash into her back.

She screamed, her injured shoulder roaring as she was slammed flat against Zhayra. Blood spurted from her lip from the impact. Her sword went flying from her grip. She didn't even hear it splash into the ocean hundreds of metres below them.

Mazen's dark laugh echoed over them.

They didn't have a moment to rest, to gather themselves, as Vaherin charged back in, his claws flashing in the light.

The world seemed to go silent to Elinta. The heavy clash of the dragons fading to the background.

She'd known from the beginning that fighting Mazen and Vaherin was a long shot, especially when she didn't want to kill them and Mazen had no such qualms. But what could she do now? So high in the air, unarmed and with her sword in the sea? Zhayra was fighting as she'd never fought before, but Elinta had begun to suspect it wouldn't be enough. Not against both Vaherin and Mazen, who still had his own *illayas* sword.

Elinta did something she had never done before. She pulled back from Zhayra's emotions, and blocked her. She'd suspected she could do it for months, had known for sure when she'd witnessed Zhayra doing it in her memories with her mother. But had never had any reason to. But now, now she did. A gulf opened up inside of her and she ached at the emptiness. The loneliness.

Zhayra grunted in surprise at Elinta's withdrawal. She broke away from Vaherin with a swipe of her tail, gaining some space. Elinta knew what she'd feel if she reached back out to the dragon. Confusion, worry, perhaps a little hurt.

"It's OK," she said to the dragon, guilt seeping in. "I just—I just need a second."

Because she'd had an idea. Seen a way to end things. But emotions would give her away, even as she merely considered it, and Zhayra would never let her do it.

But what other option was there? If Mazen won this fight over the seas, he would turn his attention to Culmar and to Lorrin before their bodies had even hit the ocean. And when he was done, he'd move on to the rest of Eldras. She couldn't allow it. Couldn't allow any more deaths. Any more suffering when she could end it now. End it with her.

"Zhayra," she said, softly enough that only the dragon would hear. "Come down on them from above."

CHAPTER
TWENTY-FOUR

T HIS WAS THE LAST thing open to her. The last option. She had no weapon—a fact she was sure Zhayra was yet to realise. Only her body.

Zhayra grunted her understanding, a tinge of her confusion slipping into the sound. But Elinta didn't reopen the bond. Didn't let the dragon feel the fear and the other thing solidifying inside her. They would both have to bear this hollowness until she was ready.

As the dragon turned around in the air, Elinta slipped her hand to the buckle keeping her anchored to the dragon and fought her shaking hands to unclip it. Fought the raging pain in her shoulder for a moment of steadiness. *Please*, she begged her body, *please*.

The fear raging inside her finally, finally let her tap into the balancing senses. The ones that she would need in these final moments if this desperate plan was going to work.

"Give me an opening on the right," she said, wrestling her voice into a calm she didn't feel. Zhayra couldn't know.

The dragon shifted her path. Elinta watched the space between them and Vaherin and Mazen close. Saw the fire in Vaherin's eyes, the triumphant grin on Mazen's beautiful yet twisted face.

It happened in a second. In an age. In a heartbeat. In a lifetime. Zhayra slammed into Vaherin from above, the way open for Elinta for only a fraction of a moment. She pushed her legs under her. And jumped from the dragon.

Mazen's eyes widened, his reactions delayed by the surprise he felt so that his sword hung uselessly beside him as she flew at him. She slammed into him, her shoulder screaming once more, wrapping her arms around him as she did, and they both slipped over the side of Vaherin's large bulk.

The whole world opened up below them, and Elinta clung to Mazen, digging her fingers into his scaled armour. His sword fell from his hand as he scrambled to hold on to her, too. No longer was there any anger or coldness in his eyes. Fear was in them now.

She pressed her cheek to his, her lips by his ear, and whispered. *"Zetayn eyan pepyan eka ayn air kli nalliyan."*

Elinta shoved away from him with both arms and legs, tearing herself from his arms. Zhayra's and Vaherin's roars echoed over them.

Her last view of Mazen was of his widening eyes, and a terror she had never seen before spreading across his face. Then she rolled over in the air, the wind tearing at her clothes and hair, to watch the dragons.

Zhayra and Vaherin were high above them, fighting each other even as they both dove toward their own *Zearla lurai.* The whites of Zhayra's eyes showed as she fought tooth and claw against

Vaherin to gain the precious space between them. Elinta's heart ached at the terror she could see so plainly written across the dragon's body. Zhayra's anguished roar filled the sky even as she slammed into Vaherin again and again.

Elinta shut off all the senses; shut off equilibrioception, shut of proprioception, the strength of Zhayra's ears. Leaving only her eyes enhanced. But there was one more thing she needed to do before she said her final goodbye to the dragon. She closed her eyes and pictured Lorrin. Pictured his bright blue eyes and that perfect smile that had brought her so much happiness even when she wasn't sure she'd ever feel it again.

His vision came easily to her this time, and she found herself watching her own body falling through the air, Mazen below her, and the two dragons fighting above her while shooting after them. She didn't reach for Lorrin's ears, but rather summoned all her feelings for him, all her love and hope and happiness, every shred of goodness he had made her feel, and she shoved it at him.

"Goodbye," she whispered, feeling a tear glide down her face. She wished Niles could be with him now. But at least Lorrin was safe. And she knew too that with him on the throne Zhayra would be safe as well. They could look after each other. She let the image fade, cracking open her eyes to look at the dragon.

Pain tugged at her heart as Zhayra finally broke free of Vaherin's large bulk, folding her wings tight against her body and shooting through the air toward her.

Too late. She could already tell the dragon would be too late. She had seconds. Seconds before her body would slam into the ocean and it would be over. She was always going to be the one who died first, but she wished they'd had more time. At least now, Mazen was gone. And Vaherin would be devastated without him. Maybe the battle would even end, but if it didn't, there was still Lorrin. Still Zhayra.

With a smile, Elinta reopened the emotional link between her and Zhayra, the dragon's fear like a shot to her heart. She felt the terror choking the dragon's throat, the tightness in her belly. And she tried to wash it all away, wishing beyond anything that the emotions she sent to Zhayra would smooth away the pain and fear. Wished she could cover it with the love she felt. The calm. Zhayra was only metres away now. But the distance could have been a lifetime.

"I love you," she whispered to the dragon.

CHAPTER
TWENTY-FIVE

L ORRIN RAN THROUGH THE streets of Culmar, an unfamiliar horn sounding behind him, the image of Elinta falling through the air on a replay in his mind. Zhayra had flown after her, but he couldn't see what had happened. A lump had settled in his throat, raw from whatever sounds had ripped from him as he'd watched one friend fall and then another. His chest gave a painful throb. Not her, too. He couldn't lose her, too.

He shoved through a wall of soldiers, finally breaking through onto the docks. Light footsteps sounded behind him, but he had no idea who had followed him. Didn't have it in him to turn and make sure it wasn't an enemy. The echo of Elinta's feelings sounded in his mind, as though she were still connected to him. But she wasn't. And he couldn't see her. Or Zhayra.

Lorrin ran to the end of a creaking, swaying jetty, his eyes fixed on the roiling water.

"No." His voice cracked. She wouldn't have survived that fall.

Vaherin was still above them, his wings faltering, his body steadily jolting downward as though some injury prevented him from staying airborne. But his long keen echoed over the city. Mazen was also gone.

A splash in the water drew Lorrin's attention back to the sea, and Zhayra's head emerged from the ocean, blowing water from her nostrils. Blood trickled from wounds on her snout and cheek. She keened.

"Zhayra!" Without a thought, Lorrin dived in the water, swimming out to her in broad, swift strokes. She glanced at him, grunting even as she looked down, toward her feet, which she seemed to be trying to raise in the water.

He frowned, a sliver of hope rising in his chest.

"I'm coming," he called, fighting the weight of his armour.

She keened again.

Lorrin reached her, his hand stroking her smooth scales.

Zhayra looked at him, panic in her amber eyes, then down again.

He took a deep breath and went under, forcing his eyes open in the murky water.

Elinta's limp form was clutched in Zhayra's claws, the dragon still struggling to raise her above the water. A bubble of air escaped Lorrin's lips, and he pushed through the salty water, pulling Elinta's body into his arms and tapping the dragon's foot to let her know he had her.

She released Elinta, and he pulled them to the surface.

"Elinta!" he gasped, holding her head above the water, her back against his chest. He kicked at the water wildly, trying to keep them above the waves. If her armour had been anything but *illayas*, they would have sunk straight to the bottom of the sea together.

"Is she breathing?"

Lorrin jolted, slipping beneath the waves for a moment before he managed to surface again. He twisted to see Tamir beside him, his wet hair clinging to his face. It must have been the Asali who'd followed him all that way.

"No."

Tamir grabbed Elinta's shoulder, which sat strangely under the armour, his healing glow spreading over her. "We must get her back to the docks."

"Hurry!" Lorrin shouted at Zhayra, kicking fiercely, dragging Elinta's still body with him, his armour threatening to drag him back down. Tamir climbed back onto the jetty first, dragging Elinta out even as Lorrin pushed her up, the healing power still shining.

Shoving at the water trickling into his eyes from his hair, Lorrin crouched over Elinta, listening for any sign of breath. Still nothing. He reached for her pulse.

"No," he whispered, pushing her sodden blonde hair back from her face. "No."

He pressed on her chest, his hands pushing up and down in a steady rhythm. Tamir's glowing hands gripped her shoulders even as he worked. From the corner of his eye, he saw Zhayra emerge from the ocean. Water, mingled with blood, cascading from her body. The dragon stopped beside them, but turned, looking up into the sky. He kept pushing, kept working, willing Elinta's heart to beat as Tamir continued to pump his healing into her. But if her heart didn't start up again, the healing would be useless. He didn't allow himself to think any further.

Zhayra loosed a long and loud roar.

Lorrin merely raised his eyebrows in question at Tamir as he kept working, not daring to turn to see what was happening behind him.

"She is challenging Vaherin. He has surrendered."

Zhayra loomed over them then, water dripping from her scales and onto him. Onto Elinta.

Lorrin paused, locking his lips with Elinta's, the iron tang of her blood in his mouth, breathing air into her lungs. Then he continued pushing, working. His body straining. Water dripping from him onto her.

She coughed.

❦❦❦

Air rushed into Elinta's lungs even as water came from them in torrents. Gentle hands pushed her onto her side, the water coming easier. Voices sounded above her, but she couldn't make them out, could barely even open her eyes as she coughed until she felt as though her chest would give out. Pain tore through her shoulder and down her arm with the violent movements.

Finally, the water stopped coming, and the hands grabbed her again, pulling her soaked body against another equally wet form.

"El?"

Lorrin.

She cracked open her eyes, peering blearily up at him through the water still running over her face.

Though tears wet his cheeks, she'd never seen him smile so widely. His arms were around her, her back now against his armoured chest. She raised a shaking hand to his face before her arm dropped back beside her. He pressed a cold kiss to her forehead.

Zhayra keened, her head tilted above them to look down at her with a large amber eye.

They were on the docks. The clanging of battle still sounding in the city. Somehow—somehow, she'd survived.

"I can do a little more," Tamir's tired voice whispered from beside her. A warm hand slid into hers, and his healing warmth spread through her.

Elinta gasped as her shoulder slid back into place, the muscles and tendons twitching around the socket. She felt skin pulling together on her legs though she couldn't remember hurting them. Her split lip sealed together.

Puffing, Tamir stopped, bags under his eyes. "I am sorry," he said, gasping, "I have no more."

"It's OK," she croaked, squeezing his hand. Her throat ached from coughing, her chest hurt, and she was exhausted, but that was the worst of it. And from the look on Lorrin's face, she knew it had been so much worse.

Elinta locked eyes with Zhayra, sending the dragon a silent message. She was sorry. Sorry to have caused the dragon such fear and pain. Sorry to have nearly ended it all without a proper chance to say goodbye.

Zhayra grumbled, lowering her snout to push gently against her. She stroked the dragon, noting the way she moved stiffly.

Elinta glanced at Lorrin, his eyes still fixed on her, drinking her up.

"You scared me," he said, his hand stroking her cheek.

"I'm sorry." Tears trickled down her face. "Niles," she whispered.

"I know," he sobbed, then took a deep, steadying breath. "I know."

"Can you—can you see him?" she choked, not wanting to say the words, but also knowing that she wouldn't be able to bear turning only to see his broken body.

"No," he whispered, gently wiping away her tears. "I think he's—he's further up."

"What's happening?" she croaked, coughing at the sting in her chest.

Lorrin sniffed and shook his head, looking around them. "I don't know," he admitted. "We need to find someone; I heard a horn blowing on my way over. I can still hear fighting in the city."

He looked back down at her. "We need to get you somewhere to rest."

But Elinta weakly shook her head. "I'm not leaving Zhayra."

Lorrin's face softened. "Alright."

"I will find someone to tell us what is happening," Tamir said, his voice strained. He stumbled to his feet.

"Tamir," she said, her voice cracking, "I had to."

He held her eyes, not an ounce of anger or hurt in them for what she'd done to his childhood friend. "I know, *tarsi*." He walked away, his feet seeming to drag, in search of news.

"Zhayra," Elinta said, looking back at Lorrin and not letting her mind linger on the image of Mazen's face as they fell through the air together. "How does she look?"

Lorrin studied the dragon for a long moment. And the dragon huffed.

"She has a few cuts on her face and body, and she also looks a little stiff. I—I think she must have caught you and taken the impact with the water."

"She did." Elinta could remember that second before impact, when Zhayra's claws had closed around her, pulling her into the dragon's body. Then it had all gone black.

"Lorrin!" a familiar voice yelled, and they both turned to see General Nash hurrying toward them.

"What's happening?" Lorrin called.

General Nash stopped beside them, her wide eyes taking them in. The general's hair had come loose sometime during the battle, and the ends were scorched. A deep cut ran the length of her arm, a graze across her cheek.

"More Asali have arrived."

Elinta's stomach sunk.

"But they are fighting Mazen's men."

Elinta and Lorrin exchanged a look.

"It's Ciar," she said, hope like a knife in her aching chest.

He nodded, sending water flying from his hair.

"Go to them. You need to tell everyone Mazen's gone."

"You can't stay here alone," he said, still holding her in his arms.

"I'll be fine."

"I'll leave a soldier with them, Lorrin."

He frowned.

"You need to do this. It's nearly over," Elinta said, squeezing his hand.

He nodded. "I'll have someone sent to heal you."

"Alright."

General Nash helped him gently move her closer to Zhayra, her limbs still too weak to support her body. Lorrin pressed another kiss to her forehead, then the two vanished back into the city. General Nash left a soldier behind as promised, but the man stood far enough away that she couldn't talk to him.

Elinta struggled to focus her mind, wanting to hear what was happening in the city. But it was in staring up at the sky that she realised.

"Where are the other dragons?" she asked Zhayra, her hoarse voice breaking over the words.

The dragon grumbled, and Elinta turned her head to look the dragon in the eye. "They're gone?" she asked.

Zhayra blinked once. A strange sensation sat in her chest.

"Because of Mazen or because of you?" she asked, pride rising in her.

Zhayra merely blinked once.

Both, she supposed. Elinta stroked the dragon's cheek, just within her reach, careful to avoid the blood.

"You were amazing," she said, breaking into a cough.

Zhayra grunted, pushing her with her muzzle.

General Nash returned half an hour later, her arm now wrapped in a bandage. Ciar strode confidently beside her. The Asali had removed his mountain gear in favour of donning a simple leather jerkin, and a large spear was slung across his back. Otherwise, he looked much the same as when she'd last seen him, his thick dark curls sitting around his ears.

She felt a small, exhausted smile tilting her lips. "Ciar," she croaked.

"It is good to see you, Elinta," his deep voice was like music to her ears in that moment. "I am sorry we could not get here earlier."

Elinta shook her head weakly. "I'm just happy you made it. We weren't expecting you for another week."

Ciar nodded, stooping beside her. "We knew things would only grow worse and hurried as best we could. Let me heal you now." He placed his hand on her forehead and his glow increased. Warmth began to spread through her again.

General Nash gave Elinta a small smile. "Mazen's army have laid down their weapons."

The words reverberated around Elinta's head.

"It's over?"

"Yes," General Nash said.

Ciar continued to push his healing over her, the warmth spreading through her like waves. Slowly, she could feel the ache in her chest disappearing, the pain in her throat lessening. But there was an emptiness within her that even his warmth couldn't reach. So much loss. So much suffering. And after all that ... she'd still had to kill Mazen. The image of his terror as he fell flashed in her mind, but it was quickly replaced by the face of another.

Elinta glanced up the docks as though she could see *him*.

"General Sonnen—is he—" she broke off, unable to form the words as silver lined her eyes again. Did he know? Was he even alive to know?

General Nash's face softened. "He's with Lorrin, but he knows," she whispered. "He wants to see you—to make sure you're OK."

Elinta gulped, nodding. "Did you—have you found him?"

"Yes," she said, and Elinta could have sworn she heard a tremor in the woman's voice. "We found him."

Elinta could do nothing but nod, as Ciar's skin dimmed and he pulled away.

"Thank you," Elinta said, her voice still trembling but no longer from damage to her throat.

Ciar looked over at Zhayra, his light grey eyes surveying her. "I can do nothing for you," he said, regret in his voice.

Zhayra grunted, a light sound that echoed the happiness in her chest that had bloomed as he'd healed Elinta.

Elinta sat, looking back at the dragon. "I'll look after her."

Zhayra blinked once, a softness in her eyes.

"I'm afraid we have to go," General Nash said. "The fighting may be over, but there is still much to be done."

"Of course," Elinta said, ignoring the stab of guilt she felt at not joining them. She was sure her presence as a *Zearla lurai* would help smooth things over with all the Asali, but she had no intention of leaving Zhayra. Besides, it would be good for all the leaders, old and new, to learn to work together. "But can you have some supplies sent here? I'll need herbs and cloths to treat Zhayra."

General Nash called out to the soldier she'd left to guard Elinta, and the man went running into the city to fetch what she needed.

"Thank you."

"I'll make sure someone keeps you updated." And with that, General Nash and Ciar disappeared back into the smoking city.

Elinta had just started treating the cut on Zhayra's face when her first update arrived.

"Illar?" she said, twisting at the sound of her own name.

"May I help you?" he said, coming to a stop in front of her. He wore similar clothing to Ciar, and his long hair had been braided tightly behind him. His short sleeves revealed strong muscles.

"Please," Elinta said, glancing back at the dragon. There was much to be done, and she was already growing tired again. While the Asali were able to heal wounds, it seemed they couldn't do much for exhaustion especially when it was caused in part by a string of emotional whiplash.

But at the sight of crimson on Illar's hands, Elinta held out a hand to stop him from coming closer. "Is that from you?" She gestured at the blood.

"No," he said. "I have no wounds on my hands. You needn't worry about her blood."

So, he joined her, following her instructions on how to clean and dress Zhayra's smaller wounds, even as he described what was happening in the city.

It seemed that the two blue dragons had disappeared as soon as they had seen Mazen's death and Vaherin's surrender. They weren't sure what had happened to the three dragons, but it was assumed they had gone back to their islands, if Vaherin could even fly that far with the injuries he'd sustained. Zhayra blinked in affirmation. Elinta had no doubt the other dragons would deal with them under Zhayra's direction.

Mazen's army had continued to fight after the dragons had left, the volunteers pushing the conscripted on. But it hadn't taken them long to lay down their weapons after Ciar's people had arrived, blowing the war horn.

Lorrin, General Nash, and Ciar were currently organising what was to be done with the volunteers. Those forced against their will to fight had already begun helping with the healing of the wounded in the city. Then there was the grey area. The ones who'd fought simply because they were loyal to the throne and whoever was on it.

After they'd cleaned and dressed Zhayra's wounds, Elinta stepped back and looked at the dragon.

"You'll need to tell me where else you're hurt," she said, studying her wings, legs, and tail. "You were looking stiff before."

Zhayra grunted, blinking once.

"Are your legs OK?"

Zhayra paused.

"Zhayra."

The dragon blinked twice.

Illar was looking between them, a smile lighting his face.

Elinta pointed at each of Zhayra's feet. "This one?"

No.

No.

Yes.

No.

She crossed to the dragon's back left foot, and ran through the questions again, asking about the joints and bones.

Zhayra's knee was sore.

Elinta had the dragon lie down so Elinta could poke and prod at it, Illar helping her when she struggled to reach certain areas properly. The Asali was grinning the entire time.

"You communicate well together," he said as she ran her hands along a muscle in the dragon's leg.

"Thanks." Elinta grinned. "I should be able to feel her pain, though, but I've never tried it before."

"You are doing fine without it."

As it turned out, Zhayra had escaped relatively unharmed given the severity of their falls and collisions with the water. Her knee was bruised and swollen, and she would need to keep off it for at least a week—though Elinta suspected two—and there was a small crack in one of the bones in her wing. Her numerous cuts and scrapes would heal quickly, though, and Elinta was confident the dragon would, ultimately, be OK.

Elinta and Illar stepped back to survey their work.

"Dragon Friend!"

Frowning, Elinta turned to follow the voice. Farrell, the soldier who had informed them of the dragons' arrival the day before, was running toward her. His filthy armour bounced with his steps.

"Yes?"

"I have another update from His Majesty," the man said, coming to a halt still several metres away.

Elinta gestured for him to continue.

"He sends word that he's meeting with his council and the Asali to organise the clean-up efforts and finalise what is to be done with Mazen's people. They are to meet in Mayor Cyril's private dining hall."

"Thank you," Elinta said, but she had no intention of going to the meetings though she knew she should. So, she instead tried to glean what she could from the man. "Will Ford and Mira be there?" She couldn't force herself to say what she really meant to ask: Were they alive?

The man gave a small nod as though he knew what she meant anyway.

There was one more question. One more she had to ask. Elinta's mouth opened and closed, no sound coming out. Farrell seemed to read that too.

"His Majesty said to tell you that the fallen are being moved. Soldiers can be found in the mayor's home, in the ballroom."

The ballroom. Their training room. She couldn't stop the sob that broke through her lips.

She nodded, unable to thank him. But the man just returned the gesture and weaved his way back into the city.

"Are you alright, *Zearla lurai?*"

"I—there's someone I need to see," she said, her voice tight.

"I will stay with Zhayra if you wish," Illar said, looking back at the dragon.

She twisted, catching Zhayra's eye. The dragon bowed her head, blinking once, a deep sadness in her.

"Thank you, Illar."

It took her fifteen minutes to walk to the mayor's home, but Elinta spent every second scanning the city, scanning the people. Looking for familiar faces. Looking to see who had survived Mazen's latest, and last, attack.

Her eyes snagged on Nakiah first, his eyes no longer vague but full of exhausted rage. Blood coated him, just like the last time she'd seen him, except that this time it was not the blood of his wife. His eyes locked on hers, and he bowed his head to her as she passed.

There were others, too, people she knew by sight but not by name. Guards from Nevira, others from Culmar's own ranks, healers, and even messenger boys. But she knew a lot would be missing. Her heart stumbled as she passed an unfamiliar maid, running between houses. Was Neva OK too?

She slipped through the gates at the mayor's home, a guard giving a nod of his head so low that it was more of a bow. She frowned, looking over her shoulder as she passed. With a shrug, she hurried up the steps, staying out of the way of the messenger boys and soldiers running in and out. The ballroom.

Her heart now pounded in her chest even as her steps slowed, her body heavy with tiredness and dread. Fear. Niles. Her throat bobbed. She forced herself on. She had to see him.

The ballroom came into view, everything else fading away around her. General Sonnen walked from the room. She couldn't see his face, wasn't sure she could bear it. But his body language spoke volumes. Elinta had always known the man to have impeccable, strong posture. But today—today there was a slight dip to his shoulders. A heaviness to his steps that she doubted many would notice. He was pushing on, just getting through the day.

She opened her mouth to call out to him, but only a whisper came, and she watched him stride off, unaware that she was there. What would she have said to him, though? What words could she possibly have for failing him? For failing Niles.

Elinta sped up, hurrying into the ballroom before her body gave up following her commands entirely. And she found rows. Rows of bodies. Each covered in a white sheet.

A startled cry tore itself from her throat. She didn't know if she could do this. Didn't know if she could even stay in that room. But before she could turn around and run, a small woman emerged from a little booth that had been set up in the far corner. Her kind face drew Elinta in.

"Ah," the woman said as though she'd been expecting her. "He's this way, dear."

Elinta gawped at the woman but followed in her small steps. She shouldn't have been surprised the woman knew who she was, if not by sight, then by stories of her eyes.

The little woman led her three rows back and four along, stopping beside one of the beds. A sheet covered the body entirely.

"This is him, dear. You take all the time you need. Give me a yell if you need anything. I'll be over there." She pointed to the booth she'd come from.

Elinta didn't respond, her eyes fixed on that sheet. She had the vague sense of the woman walking away as she stumbled closer to the table. Zhayra was in her eyes, had been since she'd left, and she felt the dragon's chest constrict just as hers did.

She raised a shaking hand toward the sheet, tears already leaking from her eyes ... and dropped her hand uselessly beside her. No. She couldn't look at him now. Couldn't stand to have her memories of him be anything more than that last cocky smile he'd given her. Instead, she lay her hand on his arm still covered by the sheet as the sobs shook her body, and her heart threatened to burst.

Elinta didn't bother going to any of the meetings being held throughout the remainder of the day. She was exhausted physically and emotionally. She had nothing left to give, and instead, stumbled back through the city to the docks, and to Zhayra. She was now in a fresh pair of clothes. Illar was still there, sitting quietly with the dragon. She thanked him profusely and told him to go and find some food for himself.

Elinta sat heavily, but gently pressed her back against the dragon's side. She had no words, and Zhayra sat quietly with her, her head on the ground and her own eyes droopy.

They listened to the city progressively grow quieter as the sun slowly began to sink. And when Zhayra fell asleep, Elinta continued to listen. Her mind wouldn't stop racing, despite the exhaustion hanging over her.

Lorrin arrived at dusk, his familiar figure stepping out from the shadows between two buildings. He sat beside her, slipping his arm around her shoulders and revealing the food he'd brought with him.

They ate in silence, a heavy weight sitting over them, smothering any thought or sound. It was a long time before he said anything, and they'd long finished their food when he did.

"I found your father," Lorrin said into the quiet. "He's OK. He fought today, but he's fine."

Elinta's throat bobbed, glad that he had done what she couldn't. "Thank you."

"Don't you dare feel guilty about him, El," Lorrin said, turning to face her fully. She knew they weren't talking about her father anymore. "There was nothing you could do."

"I know," she whispered, fresh tears sliding down her face. Tears that were reflected on Lorrin's own.

"He'd be yelling at you for what you did, but he'd be proud."

Elinta smiled. "I can already hear what he would have said."

"*Don't you ever scare me like that again! I can't believe you!*" Lorrin said, matching her thoughts word for word, his voice shaking.

"*And when was the last time you ate?*" Elinta's voice broke off as a sob tore itself from her throat.

Lorrin grabbed her, pulling her in for a hug she knew they both desperately needed. She buried her face in his shoulder, his own in her hair. And they cried for the friend they'd lost. The family they'd lost.

Elinta woke to the bright morning, the gulls calling above her. She hadn't dreamt at all, her mind too exhausted to summon images to torment her. She grunted, moving to stretch her aching back, but froze. Lorrin's arm was still around her shoulders. Elinta turned to look at him. His eyes were still closed, his chest rising and falling evenly. His face was peaceful, the exhaustion and grief lines eased in sleep.

She rummaged through her exhausted memories of the night before. They'd sat together, leaning against Zhayra for some time, his arm around her. But ... they must have fallen asleep.

Elinta carefully wriggled out from under Lorrin's arm and stood, stretching her sore muscles as she looked out over the sea.

It seemed to be a few hours after dawn, but the docks were still empty.

"Good morning," Lorrin's groggy voice sounded behind her.

She turned, finding him pushing to his feet. "Morning."

Lorrin strode over to her, looking out over the ocean as well. "There's so much to do," he said, slipping his hand into hers.

Elinta glanced at him, but her eyes settled on Zhayra's still sleeping form over his shoulder. An important memory of the day before surfacing.

"Lorrin!"

"What?"

"I know how to fix things with the dragons!"

His eyes widened, and she laughed.

"*Zearla lurai* ambassadors."

Lorrin's face had stretched into a wide smile before she had even finished getting the words out. "Of course!" He laughed. "They'd be able to move between our races easily—"

"—and they'd know what the dragons wanted," Elinta finished. "We'd all be able to communicate."

"But who?"

Elinta shook her head. "I have one or two ideas, but I'll need to think it over a bit more and talk with Zhayra."

Lorrin's eyes shone, though the shadow of grief still lingered. "We'll have to get started as soon as we can. This is amazing!"

Elinta grinned.

Lorrin's own smile faded as he looked down at her. "What about you?"

Elinta shook her head. "We'll make it work."

His face softened. "We will."

CHAPTER
TWENTY-SIX

T HE FOLLOWING DAYS WERE a whirlwind, leaving Elinta
feeling as though she'd never catch enough sleep to make
up for it all. There was much to be done in the aftermath of
the battle. Elinta spent her time between watching over Zhayra
and helping the city healers and the Asali with the injured. Long
hours were spent with her hands covered in blood as she mind-
lessly worked on cuts, stab wounds, and burns with the Asali
prioritising the severely injured. But the work kept her from
dwelling on that battle in the air, the friend taken from her, and
on the fall that had followed. The life she'd taken.

She hardly saw anyone in those days. Though Lorrin came
to visit her whenever he could wrestle a spare moment away

from the countless meetings. And Tamir dropped by on those rare minutes between healing the injured and sleeping off the resulting exhaustion. But soon Ciar's people had healed all those brought to the mayor's home, and then all those still in the streets and ruined buildings. With no more work to do, Elinta found herself winding through the streets toward Zhayra when she saw a familiar figure working in the ruins of a building.

Her father. Elinta's heart skipped a beat, but her legs rooted her to the spot as she stared at the sole remaining member of her family. The muscles in his arms rippled as he worked to dislodge a beam from the top of the rubble, another man stepping up to help him. Her father's arms were covered in soot, the back of his neck shining with sweat. She should go. She should go before he saw her. Before she would have to look into those hate-filled eyes. But she couldn't. Not even as he paused and as his body went rigid as though he knew he was being watched. Not even as he straightened, turning to look around him. And not even when his eyes landed on hers. He said nothing, and neither did she. But he merely nodded, as though greeting an old acquaintance, as though acknowledging that yes, he was alive, and yes, so was she. Then he was turning back to his work, and Elinta finally managed to move her stubborn legs.

Elinta grabbed onto Zhayra's emotions as she continued on, leaning into the comfort of the dragon as her own mind whirled. Should she have said something to her father? But she didn't know what she would have said nor what she wished he would have said. Elinta replayed the moment he'd nodded over and over. That old hatred had softened, she was sure of it; his eyes hadn't speared into her. Something eased deep inside of her, just a little.

Illar was waiting for her by Zhayra. The Asali had taken to visiting the dragon, who still hadn't been able to move away from the docks due to her injuries. But it didn't matter. Most of the workers were in the city, working hard to clean the rubble and dirt and blood. The docks would remain at minimum capacity for many more days yet.

"Elinta," Illar said, turning from Zhayra. The dragon's stomach jumped in excitement at the sight of her.

"Hello," she said. "I hear you'll be sticking around for a while."

Illar nodded. "There is still much to be done. Ciar wishes to help with the damage to the city and with Mazen's Asali."

Mazen's Asali. She hadn't seen them, hadn't been to any of the meetings about what to do with them either, but she knew Lorrin was struggling to work it out. Many had been innocent, forced to fight by the willing, while others had fought out of a misguided sense of duty. She was glad to hand that problem off to Lorrin, the generals, and even Harlan of Tremass who'd arrived with troops a week after the battle. Better late than never, she supposed. But if Ciar was helping too, yes, it was a problem they'd solve soon.

"What will you do once you return to the mountains?" Elinta asked, sharing a glance with Zhayra. She'd shared her idea with the dragon only last night, and Zhayra had been in full agreeance.

Illar tilted his head, frowning.

"I—we," Elinta said, gesturing to Zhayra, "wondered if you'd join us in the dragon isles. We'll need more *Zearla lurai* now and we think you'd be perfect."

A huge smile crossed the Asali's face, and he looked between them as though he couldn't believe what he'd heard. "I would be honoured."

"She'll need a couple more days' rest before she's ready to go."

"I will be ready."

Illar left them, grinning over his shoulder as he hurried into the city.

Elinta turned to Zhayra. "I think we can finally move you. The service will be held a little further down. I know you want to be there."

Zhayra blinked once, her heart heavy. She did not want to miss tonight.

It was the night they'd finally say goodbye to all those who'd died.

Elinta swallowed thickly. "Let's get you over there, then."

"Oh, miss," Neva said, stepping back to look her over. "It's beautiful."

Elinta offered her a small smile. One she hadn't thought she'd be able to muster today.

The dress was black after their mourning custom, with a V-neckline and loose sleeves that fell a couple inches below her shoulders. But silver threads had been woven into it, beautiful patterns tracing along the skirt. For the Asali, it was a representation of their natural light. It fit her perfectly because, unknown to her, Neva had gone into the city the very day the memorial had been announced and hired someone to make it for her. Hired them to make a mourning dress that represented the loss of both peoples.

"Thank you, Neva," Elinta said, taking the maid's hands in her own and giving them a squeeze.

"We'd better get you down there," Neva said, keeping a hold of Elinta's hand as they slowly made their way down to the sea.

Every man, woman, and child who had stayed in Culmar during the battle or had since returned was there and all were crowded along the docks and all the way back among the buildings. But their ranks were swollen by Mayor Harlan's troops, Ciar's people, and even some of the Liyarnan Asali. Everyone had arrived to say goodbye to those they'd lost.

Neva left her somewhere in the crowd as Elinta continued to push her way through. To Zhayra. To the water. Lorrin was already there, the waves gently lapping over the wood and against his feet. Elinta's breath nearly caught in her throat as she finally caught sight of him. He wore a black suit, and when he turned to face her as though he had some sixth sense only for her, she saw a silver tie. The wind was steady, and the water calm. The perfect time for it.

Lorrin held out a hand, and Elinta took it.

"Ready?"

"Ready."

Lorrin turned to face the crowd. And began.

They lit a lantern for every person who'd died. And set them loose to drift away over the sea. There were too many of the dead to bury all together, to send back to the earth, watched on by the city. So, they did it in the way that their ancestors had many years ago, a tradition Lorrin had insisted on bringing back. The lights of the dead were lost forever. Some would return to the sun, but all would live on in their memories. Lorrin held two: one for Niles and one for his father. But so did Elinta. She didn't tell anyone who that second one was for. But she knew Zhayra and Lorrin understood without her even telling them. It was for the person the ocean had already claimed. For the man who had been so like her while being her complete opposite. For the man he once was.

General Sonnen stepped up beside them, a lantern clutched in his own hands. She still hadn't talked to him, coward that she was. His eyes rose to meet hers. Eyes that should have been hard, furious, but were soft. As though there was nothing to be angry about. But drenched in pain. Elinta nodded. A silent promise that she would talk with him. About Niles and everything that he'd meant, and been, and done. But not right then. General Sonnen nodded back. And they gently set the lanterns down into the water. Their tears raced them down.

"Goodbye, brother," Lorrin whispered as his lanterns bobbed on the waves.

Elinta watched them disappear. Then she stood to the side with Lorrin and Zhayra as men, women, and Asali stepped forward with their own lanterns and let them be carried away by the waves. Elinta clutched Lorrin's hand in her own, a silent, steady anchor. Strong. They'd be strong for those grieving their own losses. Strong for Niles.

When Ford stepped forward, his suit completely silver, Elinta knew then that she had to speak with him.

Her feet moved of their own accord, and she stopped beside him. "May I?" she asked, taking one side of the lantern. The flame flickered in a light breeze but didn't go out.

"Yes," he said. And they placed the lantern in the sea for Aesira.

"Zetayn eyan pepyan eka ayn air kli nalliyan," Ford whispered, the blessing settling in the air between them.

"I believe I have a message for you," Elinta said, turning to face the man who had always been such a mystery.

Ford frowned, and so she elaborated, "From your mother."

She didn't know what she'd been expecting from him, but it was not the silver that began to line his eyes, or the slight smile that tilted his lips. His eyes drifted toward that lantern bobbing on the gentle waves.

"She wanted me to say hello the next time I saw you, but I had no idea she was talking about you," Elinta said with a soft laugh. "She loved you very much I think, Ford. And those days would have meant the world to her. You were the last thing we ever talked about."

"Thank you." A tear slipped down his cheek, but he smiled again. "I'm sorry I couldn't tell you who I was," he said quietly, his dark eyes slipping to hers. "They would have treated me like one of the Asali if anyone had discovered where I'd come from. And I wanted to help change things."

"You did," Elinta said. "You helped me. And that changed everything."

Lorrin came to see her that night. She and Zhayra had moved a little closer to the mayor's home, away from those lights, now invisible on the ocean. He settled beside her, his shoulder bumping hers.

"I have to go soon," she said, the words tumbling out as she turned to face him. Zhayra had to go home. The *queen* had to go home. There was so much still to be done. And they couldn't do it from here.

"I know," he said, resting his forehead against hers and closing his eyes. "How long until Zhayra can fly?"

"Only a few more days."

His eyes opened, locking with hers. "We'll make it work," he said, repeating her words from the aftermath of the battle.

"We will."

Those blue eyes dipped to her lips then, a question settling in them. Her answer was a hand slipping to his face, asking him, daring him.

Lorrin's lips found hers and everything around them seemed to fade until it was just them, just the warmth that spread through her, and the smile that rose despite everything and that threatened to break that kiss before she was ready.

CHAPTER
TWENTY-SEVEN

"There it is!" Elinta called over the wind, pointing toward the city shining in the early morning light even though the dragon couldn't see her.

Zhayra's stomach leapt, and she grunted in reply. Then, sensing Elinta's impatience and excitement, the dragon put on a burst of speed.

Grinning, Elinta watched as the city steadily drew closer, her eyes searching for the familiar form of the White Palace.

A lot had changed in the nearly six months they'd been gone. King Lorrin had finished overseeing the repairs at Culmar and helped with the return of the women and children who had been evacuated. Harlan and Ciar's people had been hard at work, too. Then, after destroying the sole remaining *illayas* weapon in existence—Mazen's dagger—Lorrin returned to Nevira. Elinta had watched through his eyes as they'd held a proper burial for King Aldon, and then watched as the months went by and Lorrin steadily began to change things.

Zhayra had changed things too, had brought hope back to the islands, had smoothed over tensions and anger, and Elinta was sure the pride she felt for the dragon would never fade. Those first few days, even weeks, had been some of the most challenging of Elinta's life. While the dragons had accepted Zhayra as queen, a large portion were clearly disappointed Mazen hadn't been successful in his vendetta. But that was all behind them now.

The palace came into view, and Elinta shook aside her thoughts. Lorrin had told her through their bond that the palace had been repaired while he'd been in Culmar, had begun even while she'd still been there too. And it looked just how she remembered it. It looked like home.

The city was silent as the outskirts finally began to flash past under Zhayra. No warning bells rang. No screams echoed in the streets. And that was the biggest change of all. Elinta's smile widened.

"Zhayra," she called, "do you hear that?"

The dragon grunted, confusion settling in her stomach.

"There's no warning bells!"

Zhayra's response was a happy roar that echoed over the city.

Elinta rolled her eyes and slapped the dragon's scales playfully. "Well, now there might be!"

The dragon let out a series of small grunts like a laugh.

Zhayra circled above the palace, watching as the courtyard steadily cleared. Elinta had dismissed the idea of landing outside the palace walls, hardly even giving it a thought. Lorrin wouldn't mind where they landed, and Zhayra would have trouble getting through the gates anyway.

With a flap of her large wings, the dragon queen landed in the stone courtyard of the palace of Nevira. Elinta undid the buttons on her jumper, the air only a little chilly now that spring had reared its head.

Jae stared at her from the stables and Elinta offered the stable-boy a wave. He grinned, his cheeks reddening, then disappeared inside.

"Elinta!"

Elinta's head snapped around, her eyes landing on Lorrin running down the front steps of the palace.

Laughing, Elinta unclipped her belt and slid easily from Zhayra's back.

Zhayra roared at the sight of Lorrin.

"Hello, Zhayra!" he managed to say before he crashed into Elinta, wrapping his arms around her.

She returned the embrace fiercely and her feet left the ground as he lifted her, breathing her in.

"I wasn't sure what day you were coming back," he said, setting her feet back on the ground.

"I know," Elinta said, finally pulling back, but only a little. "We were going to come tomorrow, but Illar arrived early."

"How's he doing?"

"Fantastic! He's picked up the senses quicker than I did," she said, only a touch of jealousy in her voice. "Nakiah hasn't bonded yet, but he seems really close to one of the younger ones."

Many of the dragons had been surprisingly receptive to the idea of bonding, once Elinta and Zhayra had explained their idea of the ambassadors. She suspected the idea had been key in helping soothe some of the tensions with the angrier dragons.

Lorrin grinned.

Zhayra huffed.

"I'm sorry!" the king said, running his hand along the dragon's muzzle. "It's good to see you again too, Zhayra."

The dragon's feelings soared.

"I'll send for some food. You two must be hungry." He looked at her. "I'll have them bring Blaine's sword, too. It's been waiting for you."

So, they made a picnic of it, right there in front of the White Palace. King Lorrin, Queen Zhayra, and ambassador Elinta. Elinta knew they could all feel the slight heaviness in the air, the knowledge that they were missing one key member. But the weight had become easier to bear with time. A part of them.

Lorrin's hand rested on Elinta's as they spoke, talking around mouthfuls of food. Tamir had written while she'd been away with the dragons. Liyarna was steadily recovering from Mazen's attack and rule. The men Lorrin had sent had been a great help. The new council, headed by Tamir, would be arriving tomorrow. They'd officiate the treaty sometime after.

"Ford will want to see you soon too," Lorrin said. "He's still writing down as much as he can about the dragons—filling in the blanks from Edwin's journals and the other ancient books that survived. But there's probably some of the history you know that he doesn't."

"But what about you?" Lorrin asked, his eyes sparkling. No shadow of the anger that had plagued him after his father's death remained. "How did it go with the dragons?"

Elinta smiled, taking a deep breath. "The first group will return next month."

Lorrin's mouth dropped. "Really?"

"Yes." She laughed. "Illar said Ciar and the others were more than ready for the dragons to come back. They've spread the word that the dragons are to be given space to settle in. Illar will be there when they do."

Lorrin ran a hand through his hair. "This is—this is amazing."

"We did it," she said, squeezing his hand. Zhayra nudged them both, her chest welling with pride.

"We did." Lorrin patted Zhayra's muzzle. "And Vaherin?"

Elinta sobered for a moment. "We don't see much of him. Mazen's death broke something in him. He can't fly anymore, so he'll never be a problem for Eldras again."

Indeed, the maroon dragon had separated himself from his people, a fact Elinta couldn't bring herself to feel sorry for. Not after what the dragon had done. Mazen's face still haunted her dreams, but she knew ultimately it had been the right decision. They never would have stopped.

Lorrin took her hand, dragging her back from her trailing thoughts. "How long will you be here for?"

"At least a month," Elinta said, thinking back to all that still had to be done. "But we'll need to visit the dragons when they arrive."

"And then?" Lorrin said, his eyes slipping for just a moment to her lips.

"We'll be back," she said.

Zhayra locked eyes with her, and Elinta nodded, her cheeks heating.

"Come for a ride?" she said.

"Sure."

Elinta climbed up Zhayra, a move she had now grown more accustomed to. Lorrin settled in behind her, his arms slipping around her waist.

"Ready?"

"Ready."

Zhayra launched into the air, and she heard Lorrin's breath catch. The dragon levelled out once they were just below the clouds. The city seemed to shine in the sunlight below them. Brand new. It all looked brand new.

"I'm glad you're back," Lorrin whispered in her ear.

"Me too." She twisted in her seat so that her face was right next to his. His eyes fell to her lips, and she was sure he was thinking what she was. The kiss they'd shared the day she'd left for the dragon islands. A promise, not a goodbye. With the wind in their ears and the steady beating of Zhayra's wings the only sound, they made that promise again in the sky. And Elinta smiled.

"This is the best one yet," Neva said, stepping back to look her over the next day.

Elinta grinned, looking down at herself. It was a hard-won smile. Not because of who would be there tonight, but who wouldn't be. Neva had found her puffy eyed and red-faced when she'd arrived to help her prepare for the coronation. She took a deep, steadying breath as the emotions threatened to rise again. Neva would not be happy if she had to redo Elinta's makeup.

The dress was silver with a beautiful, beaded V-neckline and a sweeping skirt that trailed gently on the floor behind her. It was one of Kalla's creations—the tailor who had made Elinta's dress for her first ball at the palace.

Neva caught her eye in the mirror. "King Lorrin won't be able to take his eyes off you."

"Neva!" Elinta said.

"Is that really such a bad thing?" Neva winked.

Grinning, Elinta ran a hand down the front of her dress. "Let's go."

But it wasn't to the throne room that they were going. The coronation would be held in perhaps the most unusual place one had ever been conducted, but then, it would be before the strangest crowd that had ever gathered.

Elinta and Neva went down to the ground floor, out the front doors, to the gates of the palace. All of Nevira had gathered along the main road, on rooftops and on side streets. But they weren't the only ones. Asali had come with Tamir and the new council from Liyarna, and even some from the White Mountains. And in the air, and on rooftops set aside for them, were dragons. The queen herself, white scales shining brightly in the sun, stood at the front of the crowd by the palace gates, her bulk taking up much of the space. But no one cared.

Elinta found her place beside Zhayra. Tamir joined her, and she pulled him in for a tight hug. She'd talk with him later. Catch up on everything she'd missed. General Sonnen joined them as did the Queen Mother, followed by General Nash's husband and two children Cassia and Aiden. But General Nash waited between the open gates, an *illayas* crown resting atop the cushion in her hands. And in the centre of the band was a single white scale. A union of the three races. A mark of their friendship, restored at last. Petals of the scarlet crown—the royal flower—were spread delicately around the crown.

Trumpets began. The song of Eldras ringing over humans, Asali, and dragons alike. And Lorrin—King Lorrin—descended the steps of the palace.

Elinta didn't hear what was said, but she knew General Nash spoke of the blessings and curses of ruling; of the friendships Lorrin had already established; and the pain they'd all fought through to be there. She didn't hear it all because her eyes were fixed on Lorrin—on the king she'd always known he'd be, finally seen by everyone.

He knelt before them all, no rug or cushion for his knees, just as he'd insisted. Instead, there were solid white stones beneath him. A king, but a servant. General Nash placed the crown upon his brow, and the people cheered and the dragons roared.

Then it was to the ballroom. Queen Mira, the generals, the advisors, Tamir and the council, Neva, and Lorrin's extended family and old friends all went inside to the final celebration.

Zhayra was in Elinta's eyes and ears, sharing the moment with the dragons who'd come with her.

The band was already playing, food and drinks against the walls. The crowd could be seen out through those arching windows, out in the city, already drinking and dancing. Elinta's eyes found Queen Mira's. They were softer than they had been in a long time. Still full of pain and loss, but happiness too. They exchanged a small smile and the queen gestured towards the dance floor. Lorrin stood in the centre, the crowd stepping back for him to start the first dance.

He found her, somehow, in that crowd. His eyes settling on her. A heaviness sat in those eyes, nearly perfectly hidden by the happiness of that moment and the face he was expected to portray, but she could see it there. The sorrow the losses he'd suffered had left behind. The same that had left a dull ache in her chest for so long. But his hand stretched out in invitation.

The people parted to let her through. The *Zearla lurai*. The Dragon Friend. No longer hated, but the very person their king loved. Elinta's heels echoed as she crossed the last of the way and took his hand. So much had happened these past six months. So much had changed in the world, and there was still so much to be done. But they'd made it work, as they'd said they would. Together. Elinta smiled.

"Ready?" he whispered.

"Ready."

PRONUNCIATION GUIDE

Names:
- Ferran pronounced FEH-RAN

- Zhayra pronounced ZAY-RUH

- Vaherin pronounced VUH-HAIR-EN

- Ciar pronounced KEER (like 'here' with a 'k')

- Raisa pronounced RAY-SUH

- Mazen Elliar pronounced MAY-ZEN EL-EE-ARE

- Aesira pronounced AY-ZEER-UH

- Aisla pronounced AY-S-LA

- Piran pronounced PEER-RAN

- Nakiah pronounced NAH-KEY-UH

Locations:
- Nevira pronounced NEV-EAR-RUH

- Liyarna pronounced LIE-YAR-NUH

- Calaza pronounced CUH-LAR-ZUH

Other:

- *Illayas* pronounced ILL-UH-YAS

- *Zearla lurai ngaran* pronounced ZEE-ARE-LA LER-EYE NG (like S**ing**apore)-ARE-AN

- *Zetayn nalliyan ayn palla kli ayn karn mai ri/ti* Pronounced ZEH-TAYN NALL-EE-ARN AIN PALL-AH KLEE AIN KARN MY REE. Meaning: "May (the) sun (present) continue to (present) shine on you (male/female)."

- *Zetayn eyan pepyan eka ayn air kli nalliyan* Pronounced ZEH-TAYN EH-YAN PEP-YARN EK-AH AIN AIR KLEE NALL-EE-ARN. Meaning: "May your light (inalienable) (present) return to (the) sun" ('eka' is used despite the contradiction. The Asali consider their light inalienable in life and the use is continued).

More extras can be found on Tiani's website at www.tianidavids.com/extras

ACKNOWLEDGEMENTS

My babies!!! *bursts into tears*

I can't believe we're here at the end of Elinta and Zhayra's story. This past year has been such a rollercoaster! Three books in one year!

There are, of course, a lot of people for me to thank for getting me here.

God, always and forever first. I couldn't do anything without you. Thank you.

My wonderful beta readers. Caroline and Beba, you two are the best cheerleaders anyone could ask for. Your feedback has made this book, and this series, grow into something I am so proud of. Thank you thank you thank you.

My editor, Carrie, thank you so much for your hard work. The time you've taken to not only provide edits and feedback, but also to explain common conventions and errors in detail has been invaluable. I'm keeping those reports forever.

Tairelei. I love you. These covers are the most amazing thing ever and all I could have asked for. Thank you. Thank you especially for working your magic with this final cover.

Number-one-fan-who-has-been-demoted.... :P

My mum and dad for telling anyone and everyone they meet about my books, thanks for making me profusely apologise every time.

My ARC readers for these books! Thank you for your enthusiasm and your reviews. Your help spreading the word is invaluable to getting this series out into the hands of other readers.

And everyone who has read TEC, who has reviewed, recommended, dm'd me, left gushing comments on socials, thank you! This series is for you.

What if Cinderella was sold to the fae to cover her father's debts, and instead of the magic wearing out at midnight she's mistaken for a fae princess and kidnapped by rebels? So, the fae prince sets out to find her.

Of Glass and Cinders features:

- Childhood friends-to-strangers-to-lovers

- No spice

- Elemental magic and shifting

- Cinderella retelling

- A war brewing in the background

- The first in a new standalone series of fae fairytale retellings

Tiani Davids grew up in Victoria reading middle-grade and young adult fantasy, a love that soon expanded to include writing. She now lives on the Far South Coast of NSW where she cultivates her passion for reading, writing and all things Tolkien.

Connect with Tiani online at:

Instagram: @tianidavids

Facebook: @authortianidavids

Website: tianidavids.com

Sign up to Tiani's newsletter on her website to keep up to date and receive exclusive content.

www.ingramcontent.com/pod-product-compliance
Lightning Source LLC
Chambersburg PA
CBHW020350120726
47904CB00002B/532